A CULLING TIDE

A CULLING TIDE
CHRONICLES OF AN URBAN DRUID™ BOOK 14

AUBURN TEMPEST
MICHAEL ANDERLE

DISRUPTIVE IMAGINATION

This book is a work of fiction. All of the characters, organizations, and events portrayed in this novel are either products of the author's imagination or are used fictitiously. Sometimes both.

Copyright © 2022 LMBPN Publishing
Cover by Fantasy Book Design
Cover copyright © LMBPN Publishing
A Michael Anderle Production

LMBPN Publishing supports the right to free expression and the value of copyright. The purpose of copyright is to encourage writers and artists to produce the creative works that enrich our culture.

The distribution of this book without permission is a theft of the author's intellectual property. If you would like permission to use material from the book (other than for review purposes), please contact support@lmbpn.com. Thank you for your support of the author's rights.

LMBPN Publishing
PMB 196, 2540 South Maryland Pkwy
Las Vegas, NV 89109

Version 1.00, February 2022
eBook ISBN: 979-8-88541-127-1
Print ISBN: 979-8-88541-128-8

THE A CULLING TIDE TEAM

Thanks to our JIT Team:

Dave Hicks
James Caplan
Kelly O'Donnell
Christopher Gilliard
Micky Cocker
Deb Mader
Dorothy Lloyd
Rachel Beckford
Paul Westman
Diane L. Smith
John Ashmore
Larry Omans

Editor
SkyFyre Editing Team

CHAPTER ONE

"Happy Anniversary, Fi," Dionysus says, raising a glass of the expensive red wine Sloan had the restaurant set aside for our romantic dinner. "Though love is new to me, and the idea of monogamy seems ridiculous, you seem to enjoy it, so I'm happy you think you're happy."

I chuckle and send Sloan an apologetic smile. "Thanks, Tarzan. That's sweet. We appreciate your support, don't we hotness?"

Sloan forces a smile. "Aye, of course, we do. Though maybe not as much as we would've appreciated havin' the romantic dinner fer two I planned all month."

Dionysus laughs. "Having to be monogamous in your love life doesn't mean you have to be monogamous in your social life. Fi loves sharing meals with family and friends. That's why I changed your reservation. You almost blew it, Irish. Tarzan for the save."

I chuckle, reaching under the table to squeeze Sloan's knee. "It was very thoughtful. You're right. I love a great meal with family and friends. I'm so glad you all could make it."

Dillan, Calum, and Emmet are finding this a little too amusing.

Knowing them, Dionysus suggested crashing our dinner, and they urged him on. My brothers will do anything for a free meal and a laugh...and if it happens to torment their little sister, all the better.

Sorry, Red, Nikon says directly into my mind. *If it's any consolation, I suggested we let you two have your private celebration but got outvoted.*

Likely by a landslide, amirite?

You know it.

I appreciate the thought, Greek. No biggie. Since Calum and Kev moved next door last month, we've had lots of dinners for two. Only, don't think you need to pick up the tab. This was our dinner plan. We've got it.

Don't be stupid. We're crashing your date. You're not paying for all of us. Besides, I owe you a mulligan night at BlueBloods.

Me, yes. Not me and ten of our closest friends.

He shrugs. *Let's just enjoy it. This might be our last chance to let loose for a while. I intend to eat my fill, drink too much, and sweet talk your brother and his groom into taking me home to take advantage of me.*

A man with a plan. You've got a good shot. Bizzy is having a sleepover with Jackson and Meg.

Sweet. This night is getting better and better.

Dionysus says something to our server, and she busts up laughing and almost drops her tray. By Dillan's expression, it must've been wildly inappropriate because he's laughing so hard, he's going red in the face. Ciara's mouth has dropped open in an unflattering gape. And Suede doesn't look at all pleased.

I don't even want to know.

"Do ye think they'd notice if we ditch?" Sloan asks, leaning close.

"I think they would, yeah." I reach across the table and snag more bread. "It's fine. We'll be alone for the afterparty. For now, let's be happy to be happy."

"It's hard to argue with that, *a ghra*."

Over the next five minutes, I check with Tad about the Heirs of the Order meeting next weekend, ask Kev how the underwater mural is coming along in Bizzy's room, and excuse myself to use the loo and say hello to a friend sitting on the other side of the restaurant.

From the outside looking in, Xavier appears to be a stern Korean businessman in a four-thousand-dollar suit. To those of us in the empowered world, the king of the Toronto Vampires is much more. He oversees all the seethes in the Greater Toronto Area, he controls the guns and drug market, and he's one scary dude.

Until you get to know him.

No…even then.

After losing control and trying to kill me, he's gone out of his way to be polite—almost friendly.

Tonight he's having dinner with his human companion, Karuna. I run into Xavier once a month at the Guild of Governors meetings but haven't talked to Karuna since our friend Laurel was killed by the rival Romanian startup seethe.

I'm about to lean in and say hello when I get hit by the brick wall of my least favorite British vamp acting the part of a feral guard dog.

He moves like a blur and knocks me back a step.

My hands come up as I totter on my heels and almost end up in the lap of a finely dressed businessman. Regaining my balance, I straighten. "Oye, Oli, back off! If you want to dance, ask nicely or keep your hands to yourself."

His lip twitches in a snarl. "It's my job to keep questionable factors at a distance. In your case, it's not a job at all. It's a pleasure."

"Yeah, well, manhandle me again without cause, and I'll put you on your ass and embarrass you. You're lucky I'm playing the part of a lady tonight." I smooth a hand over my green satin dress and brush my displaced hair out of my face.

"Playing the part doesn't make it so."

I grin. "Exactly *my* point, so watch it."

"You don't scare me, druid. You're nothing but a mouthy trollop with a few garden tricks and a big bad bear to fight your battles."

I curl my lip at him. "I've heard dominant traits heighten in the second life of your people. So, you were a dick before, and now you've magnified into an uber dick? Is that what happened?"

Oli puffs up, but this time I'm ready for him.

"Enough, Oscar. To your seat. Your dinner awaits." Xavier's tone is calm, and his voice is quiet, but there's no missing the warning in his words.

Oli is a feral dog who isn't pleased to be called off his prey. Still, he knows better than to disobey Xavier. Reluctantly, he submits and returns to his table across the aisle.

With the hostilities of the moment behind us, I turn to the vampire king and his companion, giving Oli my back. It's a bit of an F-you power play because as hard as he tries, I don't consider him a threat.

"Lady Druid, always a pleasure," Xavier says, as composed as ever. "You look lovely this evening. Are you celebrating a special occasion?"

I hold my hands out and do a little runway pose. The emerald green dress Sloan bought me for the Imbolc dinner last February is elegant, grown-up, and has a wicked slit up the side to show off my leg and hip. "It's a night to celebrate life and love."

"Well, we wish you endless quantities of both."

"Thank you. And to you both as well."

"That color is radiant on you, Fi," Karuna says, waggling her brows. "You're stunning."

"Thanks so much. It's all Sloan though. He has an eye for fashion. I love your hair like that. It's great."

Xavier seems to appreciate my compliment and his perma-stern professionalism eases a little. "Garnet says you and yours have been busy lately."

"We have. Both with training and meeting with heads of communities to gauge who's playing for which team for the coming event."

"If you think it might help you prepare to have sparring partners from my family, I can arrange that."

"Do you think we'll be coming up against members of your community? I hoped you and yours would be either onside or sitting out."

"My family will be sitting out, but I'm sorry to say many others like me won't be. There's growing discontent in my circle about living in the shadows. People are tired of discretion and want to be seen, I'm afraid."

"We're seeing that more and more lately."

Their server arrives to clear their plates, and I step back to let him in. "Enjoy the rest of your evening. I just wanted to say hello. Um…and if you think it might help, wish Benjamin my best. I think about him often."

"That's sweet of you, Fi," Karuna says. "I'm not sure it'll help him, but I'm happy to hear Laurel is in your thoughts."

"She is." I offer them both a genuine smile. "She definitely is."

Sloan stands when I return to our table and moves to tuck my chair in for me. When he catches my gaze, he checks in.

I wink and kiss his cheek. "S'all good."

Well, except the part about vampires outside the city fighting for evil during the Culling and wanting to come out and be acknowledged by society.

Those are problems for tomorrow.

Tonight is my first anniversary dinner. Sitting down, I return my attention to our table. "What did I miss?"

Nikon chuckles. "Dionysus has stumped us with a riveting question."

I turn to the god of wine and festivities and am ready for anything. "Okay, lay it on me."

"Have you ever seen a baby pigeon? I was sitting in the park the other day feeding the pigeons Timbits, and they were all big and fat. It struck me then…I've never seen a baby pigeon. Have you?"

"Well, first of all, if you're feeding them Timbits it's no wonder they're fat, but beyond that…I'm not sure I have."

Nikon chuckles. "Then Emmet followed up with never having seen a baby squirrel."

I laugh. "Nope. I don't think I've seen one of those either, but realistically, there have to be babies to grow into adults."

"The next question posed was if the adults sequester them until they're presentable."

"That sounds very medieval, doesn't it?"

With everything we've been through over the past year and everything we're readying for in the next few weeks, I love that this is what has us wondering.

That riveting dialogue halts as our server arrives, carrying a large tray of food and a tray stand. She seems to have recovered from Dionysus's comment well enough and sets up to hand out our meal orders.

As she reaches across the table to hand Calum and Kevin their steak entrees, I take in the smiles of the group. This might not have been the plan for the evening, but Dionysus is right. I do love dinners with family and friends.

Plates are handed out around the table until her tray is empty. Then her co-worker sets a second tray down, and she continues to distribute.

"Prime rib and baked?"

"Yes, thanks." I accept my plate and wait for everyone to get theirs. While we wait, Sloan tops up my wine. When we're all set and the servers clear out, I lift my glass. "A toast."

The group settles, and all eyes are on me.

"The past year held challenges, both welcome and not, enlightenment about me and the world, and more than a few hairy moments. My family had my back, new friends joined the cause, but without an ounce of hyperbole, I know I wouldn't be alive today if it weren't for Sloan Mackenzie."

"Irish! Irish! Irish!" my brothers chant, gently drumming their fingers on the table.

"Sloan has rescued me more times than I can count. He healed me when I was hexed, stabbed, poisoned, and possessed. He found me when I was lost and kidnapped. He trained me and taught me and taunted me. I'm not only a better druid because of him. I'm a better person. I lurve you, hotness. Big, mad, sappy lurve."

Sloan chuckles and raises his glass. "It's been my honor, luv. Every chaotic minute."

I *clink* our glasses together and sip.

"To Sloan and Fi and the years to come," Calum says, addressing the table.

"To Sloan and Fi," the others chime in.

We all drink to that.

"My question is, when is the wedding?" Emmet asks. "You've got the rings and the house. When are you making it official? Inquiring minds want to know."

Sloan shrugs. "What we share is official to me. If yer sister wants more, all she needs to do is say so. I'm not going anywhere, and I have Niall Horan on standby."

I chuckle. "Me either. I am blissfully content living in sin. Maybe we'll go the Kurt and Goldie route and be happily unmarried for the duration."

Sloan shrugs and lifts his glass to me. "Whatever ye want is how it shall be."

"Wow, you've got him trained," Suede says.

I wave that away. "Why mess with perfection?"

"Speaking of which," Dillan says. "If you stop rambling, we could eat before this perfect meal gets cold."

"Point to you, D." I set down my glass and pick up my cutlery. "Let the anniversary dinner begin."

I pass on dessert, unable to eat another bite. Part of me wants to say yes to crème brûlée, but a bigger part wants to avoid a repeat performance of throwing up my BlueBloods dinner into the flowerbed when we arrive home. Not that there are any flowers left in the garden in November…and not that fertilizing the flowers was my fault.

An evil grimoire possessed me at the time.

"Can we get two crème brûlées to go, please?" Sloan asks when the girl comes around to take the dessert orders.

"Of course. I'll get those packaged up for you and bring it out with the bill if that's all right."

"Wonderful." He winks at me. "I'd rather ye eat it later when ye have room than to make yerself sick. There's still the private part of the anniversary to celebrate, and I don't want ye feelin' ill."

"That's one of the things I love most about you, Sloan Mackenzie. You're always thinking."

While the others eat their desserts, we make small talk, but honestly, the two of us have already checked out and are planning the next part of our evening.

"Congratulations, you two," Eva says, leaning our way as Dillan, Kevin, and Nikon laugh about something. "It's lovely to share your special night with you. Dillan probably hasn't said it, but he's very proud of you and thinks the world of Sloan."

"Thank you for saying so."

She nods, and her fat, blonde curls spring beside her cheeks.

Her attention trails off, and I follow her line of sight over to where Xavier and Karuna are getting ready to leave.

After a moment, she shakes herself and returns to our conversation. "Anyway, it's been a lot of fun celebrating with you."

I glance toward Xavier and back at Eva. "Is something wrong?"

"Maybe…there's a displaced soul desperately trying to get the attention of the grouchy man you were speaking to earlier. She's quite animated."

"She?"

Eva nods. "Yes…about your age…blonde. She's wearing her hair pulled back in a ponytail and jeans…"

"That sounds like Laurel," Dillan says.

"*Annnd* a quarter of the local university population," Calum adds.

My dinner sinks heavily in my stomach. "Yeah, but why would any of them be trying to speak with Xavier?"

Emmet sets his cutlery down and sighs. "Maybe it's vampire business, and we should stay out of it. That guy gives me a serious case of the creeps."

"I get that, Em…and I really don't want to piss him off, but if it is Laurel, and we can do something to help her after what she's been through, we have no choice."

Emmet makes a face. "Fine. Go check it out, and we'll finish up here. Let us know if you need backup."

I toss my napkin onto the table and stand. "Eva, you're with me. Sloan too. Maybe your ring can help. The rest of you, stand by."

The three of us hustle toward the entrance, chasing down Xavier as he and Karuna leave the coat check and head for the exit.

"You're sure about this, Eva?"

"Yes. I've been dealing with displaced souls and spirits for centuries. This girl is quite agitated."

"Xavier, hold up." I jog to catch up, and Oli decides to flex his muscles again. This time, when he moves to shove me back, I'm ready.

Brute Strength. I call the force I need to hold my own against a vampire, grab his wrists tight, and bring my knee up between his legs as hard as I can.

Do vampires get sacked the same way other men do? I don't know until that moment. The answer is yes.

Yes, they do.

When he drops to the marble floor, I release his wrists and scowl. "That is on you, asshole. Stop trying to manhandle me. Use your words."

Xavier looks pissed. I can't tell if the glower is him being angry at Oscar, me, or the kerfuffle of me dropping his man in the entrance of his favorite restaurant.

"I apologize for the scene, honestly, but I need to speak to you privately. It's quite urgent."

Sloan gestures a hand toward a private alcove just off the entrance. Because of the restaurant's location within the walls of Casa Loma, it has all kinds of architectural character like that. "Will this work, ladies?"

"Perfectly. Great spot, hotness."

I step to the side as other diners come out to collect their coats. Pointing over toward the alcove, I urge them to join me. "I'll explain everything. I wouldn't want to expose anything delicate here."

Xavier nods, places a protective hand at the small of Karuna's back, and follows us into the private space. Despite the increased occurrence of exposure risk, most of the empowered community remains dedicated to our tenet of secrecy. "What's this about, Lady Druid?"

I check with Eva. "Is she here with us?"

Eva nods. "She is. She quieted down quite a lot once she saw you."

"Who are you?" Xavier turns a withering glare on Evangeline, but she doesn't seem to notice.

I field that question. "Xavier and Karuna, this is Evangeline. She's dating Dillan and is a friend and an Angel of the Choir. Her designation, up until recently, was a reaper for Death."

Xavier takes an aggressive step in front of Karuna and comes at Eva, fangs dropped and eyes wild and glowing scarlet. "You are *not* welcome here."

"Hey! What? Nonononono." I would get in between them, but there is physically no space. "Xavier, stop. Geez Louise, dude. When will you clue into the fact that you can trust me? No one wants to hurt you or Karuna."

"Then why would you invite us into a secluded spot with a reaper?"

"Because she can see Laurel...or a displaced spirit that I'm guessing is Laurel. Either way, the spirit is desperately trying to tell you something."

Xavier's gaze narrows on me.

I take Sloan's hand and thankfully, he's already activated his ring. The moment we make contact, the image of my high school friend takes form in front of me. "Hey, girlfriend."

"Fi? You can see me?"

"Yep...and you're looking good for being dead."

"Forget that...I need help. I need to tell Xavier something, and I'm running out of time."

"I've got you. Let me connect the party line here." I hold my hand out to Xavier. "Please trust I am a friend."

He hesitates for a moment until Karuna steps forward and looks at my extended hand. "Vampires aren't fond of ghosts. It's an undead thing. May I see?"

"Of course, but hurry. Laurel's panicked about something and needs help."

Karuna takes my hand and gasps as her gaze locks on Laurel. "It really is you."

Xavier takes Karuna's hand, and his serious scowl softens a little. "It's good to see you, *chingu*."

Laurel straightens. "I'd love to catch up, but there's no time. Benjamin is about to do something monumentally stupid. He's rigging up a noose of razor wire and plans to hang himself from the Bloor Viaduct."

Xavier hisses. "Idiot."

He's about to rush off when I grab his wrist. "You're fast but Sloan's faster. Allow us."

He nods, and Sloan takes Eva's hand so the five of us are linked. The power of Sloan's wayfarer gift tingles over my skin, and we materialize beneath the arched trusses of the massive bridge.

Pointing up, I spot a man perched outside the security screening and curse as he drops away from the bridge and falls…

CHAPTER TWO

"Eva, help him!"

She doesn't move.

Sloan seems stuck too.

Xavier isn't. He runs like a gazelle, then launches over the water and into the night sky.

My jaw drops as I watch him grow smaller and smaller by the second. "I didn't know he could fly."

Karuna shakes her head. "He can't, but he can jump very high, very fast."

I swallow, my heart beating wildly in my chest. "Come on…come on…"

"I'm sorry I couldn't save him, Fi," Eva says. "I could never lift him as a dove, and I can't carry souls unless they're dead."

I wave that away. "Not your fault. I couldn't help and hoped you could. No worries. Xavier's got this."

"He's coming down," Karuna says. "Sloan? Can you get us over there quickly, please?"

We group up, and Sloan *poofs* us across the ravine and into the treed area beneath the bridge. The moment we materialize,

Laurel rushes to where Xavier is kneeling on the ground. "Is he alive?"

Xavier doesn't answer, so Eva does. "He lives, and I get no sense his final death is pending."

"Unless I kill him myself." Xavier sinks back roughly to sit in the scrub. He's breathing heavily as Karuna drops down next to him.

Huh, his hands are shaking.

Either that thoroughly shook our unflappable king of vampires or exerting that level of energy weakened him to the point of vulnerability.

Fascinating.

I study the still form of Benjamin lying in the brittle grass. He's an unremarkable male who you'd likely not give a second glance if you passed him on the street. He's certainly no one you'd look at and imagine as a vampire.

Still, Laurel adored him and was devoted to him as his companion feeder.

"He hasn't been drinking," she says, brushing her fingers over his brow with no effect.

I chuckle. "Then your nose doesn't work anymore, girlfriend, because he reeks of booze. I guarantee you he's done little else but drink today."

"No, I mean he hasn't been feeding. Xavier has sent him several new companions to bond with, but he's not drinking. Tell him."

I relay the information and Xavier frowns. "Is she sure? I checked with the ladies—"

"He punctures their flesh to make it look like he is and alters their memories to make them think he fed. He keeps them in thrall for a time and sends them out to report back to Xavier."

"Sneaky." I relay that too.

Xavier curses.

Karuna looks stricken. "He's been hiding how bad it's gotten. That's on us for not realizing."

Xavier sighs, looking sad. "Thank you, Lady Druid. I appreciate you stepping in when you did. And you, *chingu*, for watching over us."

He rises to his feet with an uncharacteristic effort and straightens. "Sloan, if you don't mind, I would appreciate a transport back to the castle."

"Of course." Sloan squeezes my hand. "Would the carriage house be best?"

Xavier nods. "Perfect. Thank you."

Xavier and the descended vampires of his siring line live in a secret U-boat bunker built beneath the Casa Loma property during WWII. The entrance is through the floor of one of the horse stalls in the old carriage house, and that's where Sloan *poofs* us.

Xavier's men are milling around waiting for his return. They make quick work of opening the way for their king to escort him, Karuna, and Benjamin inside.

"What about you?" I ask Laurel when she doesn't follow. "Are you going in?"

"I will, but it's so nice to be able to talk to someone. I thought I'd say goodbye to you properly."

"That's because you're displaced," Eva says. "It would be different if you passed over to your final resting place."

I shrug. "Do you want Eva to drop you somewhere better suited to your current state?"

Laurel shoots Eva a suspicious glance and shakes her head. "No. I don't intend to go anywhere, especially when Benjamin is suffering. I'm not about to fly off to be some kind of afterlife angel when the guardian angel of *my* life's story is lost and alone."

Eva offers her one of her prize-winning sunshiny smiles. "I would never take you without your consent but know there's only a given window of time to accept the next chapter of your life. Don't wait too long."

"I'm fine. I want to stay with Benjamin."

I understand completely and would do the same thing. If I were killed and knew Sloan was in a dangerous place, there's no way I'd leave him. "Sloan and I or maybe Eva will stop by to check in with you every few days. If you have something to tell people or change your mind about moving on, let us know. Deal?"

"Deal."

"If there's an emergency, you know where I live. Come find me."

She frowns. "I know where you lived in high school. At the end of the street next to the woods. Are you still there?"

"Next door. Aiden and his wife have our old house with Dillan. Sloan and I are next door. Calum and Kevin are next door to us. And Emmet is across the road with his betrothed, living with a friend. Honestly, anywhere on that street, you can trip over a Cumhaill."

"So, they are close, but you don't end up fighting with them for the bathroom."

"Exactly. It's perfect."

"Ha! Remember that night we were trying to get ready to go dancing at Rebel?"

I roll my eyes. "Elbows up for a turn in the shower was the story of my life. Now that I've got my own ensuite…life is good."

She smiles. "I'm glad it worked out for you, Fi. My life sorta took a turn and has been a messy scramble."

Right. "Sorry. That was insensitive of me. You've had a raw deal all around."

"I thought so too until Benjamin. Fi, he took me in, protected me, and loved me. He turned everything around for me, which is why I can't leave him in his darkest hours."

"That's perfectly understandable." I smile up at Sloan. "Good men deserve our devotion. Go check on Benjamin…oh, and find the new family member, Clara. She's Parisian and can read thoughts. Maybe she can pick up your wavelength, and you won't be totally unheard."

Laurel nods and her blonde ponytail bounces behind her like it always did. Honestly, if not for her being translucent, I wouldn't know she's a ghost.

Seeing through a person is a bit of a tell.

"Go. We'll see you again soon. And Laurel…it was great to see you again."

"Thanks, Fi. It was even better to be seen."

Sloan, Evangeline, and I leave the carriage house and walk across the stately grounds of Casa Loma to reunite with our group. It's nearly nine, and Sloan wraps an arm around my shoulders, warming me from the night's chill. We left in such a rush I didn't grab my jacket from the coat check.

"Internal Warmth," he whispers close to my ear.

As heat builds in my core and radiates outward toward my extremities, I sigh. "It's good to be a druid."

Sloan's body vibrates against my side. "Aye, it is. And for more than being warm in the winter."

"True story."

"Well, if it isn't the dine and dashers," Emmet says as everyone comes out the front doors to meet us outside the entrance. He's holding my jacket and Sloan's, and Dillan has Eva's. Although I'm not sure she feels the cold because she looks as content as always.

"Here are your crème brûlées." Nikon holds up a brown bag with handles. "For the afterparty."

"There's an afterparty?" Dionysus brightens, his smile gleaming in the moonlight.

"A private one, *sham*," Sloan says.

To ensure it's very clear, I add to that. "A monogamous kind of private party, Tarzan. You'll have to sit this one out."

Dionysus shrugs. "Being friends means supporting opinions with no judgment, amirite, Jane?"

"Right you are. We all get to decide what makes us happy and there are no wrong answers."

He nods. "What would make me happy right now is having a private afterparty at my loft. Everyone here is invited. There will be much drinking and nakedness. Although, in the spirit of choice, the removal of clothing is optional. Anyone wishing to join is welcome no matter what the apparel."

He extends his hand in front of his body and smiles at the group. "All aboard!"

Everyone stacks a hand on the pile except Sloan and me. "Have a fun night, guys. We'll catch up tomorrow at brunch."

"Mmm, brunch. What's on the menu?" Emmet asks.

"Raspberry pancakes and back bacon."

"Noice." Emmet waggles his brows. "Have you got enough syrup?"

Tad snorts. "What is it with you and the fear of running out of syrup? It's weird, *sham*. Really weird."

"Don't mock me. Did you have to live through the syrup shortage of 2012? No, you didn't."

Tad looks at him as if he's crazy, but I shake my head. "No, for reals, look it up. The great Canadian maple syrup heist. To this day it's the number one biggest theft in all of Canadian history, and it left us in a syrup shortage. It scarred Emmet for life."

Emmet nods. "For Canadians, a syrup shortage is a very big deal. So, I repeat…don't mock me."

Sloan waves. "Okay. Goodbye. Luv ye. Off ye go."

Nikon snorts. "I think that's our cue to get lost. Irish has had enough of team sports for the night."

Dionysus chuffs. "Team sports are the best."

Suede smacks his arm and gives him a look. "One-on-one is nice too."

Dionysus catches his mistake and nods. "Yep, that's what I meant. Look at that. Time to go."

With that, our entourage disappears, and Sloan and I are finally alone on our anniversary.

CHAPTER THREE

"Emmet, you better stop eating, or you won't be able to move in training." I peg my brother with a serious look. "Merlin is bringing some ancient warrior friend to spar with us. You'll make us look bad if you waddle into the match and can't rally an attack or defense."

I reach for the platter, and he gives me a defiant look, spearing the last piece of back bacon with his fork. "Let no food go to waste. Geez, it's perfectly good."

"It doesn't go to waste if I wrap it up and put it in the fridge for later. You don't have to eat it now."

"Oh, I think I do." He takes an exaggerated bite and chews it smiling up at me. "Delish."

I smile at Ciara. "You picked him."

"I was heavily altered and under a fertility spell at the time. I can't be held responsible."

I laugh. "Yet you married him months later."

"Handfasted. I left myself an out."

I laugh harder and head to the sink.

"Hey," Emmet grumbles. "Both of you be nice, or I might think you don't love me."

Ciara laughs and leans over to kiss his cheek. "Och, if I could quit ye, I would but yer just too damn adorable. I'm afraid I'm a lost cause."

"Good. That's right where I want you. Well...in public. In private, I like you somewhere else entirely."

I roll my eyes and rinse the now empty platter. "Don't come complaining to me when we start the first drills, and you feel like you're gonna puke. There will be no mercy."

"No mercy!" Calum and Dillan repeat.

I laugh. "See. Told you."

Over the past month and a half, Merlin has been schooling my brothers, Sloan, Tad, Ciara, and me on all things druid-y both offensive and defensive. Nikon and Dionysus have shown up on the regular to brush up on skills and stay current, and even Garnet and Anyx have joined us during a couple of the late-night sessions.

My instincts say they come to work with Dart. Having a dragon in the city has created a buzz among the empowered community, and I think Garnet likes to keep his finger on the pulse.

Now that Saxa has joined the training crew, I'm sure things will get even more interesting.

During this time, Merlin has led the way and has been driving us hard. The last Culling happened when he was mourning Cazzie and had cut himself off from the world. He was in a drunken fog and turned his back on the world for centuries.

Working out for hours a day with us has leveled up his skills rapidly. He says he only needed to knock the rust off, but it's much more impressive than that.

He's a freaking phenom.

Well, duh...he's Merlin.

We *poof* as a group to the druid circle we confiscated from the Barghest last year. They created a replica of the sacred Druid's Altar at Drombeg, then perverted it with necromancy and human sacrifice.

Yeah no, I don't think so.

We liberated the stone circle and restored the natural juju of the place. It's become a touchstone for our growth into the druids we are today.

Merlin waves us in when we arrive and gestures at the androgynous warrior standing next to him. "Everyone, this is Renis D'Jarron. They've agreed to be the offensive force for today. Take a few minutes to stretch and get ready for the battle, and when Nikon gets here with Niall, we'll get started."

I'm jazzed about Da joining us today. As much as I support the oul man enjoying retirement life in Ireland, we miss him and need him on our squad.

After all, when we entered Fionn's battle bunker, there were six statues to bequeath our enhancements. If Brenny were alive, maybe he would've been called as our sixth, but he wasn't.

For better or worse, Da is part of this.

For us...it's better. I hope it is for him too.

As I stretch, I think about that afternoon. Fionn sent us to Ireland to reclaim the Fianna treasures from his ancient fortress beneath the Hill of Allen. To his horror, they were in danger of being discovered or destroyed by the gravel company excavating the land.

It was our first family druid adventure.

As we explored the Grand Hall of the Fianna, we found the statues and were gifted designations and weapons.

Fionn's statue drew me in and gave me an iron crown and my body armor. Birga had already found her way to me through a Barghest kidnapping, so I was all set.

I never did figure out what the crown was about.

The scout rogue statue called Dillan. He received a Cloak of

Concealment and his dual daggers. He's our stealth fighter, and with the hood of his cloak up he gets a flood of information about his surroundings.

Calum is our range fighter. He was gifted his bow and an Eternalfull Quiver. Very cool.

Aiden, the biggest and bulkiest of us, is our party tank. He received a curved blade sword and a buckler and is one of our defensive fighters.

Da received a wicked cool staff made from snakewood. He was jazzed about that because the staff was his weapon of choice in his youth. He's happy to be a defensive fighter working to protect our party as well.

Then there's Emmet.

I laugh aloud as I picture him standing in front of the sixth statue. The guy had no weapons but even worse…no clothes.

"Seriously? I'm the naked guy? What the hell?"

I cover my giggles and switch from shoulder stretches to lunges. Emmet's primary discipline was healing at the time… since then, he took a bath in the pink waters of raw, fae prana.

He's got great things percolating in him—I know it.

When Da arrives with Nikon, I head over to say hello. My father's been stumbling through a rough patch the past year. After our second-oldest brother Brendan was killed in an off-duty shooting, Da has suffered what I think is both a parent's loss as well as survivor's guilt.

Whatever it is, it's taken a toll on him.

"Hey, Daddio. What's the craic?" I reach around his ribs and hug him.

"Och, not much craic these days, I'm afraid."

I give him an extra squeeze before I ease back. "About that…I was thinking. When things settle down, I could take you into my happy place to spend some time with Brendan. I know it's not the real Brendan, but it helps me sometimes to talk to him and tell him things I would've told the real him."

My father looks torn between sorrow and horror. "I don't know if that's an answer for me, *mo chroi*, but I'll think about it."

I nod and step back. "Well, as long as you know it's an option. You can let me know. Now, get stretching. We have butts to kick."

Turning toward Merlin and his friend, I swing my arms around in a windmill and head over to join them. "Once my father and Nikon are ready to roll, how do you want to do this? What are your affinities, Renis?"

Merlin casts me a sidelong glance and grins. "Oh, we're not telling you that. It would ruin the surprise."

I read the amusement in Merlin's expression and a rush of trepidation hits. What can one person do to challenge all of us? I'm almost afraid to find out.

"Fi, behind you!" I hear Dillan's girly screech right before the eight-foot spider pincers my arm and lifts me off my feet. My armor keeps the hold from hurting, but its grip is tight, and I'm seriously stuck. I grunt, flailing at first, then swing back to kick it squarely in the jaw.

My boots connect with its creepy face.

Nothing.

"Bestial Strength." As the rush of power feeds my cells and my strength multiplies, I leverage the beast's hold on my arm, throw my body backward, and kick the giant insect squarely in the mandible.

This time, it takes me seriously.

Flipping its ugly head, it tosses me into the air. I tumble head over heels, find the target to focus on, and orient myself to attack as I descend.

Dillan has always hated spiders.

As I drop into position to strike, the manifestation of Dillan's fear is distracted by Calum and Nikon fighting a great white shark on the grass next to us.

Yeah, it's a crazy Sharknado moment, but hey—magic—amirite?

The beauty of Aiden's fear of *Jaws* is that Dillan's spider is distracted, and I manage to thrust Birga's jagged marble spear tip through its eye.

The spider reels, wildly scuttling as it throws its head this way and that. I lose my footing for the second time in minutes but still have hold of Birga. Dangling by both hands, the beast whips me back and forth, and I hang on for dear life.

Dammit...the spider's screech draws the attention of the ghost that manifested Sloan's fear.

The poltergeist guns it for me, and there's no way I can defend myself without my hands or feet to fight.

"Oh, no you don't, Casper." Aiden casts a solidifying spell and rams the ghost into the void of darkness sucking everything up like a black hole.

Oops...that opponent is on me.

I was always afraid of the dark as a kid.

The spider is winding down but is still swinging me around like a flag hanging from its eyeball. Birga and I are good to ride it out, but then an army of zombie porcelain dolls start grabbing my feet.

"Dammit. These undead dolls are freaking me out."

I get that we're battling everyone's childhood fear but who the hell thought up zombie dolls?

With those painted-on faces...yikes, they're creepy.

"Nikon, watch out for—" Pennywise the Clown takes down the Greek, but Da is quick to assist. That is until the clown turns on him and sprays knockout gas from the flower in his lapel.

Nikon and Da both drop like rocks and faceplant on the frosty ground.

I don't know who was reading Stephen King when we were kids, but *IT* is terrifying in the flesh, and I'm twenty-four.

One of the zombie dolls makes it onto my boot, and I scissor my feet to get rid of it.

Crap on a cracker. So creepy.

Da and Nikon are still down when a giant earthworm comes out of the ground and breaches its hole right next to where they're lying. Its arrival pushes back Pennywise, leaving a long trail of sticky silk all over the two of them.

Sloan raises his hands and runs to their rescue.

I wonder what he's conjuring until a massive shadow blocks out the sun above me. For a moment, I think I've lost track of my black hole of darkness. No, that's not it. Emmet and Calum are shoving the great white into it as we speak.

I glance up at the gray sky, and my mind fritzes out like my wiring is faulty. "Is that a robin?"

Yep. It is.

A robin the size of my SUV swoops down, grips the earthworm in its beak, and flips it into its gullet. A swallow later, it eyes the spider and rushes forward to do the same thing.

I barely pull Birga free and drop to the ground before the robin snaps up the spider, pushes off the ground, and flies away.

"Good one, Mackenzie," I say, now totally overrun by zombie dolls. Swinging Birga, I'm bowling them over, but they keep pulling themselves back together to resume their attack.

"Did someone get rid of my feckin' ghost?"

"I think Aiden shoved it into my darkness."

"Nope. It ghosted me." Aiden rushes over to help me with the zombie dolls. "See what I did there? Ghosted me…"

I snort and try to stay focused.

"I've got an idea about the ghost," Dillan says, racing past me. "Fi, you need to help Emmet with the psycho *IT* clown. He's hiding behind the cotton balls."

I laugh. Since we were kids, we've tormented Em endlessly

about being freaked out by cotton balls. At this moment, it's the best. Even when worst fears come to life, they're still cotton balls—only supersized. "What if I get the clown over to the black hole?"

"The darkness is currently occupied," Calum shouts, fighting to force *Jaws* into the void.

"Fi, zombie doll coming for ye, luv."

I groan, running to bounce on one of the cotton balls to gain distance from the creepy dolls. "Whose fear is this because it's terrible. I hate these things."

"Sorry," Calum shouts, pushing the last of the shark's tailfin into the black hole. "When they said they were going to pit us against our childhood fear, I couldn't decide between zombies and those porcelain dolls Mrs. Graham used to collect in her spare room."

"Yeah, tough choice. They always freaked me out."

"Right?"

"Clown down!" Da huffs and uses his staff for support.

"The ghost is clear, Irish." Emmet chuckles. "See what I did there, Aiden? The *ghost* is clear…"

He laughs. "Yeah, good one, Em."

Hilarious. It's a good thing we all get along because no one else would think we're half as funny as we do.

Straightening, I take inventory of what's left. All we have is the darkness swallowing everything and Emmet's cotton balls. "Does anyone think we can stuff the black hole with cotton balls?"

Da chuckles. "It's worth a try."

Da and Sloan take that on, and I flop on the grass, heaving for breath. Nikon drops beside me, then Emmet and Calum join in.

"Dayam, I'm gassed." Emmet is panting. "How will we fight the Culling battles for four or five days when we're wiped after half an hour?"

"Maybe we get Dionysus to pivot Newgrange a few ticks

toward the river and change the line of the sun. If it doesn't light up the chamber, there's no Culling period, right? Do you think that will work?"

I hear the hopeful excitement in Dillan's voice, but my instincts say no. "Sadly, I don't. Sorry, D."

"Well, it was worth a shot. Don't say I don't participate in the brainstorming."

I'm still catching my breath when the tribal song of the Lion King breaks the silence, and I groan and roll to my hands and knees.

My phone is *sooo* far away…

And my body is *sooo* broken.

"Gust of Air." My call to the elements inspires a surge of wind to my aid. The force of the air catches my purse and deposits it in front of me.

I flop back onto the ground, reach into my purse, and answer the call. "Hey, boss man. What's the sitch?"

"I need you and the team to saddle up and head over to the aquarium. We have a group of empowered protesters tired of hiding who they are."

"There has been a lot of that going on lately."

"There has. As much as I have always maintained that the empowered community remains unseen, if the members of the dark species continue this way, we might not be able to keep a lid on it."

"For now, you want us to give it a try?"

"I do. I know you have a lot to deal with, Lady Druid, but no matter what's coming up next month, there's still the here and now to worry about."

I draw a deep breath and force myself to get to my feet. "Got it. On our way."

CHAPTER FOUR

"Water nixies. Weren't those twins who tried to claim Maxwell as their betrothed water nixies?" Calum asks as we arrive at Ripley's Aquarium.

"They were...specifically swamp nixies."

Emmett chuckles. "Didn't you have to go to their swamp territory and eat crow?"

I roll my eyes at my brothers and sigh. "Yes, Garnet and Andromeda said it was the only way to make peace and get Maxwell off the hook for a nixie ménage marriage. I still don't think I did anything wrong—those nixie bitches spit in my face and came at me—but Garnet insisted that me making a formal apology was the politically correct thing to do."

Da smiles at me, his bright blue eyes dancing with amusement. "Adultin' is hard, *mo chroi*. Often, we must do things we're not keen to do in order to keep the peace. I'm proud ye can take it on the chin when needed."

"Yeah, it wasn't much fun, but it got Maxwell out of hot water."

"Mad Max rules!" Emmet pumps his fist. "Man, I wish I could've seen that firsthand."

"Which part?" Calum asks. "The clusterfuck of Dionysus slipping Maxwell ecstasy or him rushing around naked and hugging everyone?"

Emmet laughs. "No, I got to see the pictures of him groping Sloan back at our place. That was fun for me."

I laugh. "That was fun for me too."

Sloan mumbles something about us all being eejits and gestures at the aquarium door. "Not to put a fire under any of yer arses, but weren't we asked to come here to stop an exposure event?"

His bah-humbug routine only makes me laugh harder. "Remind me to have that picture framed to put on our mantle for when times get rough."

"Yer ridiculous. I'll not have a picture of a naked Maxwell and me on my fireplace mantle. If ye remember, I do still own the place."

My response to that is interrupted as we enter the front doors of the aquarium and take in the scene. "Okay, I see the problem."

Before us, there is a spiral of chaos.

Tourists and visitors are crouched in the corners and staring wide-eyed as two pale green women with webbed fingers and pointed ears dance and twirl with their hands up.

They've called upon their connection with water and have tidal waves swirling and sloshing all around the front entrance.

Nikon jogs in to join us and blinks at the public display. "Garnet thought you might need help."

"As usual, he knows best." I figure out our best course of action. "Greek, see if you can snap those girls out of here and back to Stephenson's Swamp. It's the wetland at the mouth of the Highland Creek Watershed."

"I'll try, but it doesn't look like they're ready to leave the party."

As Nikon advances toward them, the girls squeal, spew a

fountain of water into his face, and run deeper inside the building.

"Sorry, Greek, I forgot to warn you they spit."

Nikon turns to give me a droll stare as he wipes a hand over his face. "Yeah, thanks, Red. Got it."

I giggle and check in with the others. "Calum, text Garnet and find out if the djinn are coming. There is definite exposure here. Sloan, if you can alter the memories of these people and get them out of here, that would be a start to cleaning up this mess."

Sloan glances at me and arches a brow. "If I remove the memory of swamp nixies, how do I explain the fact that once they leave, they're outside in November soaking wet?"

"Caught in a rainstorm?" I offer.

"No. The sprinkler system at the aquarium broke," Dillan says. "It was a freak electronic malfunction, and everyone in the building got soaked."

I give Dillan a thumbs-up for that one. "Great explanation, D. I totally buy that. You're on fire today with the good ideas."

A shrill shriek deeper in the building has me moving out to investigate. "Somebody stay back and help Sloan with the evacuation. We'll try to send more your way."

As we get to the entrance desk, the boy behind the glass screen raises his hand to stop our entrance. "You can't go in there. You haven't paid for tickets."

Hubba-wha? "Seriously, dude? I'm not sure if you've noticed this, but crazy nixies have invaded the aquarium. We're here to help you, *not* to enjoy the wonder of your exhibits."

He doesn't seem to know how to respond to that, but I don't give him the chance to argue. Hopping over the turnstile, I rush into the aquarium proper. "Does anyone know where we're going?"

Aiden snorts. "There's only one option. Down the ramp to the right and into the exhibits."

He points the way, and yeah, now that he mentions it, it's

obvious that it's a one-way traffic flow. We rush off to our right, pass guest services, an entrance tank with a coral reef and tropical fish, and a marine education center.

Visitors and staff are running against traffic flow, forcing us to scatter to the sides as they flee the chaos of the lower level.

Our group runs down the ramp dodging tourists, turns a hard one-eighty to continue the descent, and another one-eighty to wind back to the original direction.

"Where are the actual exhibits?" I ask.

"On the lower level," Aiden says.

"What's with the downward maze?" Emmet asks.

Aiden and Dillan have given up on winding back and forth and are jumping up and over the half-walls dividing the ramp. "You've obviously never been here during the summer," Aiden says.

"I've never been here at all," I correct him.

"Well, it's packed...like can't move the stroller, can't see anything, stupid busy packed. This whole section of winding back and forth is crowd control."

We reach the bottom of the ramp and run smack into our green-skinned girlies outside the Fancy Fins Mermaid Boutique. They have swirling balls of water dancing on their palms with their fingers curled up to expose the webbing of their hands.

As we approach, they draw their arms back and start shooting water balls like this is a snowball fight.

I duck the globe that flies at my head and bat the second one out of the air. There's no way we're getting out of here without being drenched, so why try?

Tourists screech and run past us to get back up the ramp. I hope Sloan and Calum are doing okay catching people at the door but honestly, there's no way we're capping the exposure on this.

Sure, Sloan's handling the panic at the entrance but if this is one-way traffic, there must be an entirely different stream of people rushing out the exit.

Our only hope to make this go away is that Dan the djinn is here and he's clearing the memories of the people rushing out the other door.

A water ball hits me in the shoulder and splashes in my face. "What the hell? You girls realize this is blatant exposure, right? Garnet is going to come after you and your leader hard. Does Malachi even know you're here?"

The two of them break out into a fit of giggles and run off deeper into the aquarium.

The leader of the water nixies of Toronto is a putztastic schmuck named Malachi. The first time I met him on the riverboat luncheon of Lakeshore Guild members, he got royally put out because I wouldn't let him play with Bruin.

In hindsight, I should've let him and given Bruin permission to eat the bastard.

He was also the one who insisted I slighted him by saying Maxwell didn't have to marry the nixie twins when Dionysus accidentally roofied him.

He's a schmuck with an inflated ego and a need to feel important.

We chase after the nixie girls into the water tunnel, and I admit, it's kinda spectacular. There's a six-foot arched pathway meandering through a massive water world. It's glass on all sides and arched overhead so the sea life completely surrounds us.

Colorful fish, jellyfish, sharks, stingrays, and thousands of other waterborne creatures are swimming beside us, above us, and around us.

"Are those sea turtles?"

Dillan chuffs beside me. "Here's another great idea. Let's focus on everything going to shit around us and look at the fishies later."

"Sea turtles are reptiles, but I get your point."

"Alligator!" Emmet shouts.

I'm about to explain to him that there's no way an alligator could live in a giant fish tank when I realize he's not pointing up at the aquarium. He's pointing down the pathway at the ten-foot reptile scrambling toward us and snapping its jaws.

"Beast Bond," I say, focused on making a connection with the beast before he's in chomping range.

Usually, when I reach out with my druid connection, I get a sense of the animal and its willingness to bond or not. In this case, my intention to bond goes out, but nothing comes back at me except a metaphorically magical brick wall. I try again.

"Animal Friendship." Our group has stopped chasing the nixies and is now backing up step-by-step. "Is anyone getting a sense of this alligator? It's not responding to me at all."

"That's because it's not an alligator," Da says, frowning. "It's a shapeshifter here to cause trouble."

I'm not sure how my father knows that, but there's no time to ask him. If this is a shapeshifter here to amplify the chaos, this isn't a nixie prank—this is an outright assault on the secrecy of the empowered community.

"Well, that changes things. There's no need for us to protect the animal and go on the defensive. If you want trouble, asshat, we'll give you some."

Since there are no other humans in the tunnel, I raise my palm and advance. *"Control Animal."*

I take his control from him and lock him down. In human form, this wouldn't work, but in his shifted form, he's as much animal as any other. The moment my spell hits him, I freeze him on the spot and hold him prisoner.

Grabbing his tail, I secure it against my hip and start dragging him toward the others. "You're gonna make a nice pair of boots, dumbass. Nikon, snap him to the holding cell at the Batcave. I'll deal with him after I take care of the nixie uprising."

"You got it, Red." Nikon strides over.

Before the Greek takes possession of the alligator's tail, a surge of magic snaps in the air, and I'm holding the feet of a very annoyed man. "Let go of me."

I do as he asks, but there's no worry of him getting away. There are enough of us down here that he's surrounded. In fact, there are too many of us. "Who wants to take care of alligator boy?"

"I've got him," Dillan says. "Hey Greek, how about that lift to the Batcave?"

"Yep. Meet you guys back—what the hell is that?"

All eyes sweep toward the aquatic wonderland beside us, and yep...today is full of surprises.

"Is that a merman?" I stare at the guy with a blue, glittery tail doing corkscrew spins in the water of the tank. "Huh...I didn't know we have those."

"Believe it or not, no, I wasn't talking about him." Nikon points at what looks like a cat-sized rat with clothes swimming inside the aquarium water. "Him! What the hell is that?"

"That's a Fir Darrig," Da says. "Nasty buggers."

As we watch, the rat thing swims over to the glass next to us, flips in the water, and backs up to the thick glass wall.

"What is ugly rat boy doing?" Dillan asks.

In answer, a bass sound reverberates against the glass, and a rush of bubbles rise from his ass.

"Charming." I blink, wide-eyed. "Nikon, any chance you want to snap in there and grab Mr. Fart Bubbles to take with you?"

"Hard pass, Red," Nikon says. "I heart you huge, but a man has gotta have limits."

"Farting rat fae is over that line?"

"By quite a bit, yes."

I laugh and give him that one. "I accept that. We'll fish him and the merman out of there once we get control of the nixies."

Emmet has his phone out and is now taking a video of Mr. Fart Bubbles sending us a second message.

As the vibration of his ass-air rumbles in the tunnel, I roll my eyes at my brother. "Really? Have you never heard Kinu say we're supposed to ignore bad behavior, so it stops?"

Emmet laughs. "You never know. We might need this as evidence of his behavior later."

I roll my eyes and wave away Nikon, Dillan, and the man formerly identifying as an alligator. "Hurry back, boys. There's still plenty of fun to be had."

After they snap out, the rest of us continue through to the end of the aquarium tunnel and end up in the discovery center looking at a bunch of nixies playing in the touch pond of the stingrays.

"Should they be in there with them?" Emmet asks. "I'm quite sure if you're not supposed to tap on the glass, then you shouldn't be jumping around in the touch tank when it's filled with baby rays."

"Agreed. Let's get them out of there." Rushing forward, I scan the room. When I'm sure no innocents are hiding in any of the corners, I raise my hands. *"Tidal Wave."*

A wall of water rises from the touch pond and knocks the nixies flying out of the shallow basin and onto the floor.

The scene reminds me of my last fight with irate nixies, but this time there are no fun inflatables to catch the rush of water and no skinny-dippers in Dionysus' indoor kiddy pool.

One of the male nixies scrambles along the tile and regains his footing quicker than I expect. He rights himself and launches at me, spewing saltwater.

As the stream of saltwater hits my mouth and burns my nostrils, I twist my head and spit it out. "What is it about nixies and spitting in my face?"

"It's a thing." Nikon returns from his trip to the Batcave. "I learned that myself earlier."

I barely hear the amusement in Nikon's words as I backhand the guy across the face and knock him on his ass. "Spitting is gross and will never win a fight. Stop doing it and sack up."

Nikon barks a laugh.

I turn to scowl at him, and he's biting his bottom lip, chuckling. "I'm glad you find this amusing, Greek. Maybe I should've made you go get the farting rat-man out of the fish tank after all."

That only makes him laugh harder.

Thankfully, Emmet has put away his phone and is wrestling nixie protesters to the ground. *"Hold Foe."* He immobilizes them as he moves through the opposition with my father and brothers.

"Do you want all these troublemakers taken to the Batcave too, Red?" Nikon asks.

"Yeah. We'll let Garnet sort them out and decide what he wants to do with them."

"You can't do anything with us," one of the females says. "In a few weeks, it won't matter. Once we shift the balance of power, we won't have to hide in the shadows any longer."

I chuckle. "So, what? Do you honestly think Team Evil will get the upper hand, and all of a sudden the humans will welcome you into their society?"

"It doesn't matter what humans want or don't want. The fact is we live here too and are tired of being considered second-rate citizens."

I push her toward Emmet to subdue her with the others. The boys have them under control, so I assess where we are. "Aiden? How much more aquarium is there for us to secure?"

"Not much. That's the ramp to go back upstairs."

"Cool, can you and Dillan go up and make sure the rest of this place is locked down? We'll be right up as soon as Nikon transports these to Garnet. Oh, and ask a staff member how to access the aquarium waters. The merman and the rat boy still need to be gathered."

"On it."

Aiden and Dillan jog up the ramp and I frown at our captives.

"What's with the face, *mo chroi*? Ye look upset."

"Yes and no. As much as I object to this whole display of fear-mongering and shock value, the truth is I don't disagree with the reason they did this. People deserve to live freely and be who they are. If communities of citizens aren't hurting anyone and only want equality among their peers, is it wrong to fight for change?"

"I suppose that depends on how they go about putting change into effect."

"Oh, yeah. I'm with you on that. There's not one part of this childish tantrum that garners any sympathy from me. These people aren't fighting for equality. They're thumbing their noses at Garnet and the Guild and everything it stands for."

"Agreed. It's a complex problem."

"Yeah, but we don't have time to spend on it right now. There are life and death issues on the horizon."

"Maybe time is runnin' out on their patience. There's only so long ye can push a beach ball beneath the surface before it bursts out of the water."

I think about that and nod. "Do you think the secrecy of the empowered community has served its purpose, and we need to reevaluate it?"

Da shrugs. "That's above my pay grade, baby girl. I'm retired, remember? I spent the last thirty years playing the part of the peacekeeper, the referee, and the guardian. I passed that mantle on. Now it's yer turn to help shape the world into a better place."

I glance around the mess of the aquarium and wonder where to begin to make this better.

"Okay, you stay here while Em and Nikon work on taking the nixies to the holding cell. I'll continue upstairs and see how Dillan and Aiden are doing."

Da nods. "Let's clean up this mess."

Emmet snorts. "Do you think that's possible, Da? I mean, how many people ran out the exit while we were still coming through from the entrance? Hell, how many left before we even got here?"

He's not wrong.

"Maybe Dan the djinn can fix things with a blanket mind sweep," I say.

Da frowns. "It feels like we're patching up a leaky boat more and more."

"True story. For now, we sweep what we can back under the rug. We'll revisit the secrecy of the empowered world in a couple of weeks. We have enough to worry about at the moment."

"Preach." Emmet pulls one of the males to his feet. "One day at a time, my peeps. One day at a time."

CHAPTER FIVE

"What the hell happened, Fi?" Garnet points at the wall of monitors lit up with all kinds of aquarium chaos. "We have confirmed exposure popping up all over the place."

I scan the images and yep, it's as bad as I feared. Videos of green girls with gills and a merman and all kinds of magical mischief have been posted all over social media.

"Sorry, boss man. It was a big place, and we had a dozen empowered actively sending up magic flares trying to get attention. I hoped the djinn squad could clean up anyone who got through the cracks."

"Dan did his best, but several people had already posted videos before the djinn arrived."

"Stupid cellphones."

He nods. "They're an inescapable part of our world now. It doesn't matter what's going on. We have to assume someone is hanging around, witnessing it, and likely videoing it."

"Oh, look, I'm famous." I point at the video of me calling the tidal wave and frown. "There was no one in the room when I did that. I double-checked."

"That lovely addition to the insanity came directly from the aquarium security feed."

I close my eyes and draw a deep breath. *Dammit.* "That's one hundy percent my fault. With all the excitement, I gapped out on the recordings from the security cameras. I'm sorry."

Garnet doesn't look angry. He lifts a muscled shoulder and shrugs. "It happens. Anyx got to them before you guys left, but the video was already out. Everyone wants to be the one to go viral these days."

I scan the proof of myth and magic, live and in color, and sigh. "What do we do now?"

"I'll put Emmet and Tad on removing what they can from the web and tracking down anyone posting. Then, I'll send Dan and the djinns around to wipe memories."

"And if that doesn't clean it all up?"

"Then we claim fake news and discredit what people think they're seeing. The world is unreliable. People are unsure what to believe on a good day."

"Today isn't one of those."

"No. Unfortunately, it's not."

I watch the video I'm starring in again and grin. It's a total clusterfuck, no denying that, but *dayam*...I look good getting my druid on.

Of course, I don't say that in front of Garnet.

"What can I do to help?" I ask.

He waggles his brows at me. "You're coming with Andromeda, Maxwell, and me to speak to Malachi about the involvement of the nixies."

I groan. "Malachi? He's my punishment for failing you, isn't he?"

He growls, his lion weighing in. "You *didn't* fail me, Fi. I'd never think that. You and yours did your best to navigate a tough situation, and the wind blew against us this time around. We can't win them all."

"*Buuut?*"

"But you did overlook an important aspect of our security protocols."

"And you're punishing me."

"No. I'm reinforcing the importance of excellence by introducing a negative consequence."

I chuckle. "You can put lipstick on a pig, boss man, but it's still a pig."

Garnet's mouth curls up at the sides. It's not quite a smile, but it's definitely more amusement than when I first got here. "Fine. Malachi is your atonement pig. We will go question him, you will be twice as diplomatic as you think you're capable of, and I will decide what I want to do about his involvement."

"Why me? You know he hates me?"

He grins. "Exactly right, Lady Druid. Nixies are devious and untrustworthy bastards. They are so content to lie that even shifters can't always scent the deception."

"My presence will make him tell the truth?"

"No. With you there, he'll be so emotional and focused on making me punish you for once again picking on his people that he'll forget to guard his deceptions."

"*Noice.* So, my mere presence makes me the bad cop in this interrogation and will rattle his cage."

Garnet chuckles. "Now you're getting it. Still, you have to try to make it seem like we're being diplomatic. He's not the brightest star in the night sky, but he's an important one."

I snort. "Yeah right."

"No. I'm serious."

I gauge his expression, and yeah, he is serious. "How is Malachi important? Are the water nixies more powerful than I'm aware of? Malachi sits way down at the far end of the table during monthly meetings."

"That's true, but do you know who Malachi is bonded with and has been sleeping with for almost three years?"

I picture the man in a romantic light and scrunch my face up at him. "Ew...thankfully, no."

"Are you curious?"

I roll my eyes. "Well, I am now. Okay, hit me. Who is Malachi's special squeeze?"

"Janeera Hanlon."

I stare at him. "Well, that was anticlimactic. I thought it would be someone I know. Should I know who that is?"

Garnet pegs me with a patient stare and lets out a soft growl. "She's the woman you refer to as High Priestess Drippy Face."

I chuckle. "Oh! Yeah, sorry. I do know her."

"Yes, you do. Do you recall where she sits at the table during the monthly meetings?"

"Right next to Nikon and me."

"Exactly. Nikon's powers are pure and strong, gifted by the fae Source itself. Yours are active and growing, gifted to you by Fionn. Hers are learned and bolstered by the witches in her coven. It's not the same kind of power, but it's power all the same."

"So, why is she sleeping with Malachi? That makes no sense to me."

He shrugs. "Maybe he's a dynamo in the sheets. I couldn't tell you. What's important is that the two of them have been an item for years. If we're accusing him and the nixies of something, we better be very sure of ourselves because to piss him off means we're also alienating the Toronto Coven of Witches."

"Ugh, why does everything have to be so political?"

"Because we're talking about politics."

"Right. There's that."

Andromeda and Maxwell come out of their offices. Maxwell is shrugging on his jacket, and Andy is already dolled up and looking like a power player with her long, cashmere coat and her briefcase in hand. "All right." She strides over to join us. "Are we ready to do this?"

Maxwell nods. "Can't wait. Looking forward to it. Still not sure why I have to come."

I chuckle at the total lack of enthusiasm and feel for the guy. His last legal run-in with the nixie community was a big embarrassment for him and indirectly my fault.

Oops. I didn't anticipate how long Dionysus' learning curve would be while integrating him into modern society.

Garnet extends his hands to touch my shoulder and Andromeda's. She reaches to take Maxwell's hand, and a surge of Garnet's magical signature builds. "Here's to a successful and uneventful afternoon."

I laugh. "I'm sure that's what we have to look forward to. After all, in my life, everything goes according to Hoyle."

Garnet flashes us to Stephenson's Swamp, the wetland at the mouth of the Highland Creek Watershed. It's about twenty minutes from my house, but not somewhere I had gone before he brought me here to formally apologize for pissing off a pair of entitled nixie twins.

"So, where do you think they meet up for the horizontal hijinks?" I ask, my curiosity piqued. "Does the high priestess slum it in the swamp bogs or does her frog prince come to her?"

The soft rumble of Garnet's lion vibrates in my chest. "Not the time or the place, Lady Druid."

I hear what he's saying, but honestly, we haven't even started approaching Malachi's meeting house yet. "Yes, boss. Consider me on my best behavior."

"I could only hope."

"Do they know we're coming?" I ask.

"They know *I'm* coming and bringing Guild counsel. I'm entitled to bring whoever I choose to accompany me, but figured I'd leave your attendance as a surprise."

I chuckle. "The unwelcome surprise meant to knock him off-balance."

"Something like that."

The four of us meander up the natural path from the edge of Lake Ontario. As we work our way inland toward the reserve land where the water nixies live, the evergreen growth blocks the bite of the breeze. A decent tree-filled area creates a green belt between the wetland and the urban cityscape on the other side.

"What about the nixies we arrested?" I ask. "Will you release them back to Malachi?"

"That depends on how this meeting goes. We need to ascertain how much knowledge Malachi had of the aquarium plan. Was it his subjects acting out of line or was he behind it and making a play?"

I consider that. "That's what still isn't adding up for me. If all this was about fighting for the right to live life out in the open—"

My words cut off as my shield flares hot.

I call my armor forward and shift closer to Andromeda. "On your toes, people. We have trouble."

Maxwell stiffens and Garnet curses.

Searching for what tripped my warning, I point. "Incoming."

Blow darts suddenly pepper the air, coming at us hard and fast.

"Gale Force." I swipe my hands through the air and direct the sudden surge of wind to the side and away from us. "Based on my shield's fiery intensity, I'd say they tipped those darts with something nasty."

Garnet pulls his Sig Sauers from his dual shoulder holsters, and we tighten the ranks. "Maxwell, you've got Andromeda. Fi, you're with me. If Bruin's here, he can take point. I want him to maim, not kill."

"Yep, cover me for two secs."

"Do your thing."

Bruin, did you hear that, buddy? We've got trouble.

Maim? That's no fun.

Sorry. Not my call.

The sensation of my bear fluttering around in my chest is always a comfort to me. I release him and smile as he swirls once around me before shooting off into the distance to take out the trash.

With him deployed, I step back from Maxwell and Andy, hold up my free hands, and focus on encasing them in a bubble of protection. *"Impenetrable Sphere."*

When the iridescent bubble of my shielding surrounds them, I fall in behind Garnet, call Birga to my palm, and nod. "S'all good. On your six."

Garnet eyes the sphere and grins. "That's new."

"A month or two now. We've been working our asses off. Lots of new little tricks in my bag."

Another round of projectiles flies through the winter-bare foliage. I blow them into the trees and render them useless like the first ones. Scanning the evergreen screen in front of us, I search for whoever is behind this.

"A-hunting we will go. A-hunting we will go. Heigh-ho the derry-o." I pause and take stock of the surroundings. "What actually *is* a derry-o?"

Garnet flashes me his teeth and tilts his head toward the trees. "Let's go find out."

I've fought with Garnet Grant a bunch of times over the eighteen months since Fionn woke my druid powers and named me as his successor. In those times, I've fought *with* him, and on occasion, *against* him.

I much prefer the former.

Garnet comes off as a brutally dangerous man who can snap a

man's neck then play unicorn dance party with his little girl without a second thought.

That's because he *is* that man.

True story. I've seen it happen.

Beyond the man's lethal predilections, there are the savage instincts of the alpha lion within. I met head-to-head with his animal side while Eros' love spell possessed him. The beast is a foe to be respected and avoided.

So, why attack the lion who runs your world?

The only answer I can come up with is that whoever is ambushing us doesn't intend to live in that world much longer—one way or another.

Either they plan to die trying to kill the apex predator who runs their empowered community, or they think the empowered community needs new leadership to take it in a different direction.

"Is this a Team Evil *coup d'état*?" I scan the snow-dusted landscape between the fir and spruce trees.

"Maybe." Garnet's voice is a growl, and his eyes are no longer the normal amethyst purple I'm used to but the cool amber of his lion ascending. "And here I thought today would be just another day."

"Best laid plans, my friend. Like they say...always wear your good undies when you go out. You never know what the night will bring."

Garnet chuckles. "I'll remember that."

We stalk forward and are barely a hundred feet deeper into the forest when the next barrage of attacks hit. This round of assault is magical. Green balls and purple bolts of crackling energy shoot out from behind the trees and finally give us a target to focus on.

I don't need to check with Garnet to see if he traced the trajectory back to the source. He's as quick as I am at deducing where our enemy lies in wait.

The two of us break left and right and race through the trees toward whoever thinks they can take us out. There's a moment when I'm maneuvering behind a thick cluster of evergreen growth when I lose sight of Garnet.

The sharp crack of his gun discharging has me pushing harder on my muscles and digging in on my run. Then I hear Bruin roar in the same area, and my heart rate calms a little. If Bruin's on the scene, Garnet doesn't need me to back him up.

I continue alone to where the green globes fired through the trees. High Priestess Drippy Face has never interested me, but if she's entangled in this mess and her witches are coming after us, consider me intrigued.

My breath escapes in clouds of white condensation with each quick stride forward. The wetland has gone quiet, the whippoorwill's song silenced by the disturbance of battle. My thumping boot falls are the only sound as I close the distance.

An energy bolt hits my side, but with my armor up it does nothing more than spin me on my feet as I run. It also changes my focus because the hit came from a different direction entirely.

My witch bitch is on the move.

I alter my course and race around a fluffy blue spruce. Four attackers drop from the branches above to surround me.

Good. I'm tired of chasing these asshats. Let the melee begin. "Running around to find a foe is tiring. Thanks for dropping in so we could get things started."

By their creased brows, I take it that wasn't the reaction they were expecting.

What? Was I supposed to cower? Not bloody likely.

A quick assessment of my attackers gives me two male nixies and two witches. By their stances, it seems the witches might be in charge of my ambush.

Huh...maybe High Priestess Drippy Face is more involved in this uprising than Garnet suspected.

Twirling Birga in my hands, I shift my stance, making a slow circle as I take in my competition. "I don't know who pissed in your cornflakes this morning, boys and girls, but you chose the wrong people to take it out on. I suggest you walk away while you're still able to walk at all."

The witches are far more confident than the nixies—or I suppose arrogant would be more accurate. The two women stand opposite one another, and as I rotate to keep everyone in my sights, it's them who I size up as the larger threat.

"Are you sure you want to do this, ladies? I'll tell you right now that it won't end well for you. How about you stand down, and I tell Garnet you saw reason and he should be lenient with you? This is you following your leadership, amirite?"

My welcoming committee doesn't feel like talking at the moment. They also don't seem to feel like standing down. I sense the buildup of their next attack before the sparks of power begin to swirl in their palms.

Whatevs. We can do this the hard way too.

I watch the glances exchanged between the four and soon understand their unspoken conversation. The witch in charge wants the nixie with the seaweed hair to charge me, but he wants her to start her magical assault first, so he has a better chance of taking me down.

"Are you afraid to fight me, big guy?" I hold up a finger to qualify my question. "Sorry, did that come out judgy? I didn't mean it to. What I meant was, are your instincts warning you not to engage?"

"Don't listen to her," the witch says. "She's trying to get in your head."

I wave that away. "No, for reals. I didn't mean it as a jab. It's smart for you to assess me as a foe and if you're any good at it, you already figured out I'm gonna kick your ass."

That slaps him right in the ego. "Maybe you overestimate yourself, druid. Or maybe you're the one who isn't good at assessing your opponent."

I shake my head, continuing to shift my footing to keep everyone in sight. "No. Let's go over it for our viewers at home so we're all on the same page. You have two choices of attack. As a nixie, your connection is with water, and you could come at me with either snow or ice since that's what we have around us. Your other choice is to use physical force."

His gaze narrows and I fight not to chuckle. Did he honestly think I couldn't figure that out?

"If you go with snow or ice, I'll counter and render your attack useless. I can do that because I'm a druid and my dominion is *all* of nature. I'll dispel your attack, then use the ground, the trees, the wind, and everything around me to take you down."

His expression tells me he hadn't thought of that.

"So that leaves physical force. I'm not being a bitch by saying so, but I've got you there too."

I hold up a finger when they look skeptical. "I know you're thinking, you're men, and I'm a five-and-a-half-foot girl. True story, but I can call *Bestial Strength* and take you all to town. Also, with my armor activated, there's nothing you can do to hurt me or bring me down. Sorry, dudes, you're outmatched."

"You talk too much, female."

"You're not the first person to tell me that. The point is, I'm not wrong."

His expression darkens. "Call whatever spell you want, bitch. You're not making it out of this forest." He lifts his chin and brushes back his seaweed hair.

Then, he bends his knees and launches.

"Bestial Strength." The power of my spell feeds my cells, and I launch forward to meet his attack. As we engage, I reach back and plow a solid punch into the softness of his belly. A rush of breath and a groan leak out of him as he doubles over.

The witch to my right lets loose with her ball of energy. I shift to face her, choke up on Birga's staff, and line-drive it into the second nixie male.

As he screams and throws himself onto the crust of the snow, I raise Birga, brace her with both hands, and ready for the first nixie male to grab at me.

He's recovered from getting hand-hammered to the breadbasket and is angry.

When he grabs Birga's staff, I use his forward momentum to my advantage. Rolling backward, I get my boots up to brace against his hips and give him a druid super-duper airplane ride.

As he rises over me, instead of balancing him in the air with my feet, I thrust my legs and launch him. He sails eight feet behind me and cracks into the wide trunk of an elm tree.

The hollow *thunk* as he hits is satisfying, and I roll back to my feet. No time to enjoy that because one of the witch's green energy bombs hits my shoulder and explodes in my face.

Rude.

I twist, smacking the spent spell away. The rancid smell of burning nylon singes my nose. "Dammit. I liked this coat, too."

Diving out of the line of fire from the next assault, I grab a handful of snow and rub it across the shriveling fabric. I find I fight better when I'm not on fire.

Once I put out the smoldering, I get a proper hold on Birga and—since the nixie males are both down and out—go after the witches.

The two of them are confident, but that's fine. Once I drop one of them, the other will lose her nerve. I target the one who pits herself as the leader and move in fast.

Running forward, I drop and slide on my hip. With my hand running along the ground, I call my connection to the earth. *"Erupting Earth. Ice Storm. Vine Whip."*

As the snow around us lifts in a cyclone of ice pellets, the earth heaves, and I reinvigorate the twigs and vines dying on the ground and call them into service.

The witch might have been able to defend against one or maybe two of my spells, but three draws her focus enough that I launch to my feet with my *Bestial Strength* still in play and ram Birga into her thigh.

The sound of bone cracking echoes loud enough it's heard over the force of my winter storm, and I grin.

Yanking my knife out of my thigh sheath, I grab the downed witch's hands and peg her friend with a glare. "Witches don't need hands to cast magic, do you? Drop it, or your friend here becomes a stump sorceress."

The terror in their eyes is real.

The second witch drops her hands and her orbs of energy dissipate.

"What say you, ladies? Are you ready to tell me what the hell is going on? Who put you up to this?"

They look at me and say nothing.

"Okay, blink when I get close. Your high priestess brought you here to defend the nixies."

Still nothing.

I tug the witch's hands out from her body and level my knife on her wrists. "I gave you a chance. Don't say I didn't warn you."

Blinking…blinking…lots of blinking.

"Okay, good. I'm glad you decided to play my game. So, High Priestess Drippy Face said let's help the nixies. If we take out Garnet, we won't have to live in the shadows any longer. Am I close?"

No blinking.

"You were trying to take out Garnet, right?"

No blinking.

"Is it me you're after?"

No blinking.

I frown. "Are you playing *no hablo nada*? Because if you think I'm bluffing about your hands—"

"It's not about you two," the girl blurts.

"Not us? But the only other people here were…" My mind spins at double time and my heart sinks. "Shit. "Who are you after, Andromeda or Maxwell?"

"The Greek lawyer."

Andromeda. "Why? What do you want with her?"

The witch pants and I can see she's fighting not to lose consciousness. "I don't know the details. It's something about her being a conduit of Source magic."

Fuckety-fuck. Dropping her to the frozen ground, I turn and run like the wind. Reaching into my jacket, I grab my Team Trouble pendant and press it as my feet crunch through the frozen crust of the forest.

"Bruin! Protect Andromeda!" I'm not sure if he can hear me or where the hell he is. I don't stop to find out.

Pumping my arms, I push hard to get back to where all this started. "She'll be fine," I say, trying to reassure myself. "I put her in a sphere…"

I round the last of the evergreens and stumble to a stop. Dropping to my knees, I pant for breath and stare at the empty pathway.

Nikon appears thirty feet closer to the lake with Calum, Sloan, Dionysus, Tad, and Emmet. "Red, what's wrong?"

"They took her, Greek. I'm so sorry."

"Sorry? Who, Fi? What are you talking about?"

"Andromeda…they took your sister."

CHAPTER SIX

Nikon grows eerily still as that sinks in, then he scans the pathway. "Tell me what happened. Who took her?"

My mental hamster is starting to put things together. "I think the aquarium outburst was a decoy. Someone here wanted to cause a major event that breached the rules so Garnet would bring Andromeda to explain next steps and reparations."

"Why would they want Andy?" Calum asks. "Are they trying to blackmail Garnet into something?"

"I don't think so. The witch bitch I questioned said they want her because she's a conduit for Source power."

Nikon curses. "How the fuck did they find that out?"

There is a very small group of people aware of the origin story of how the Tsambikos family gained immortality, and most of that circle is here with us. "Well, *I* certainly didn't tell them, and neither would anyone in my family."

Nikon catches his temper and scrubs his fingers over the back of his neck. "No. Of course, you wouldn't. Forgive me."

I let the tension go and shake it off. "No worries, Greek. I wrote the book on overprotective cray-cray when it comes to siblings."

Calum and Emmet both nod. "True story."

"Who told ye about Andromeda, *a ghra?*" Sloan asks. "Start from the beginning, luv."

I twist and point into the trees. "Walk and talk."

As the seven of us storm through the trees of the wetland, I relay the past half hour to catch everyone up. How Garnet enlisted me to play bad cop and figure out what the aquarium exposure was about, how Andromeda and Maxwell were here to represent the legal side of things, and how we thought the attack was on Garnet.

"Where is Garnet?" Calum asks.

"He ran off that way shooting at people. Bruin was with him at some point, but I haven't seen them in a bit."

Sloan nods. "Go. We'll be here when ye get back."

Dionysus, Calum, and Emmet go to find Garnet and offer him backup. Sloan, Nikon, and I continue toward the spot where I fought my four.

"I enclosed them in an impenetrable sphere before I left them. I thought they would be safe. Nikon, I swear, if I thought there was any danger to her, I never would have left her."

"I know that, Fi. I do."

I blink against the tears stinging my eyes. "I thought the nixies and witches were taking a run at Garnet and Guild leadership. It's been that kind of a week."

"It has."

"The good news is she's not alone," Sloan says. "If both Andromeda and Maxwell were in Fi's sphere, then whoever took them took both of them."

I nod. "While he might seem like a no-nonsense Anderson Cooper, Maxwell climbed the ranks of the policing system as a Mountie. He's got skills."

Sloan untucks the tail of his scarf and brushes it under my eyes to catch the few tears that leaked out. "Maxwell is a smart man and very capable. Let's focus on finding out who took them, where they are now, and how to get them back."

Nikon is still all kinds of stiff and angry but offers me a smile. "Yes, let's."

The three of us make our way back to the spot where I left my opponents, but they've all cleared out. We course-correct to find Garnet and the others, and my beloved bear soon joins us.

"Are ye all right, Red?" He materializes among us as we walk.

"Yeah. Did the boys tell you about Andromeda?"

"They did. Give my regrets to Nikon."

I relay Bruin's condolences, but I don't think it offers Nikon any comfort.

As we jog through the windswept landscape, I send Nikon a reassuring smile. "We'll gather Garnet, get back to the Batcave, track Maxwell and Andromeda's pendants, and thoroughly kick the asses of whoever dared to take one of ours."

"This way, Red." Bruin trots off to the left.

I release Birga to her resting place and tuck my pendant into my sweater. One of the smartest things Garnet did was develop these security pendants. Not only do they unlock the front doors and call for help, but they also have a GPS tracker with almost pinpoint accuracy.

"There." I point at a flash of blue between the trees. "If nothing else, Emmet's coat is visible a mile away."

Sloan chuckles. "If nothing else…I'm sure it's warm too, luv. It does serve a purpose."

"I should hope so. If he's subjecting us to looking at that Stay Puft monstrosity, it better at least be warm."

Emmet straightens from where he's leaning against a tree and scowls at us. "Are you dumbasses bad-mouthing my coat again?"

"Who, us?" I press my hand against my chest and look innocent. "No, why? What's wrong with your coat? It's so puffy and blue."

Emmet middle-fingers me and tilts his head to where Garnet and Calum are questioning a nixie male. Nikon rushes over to see what's happening and sucker-punches the guy in the gut.

As the nixie doubles over sputtering, I recognize him as one of the males I took down earlier. "Hey, dude. How's things? Is your day improving any?"

He glares at me.

"Remember what I said about assessing your foe to determine if you're man enough to come out on top? I'll give you a hint. There's no one here you want to take on. So, considering you're outnumbered eight to one, not including my very cantankerous battle bear, give it up now and answer the questions."

The guy sneers at me. "Such an annoying female."

I chuckle. "Yeah, well, I grow on people."

Emmet snorts. "Like fungus."

"Or mold," Calum adds.

I flick my hand at them, and the tree above them shakes its limbs and dumps snow down the necks of their jackets. "How about, I'm an acquired taste. Like a rare vintage of fine wine."

"How about we find out who the fuck wants to take me down?" Garnet growls.

"You weren't the target, boss man. They drew us away while they snatched Andromeda. I went back when I found out, but they'd already taken her and Maxwell."

Garnet's ebony brows furrow. "Everyone, back to the office. I will deal with Malachi and Janeera later."

My brothers look blank.

"Who's Janeera?" Calum asks. "Have we got a new player on the board?"

I shake my head. "It's High Priestess Drippy Face."

Everyone nods, Garnet growls at me, and we all close

in. When everyone is connected, we flash into the elevator bank outside the Batcave, and Dionysus opens things up.

Technically, he's the only one of us with the juice to transport straight into our clubhouse, but he loves to use his pendant to let us in.

To him, it's a symbol of belonging. He thinks he's lucky to have us.

Nope. For reals, it's the other way around.

When we get inside, Garnet hands the nixie off to Dionysus. "Put him in the holding cell with his friends from the aquarium. Boys, do your computer magic and get us a location."

While Dionysus frog-marches the nixie off to the back, Emmet and Tad jog over to the computer terminal and call up the locators in Andromeda's and Maxwell's pendants.

"They're together," Emmet shouts, his fingers gliding over the electronic keyboard on the surface of the table. "And still in Toronto."

"Good." Garnet turns with his phone in hand and flashes his teeth. "That means I have jurisdiction and can handle this my way."

With the growl of that statement still rumbling in the air around us, he hits send and presses his phone against his ear. "It's me. Round up the pride and be ready to battle. I'll send you an address in a moment."

He hangs up and meets my curious gaze. "Andromeda might be Nikon's sister and your friend, but she's a key player in the structure of my world and mine to protect. We will handle this as an assault on my family."

Oh, this is going to get bloody.

"Does that mean we're part of the lion pride too?" Dionysus materializes and whispers in my ear as Garnet jogs to his office.

"I guess so. We're part of his team and key players in the empowered policing world."

Dionysus grins, and his clothes change from jeans and a

cream cable-knit sweater to black khakis and a military vest like Garnet's team wears. "My life has gotten much more interesting since you came into it, Jane."

"That's what happens when you spend more than ten minutes at a time sober."

"What was the point of being sober when life was boring? Potato-tomato."

I chuckle. I don't think he understands that idiom but why ruin his fun?

"Fi? What's happened?" Aiden pushes through the entrance with Dillan hot on his heels.

They're both in uniform and had to drive here while on duty. Thankfully, because of Maxwell's SITFU task force, they can tap out of beat duty any time we need them.

Dillan scans the room, and I know he's taking inventory of our friends and family. It's what we all do when there's trouble. "We got the all-call, but no one came to get us, so we came here."

"Sorry, good call. We're figuring out where we need to go. Witches took Andromeda and Maxwell."

They both react to that the same way we did.

"Why them?" Dillan asks.

I give them the Cliff Notes version and get them up to speed.

"We're ready to move," Calum says, joining us.

"Can you go like that?" I ask. "There's really no time to waste *poofing* home to change."

Aiden chuffs. "We go into battle every day on the streets dressed like this. We don't need to wear khakis and weapons vests to take on empowered assholes."

"No. I suppose not."

"How's Nikon hanging in?" Aiden asks.

I turn to study Nikon over by Emmet and Tad. The Greek is wired. He's wringing his hands together and looks ready to burst. "He's understandably worried."

When Garnet comes back from his office, he hesitates for a

moment, takes in the arrival of Dillan and Aiden, and closes ranks. "All right, Anyx and my team are in position on the rooftop of the building across the street here." He points at the map. "Prepare to join them to assist in the takedown."

Emmet sends one last *ping* to ensure the signal is active and still located where we expect it to be. When the responding intel comes back, he nods. "Game on."

We gather 'round and make contact to travel.

I hug Nikon's arm and squeeze him. "Right and tight, Greek. It'll be over in a few minutes. There's no way these assholes could predict we'd track them down so quickly. We've got this."

He glances down at me, genuine fear clouding his eyes. "I hope so, Fi. I can't lose her. In a world that's taken so much from me, Andromeda and Politimi are my touchstones. They're my everything."

I'm more determined than ever to ensure Nikon gets a happy ending on this one.

Thankfully, I'm right about us having the element of surprise on our side. The women coming and going from the building below seem oblivious to the fact that they're about to get their lungs ripped out their vajayjays. Then again, they don't look much like witches, so maybe they're ordinary people going to the library, and their vajayjays are safe.

"What are we lookin' at down there?" Sloan asks.

Emmet's already got the Google search underway and reads it out for us. "The Yorkville Branch of the Toronto Library System opened in 1907 and is one of the hundreds of 'Carnegie' libraries built across North America in the early part of the century."

"That's all well and good, Em," Aiden says, "but is there anything useful? Are there hidden passages? Underground tunnels? Hidden entrances?"

"It doesn't say." He flips through a few other articles and searches for a map or a floorplan or anything that will help.

Nothing.

"Here, try this." Garnet calls up something on his phone and taps it against Emmet's. When he steps back, Emmet's eyes widen. "What the what? Where did… How did…"

"Full sentences, Em," Aiden says.

Emmet clamps his mouth shut, scrolls through his screens, then holds up his phone so we can all see. "Well, now that I have Garnet's wonder-app—which is probably illegal in twenty different ways—it looks like it's one big open main floor with bookshelves and computer tables set up."

"That can't be right," I move in. But it is. The images on Emmet's screen are exactly what he described. "It looks like an ordinary library."

"Then we should have no problem walking in the front door to take a look around," Garnet says.

"The witches must be in the basement," Emmet says. "The ceilings are open pitched. It doesn't look like there's an attic or anything above. They've gotta have them below."

As much as I hate going in blind, the fact that the library is open to the public and busy means we can access the building without a fuss.

Garnet leaves a man on the roof, one stationed at the front entrance, and two at the emergency exits.

The rest of us head inside.

"Good afternoon," the woman behind the desk says, standing as twenty of us come through the door at once. "Can I help you find something?"

Aiden and Dillan field that one. They're in uniform and look the most official. "Nothing to be alarmed about, ma'am," Aiden says. "We're looking for a couple who we traced to this area."

Her eyes widen, and she lifts her glasses from where they

hang on the gold granny chain around her neck. "Are they dangerous?"

"No. It's nothing like that. They simply went missing quite abruptly, and we need to ensure they're all right. Their family is understandably upset."

She eyes us, but we're already spreading out to search the place.

"Is there a basement or any kind of secret tunnel system?" Emmet asks as he passes.

She blinks, looking startled by the question. "A basement, yes. It's not part of the book display space, but the washrooms are down there. It only has a three-quarter ceiling in some areas, so people tend to hit their heads. It's where we store books off rotation."

"And tunnels or access to hidden exits?"

"None that I'm aware of, no."

"Access to the basement is where?"

She lifts her hand to point, and I follow the gesture. "Around the computer carrels and to the left."

While they finish the nicey-nice, I strike off and catch sight of a woman racing through a wooden door. "We have a runner."

I take off in pursuit, rushing after her and getting to the door a split second after it slams shut. I try the knob, and the jolt of power that shoots up my arm knocks me staggering back.

"Fucking bitch!" I shout, shaking out my arm.

The outburst goes over amazingly well with the library crowd. Everyone is staring. I want to yell at them to mind their own, but I'm more concerned with not being able to feel my fingers and my arm hanging like a dead branch.

Sloan is at my side a second later, and he can tell by the look on my face I am *not* all right because he doesn't ask. He gives my arm a cursory exam and steps back. "Emmet, stay with yer sister for a moment while Tad and I disarm the door."

"Disarm the door?" Emmet chuckles. "Fi's been disarmed."

I frown at him. "Too soon, Em."

He sobers and sends me a look of apology.

While Sloan and Tad study the doorknob of doom, I go back to freaking out that I can't control my arm.

Emmet grabs my elbow, and a rush of healing warmth flows through my cells. "Zapped you good, eh?"

"Yeah," I pant. "My arm is being a disobedient child. No matter what I tell it to do, it doesn't listen."

Em's healing abilities aren't at the level of Sloan's or Wallace's, but whatever he's doing helps. As the warm tinglies ease my panic, he continues to massage magic into my muscles. "Remember when we went to that farm as kids and Dillan tricked you into grabbing the electric fence? Your fingers tingled for an hour, and you were sure he'd stolen your chance to play the banjo professionally."

I pull a breath into my panicked lungs. "I really wanted to play the banjo."

"You did…until you found out you'd have to take lessons and practice."

"Yeah, so I switched gears and decided to be a professional road hockey player."

"Exactly. My point is, your hand got better, and you went on to slapshot us for years to come. The same will happen here too, Fi. S'all good. You'll see."

"We're in." Tad swings the door open.

Tad, Calum, Aiden, and Dillan rush down ahead of us, and I glance around and notice Garnet, Nikon, and Anyx are already gone. "Did they flash through the door right here in plain sight?"

Sloan nods, wrapping an arm around my back and ushering me toward the basement door. "Believe it or not, yer outburst of profanity served as an effective distraction."

"Sorry not sorry."

I cradle my arm with my good hand and hurry down the stairs with Sloan ahead of me and Emmet at my back. There's a moment during our hasty descent when my stomach lurches and the world spins.

I think my jolt might make me pass out.

We reach the bottom of the stairs and move into the space when it dawns on me. We aren't in the basement the librarian described.

The ceilings are eight feet above our heads if not ten, the floor is dirt and pebbled stone, and the corridor we're rushing through smells like earth and is lit by golden swaths of light from fire-lit torches.

"Am I going into shock?"

Sloan stops walking and takes a moment to look into my eyes. "What makes ye ask that, *a ghra?*"

I scan the corridor, my disorientation growing. "My sense of grounding just got shaky."

"Shaky like how, Fi?" Emmet asks.

"Like a tornado barfed me out, and we're not in Yorkville anymore, Toto." I scan the corridor again, trying to align my reality, but nope.

Something is definitely not right.

CHAPTER SEVEN

The reality of my surroundings settles, and I'm more convinced than ever we've taken a wrong turn. "We're no longer in the basement of the Yorkville Library."

Sloan nods. "Agreed. Tad and I fought with a portal layer in the door. It was tricky to get it to open to the witch's entrance instead of the library, but we got there."

"What do you mean, the witch's entrance?"

"From what we gathered, the witches use the library as a front fer their coven. When they open the door, it seems like they're goin' downstairs but in reality, they portal somewhere else."

"Now we hijacked their portal?"

"Aye, that's the gist of it."

That makes sense, but... "Did Nikon and the lions make it down to this basement or the basement of the library?"

"I'd guess the real library." Tad comes out of a tunnel offshoot ahead of us. "We haven't seen them, or Andromeda and Maxwell, or any witches for that matter. But it's a feckin' maze down here, so there's plenty of ground to cover."

We get moving again, and I try to shake off my haze of mystification. It does no good. Something has gone squirrely inside me, and I can't get rid of the feeling there's more going on here than we understand.

The boys lead the way, and I work on being present in the moment. Maybe it *is* shock from the jolt to my arm. I accept that as a possibility and get with the previously scheduled program—

We need to find Andromeda and Maxwell.

My boots crunch on the pebbled stone floor, and the sound sparks something inside me. I'm whammied by a rush of *déjà vu*. "Whoa, hold up." I stare at an upright chest against the wall. "Yep. It's definitely time for an all-stop here, boys."

I glance back the way we came and forward into the corridor ahead. My instincts are firing like crazy, and I'm still a little light-headed from being witch-smacked.

Sloan steps in beside me and frowns. "Ye look a little sickly, *a ghra*. Are ye sure yer just out of sorts from the witch's shock?"

I take another step closer to the chest and look at the snake carvings twining the edges of the two long doors.

My voice echoes in my head, and I'm revisited by a memory of over a year ago. *"There should be an upright chest on the left that releases poisonous snakes. We have to render them harmless to pass. It says they'll spill out onto the stone of the floor and need to be tamed or convinced we belong here."*

"Crap on a cracker." My jaw drops and I take a quick step back. "I'm finally piecing things together. I think I'm getting it now."

"Getting what, baby girl?" Aiden says. "You're not making much sense."

I point at the chest and look back at them. "Don't you remember? Doesn't this passageway and this chest look familiar to anyone but me?"

They all look rather blank.

I wonder if poisonous snakes are going to pour out and try to kill us but when I decide to walk on, my shield doesn't object so I assume the booby-trap isn't set.

"Follow me." We pass the upright chest and follow the corridor down and to the left. When we make the next turn, I point to the corridor ahead of us. "Picture a landslide of rubble and stone blocking our path. Does that ring any bells for anyone?"

"Och, no," Sloan searches the corridor back the way we came. "Ye don't think…"

"Where the hell are we, Red?" Tad asks.

I nod at Sloan. "Oh, I more than think, hotness. We're in the Fianna fortress. And Tad…the better question is…*when* the hell are we."

My brothers have caught up and seem to agree with my assessment of things.

Dillan pats Aiden's shoulder. "I think you're going to be late for dinner, bro. Either that or really, really early."

I point at the ground as I continue toward the Grand Hall of the Fianna sanctuary. "Aiden, if I'm right, you broke your ribs right around here."

Emmet chuckles. "Then Fi fainted right here." He points to the floor at my feet.

Man, this trip down memory lane is getting trippy.

We continue farther along and pause when we hear muffled male voices. The sound sets the guys all on edge, but not me. "Relax. We're kin to Fionn, we're druids, and he obviously brought us here for a reason."

I pat Sloan's chest with my good hand and take the lead. The closer we get to the Grand Hall, the deeper and gruffer the voices sound. I worry I might have oversold our place here.

Imposter syndrome is real.

Still, I draw a deep breath, lift my chin and step into the entranceway of the main room. "Hello, the house."

Cue the sharp turning of heads and half a dozen men seizing their swords and readying to attack.

"Hold." I try to raise my hand to slow their roll, but my damned arm is still limp-noodling it down my side. "Where's Fionn? He sent for us. We're his kin."

The lead man must be close to six-foot-six and is a beast of a warrior. He has a bushy mane of chestnut hair, a russet red beard, and his eyebrows are as fuzzy as the fuzziest caterpillars.

When he sizes me up, he purses his lips and takes three quick strides at me. "Fionn's only kin are his father's siblings and their young ones. I know the lot of them and have never laid eyes on any of yer lot."

I try to hold out my right arm to show him Birga and call her, but I've got nothing. It's an inconvenient time to lose the function of my arm. "I assure you, we *are* kin. I'm Fiona mac Cumhaill, and these are my brothers, Aiden, Calum, Dillan, and Emmet."

The other men have fanned out and are jiggling their swords in their hands.

"Ye let a woman speak fer yer group?" a guy in the back asks. I recognize the green cloak he wears. Dillan has the same one at home.

"They do at the moment. We've come from a land far from here. They don't speak the language yet, so you'll have to settle for talking to me."

"Well, Fiona," the first man says. "If Fionn truly is yer kin—" his eyes catch on Sloan's hand resting on my shoulder, and he glowers. "Koen, come here to me."

A wiry man with long, mutton chop sideburns and braids in his beard comes to the front of the group.

"Have ye got yer ring or did this fud steal it when we were deep in the ale?"

Koen lifts his hand and uses his thumb to turn the bone ring around his finger.

It's the same bone ring that Sloan is wearing.

"How do paradoxes work?" I ask, suddenly revisiting the plotline of a dozen movies where two of the same people or same things can't exist in the same space or cataclysmic events take hold. "We aren't about to end the world or anything, are we?"

My question ruffles the Fianna warrior and the lead man grunts and grips my chin. With bruising force, he turns my head to look at him. My brothers and Sloan push forward, shouting for him to let me go.

Their escalating aggression has the Fianna doing the same. The tension in the room explodes.

Bruin, be big and scary. Shock these men into backing the hell off. I release my bear, and he takes form beside me. He swipes a massive paw through the air, and I expect that to convince the Fianna to back the fuck up and give us some space.

It doesn't.

Magic snaps in the air. Two of them shift into bears, and now we have a massive bear clusterfuck.

"Well, that wasn't supposed to happen."

This is about to go very badly.

Holding up my hand, I push with everything I have to emit an energy pulse that will send these guys back a few feet and keep this from escalating.

As the force of my intention surges in the air, I shout at the top of my lungs. "Fionn! Where the hell are you, oul man! I need you. Fionn!"

I still can't lift my arm, but I fight through the pain and flex my fingers enough to call Birga. When she answers my call, I struggle to close my palm around her staff and reach across my body to lift her with my other hand.

Yeah, it's a gimpy move, but at least I've got a weapon when this goes to shit.

"Birga?" Koen scowls. "How in blazes did ye manage to take her from Fionn?"

"I didn't take her," I snap. "That's what I'm trying to tell you. I'm his great-great-granddaughter, and he gifted me with the weapons of the Fianna to bring them back to their former glory. We're not from this place, and we're also not from this time."

"Horseshit," the tall one says. "Steamin' horseshit."

I shrug. "Believe what you want, but I swear to you, if you so much as scratch any one of us, Fionn will have your heads."

The threat of Fionn's displeasure impacts them more than anything I've said or done so far, so I go with it. "I'm going to have my bear stand down. I would appreciate it if you would do the same."

After a moment of consideration, the leader nods. "Let's see what the lass has to say, lads. We can always string 'em up after that."

I draw a deep breath. "Boys, show the warriors your weapons, please."

My brothers each called forward their weapons during the standoff, so all I have to do is step aside to let them see. "In my time, this fortress was about to be leveled and destroyed. Fionn tasked us to retrieve them and take them for our own."

The one with the chestnut curls and red beard chuffs. "Ye realize ye sound as looney as a lark, aye?"

"I'm sure to you it seems like that. How do you explain our weapons and us being here?"

The man takes a step back and scrubs his beard with curled fingers. "I've seen a great many unexplainable things when gone with drink."

"You're not drunk now, so try again."

He frowns at me. "I can't say just now, but ye bein' Fionn's kin from another time is bunk."

"We'll agree to disagree. Now, where's Fionn?"

"He's up top. Went to check the traps and fetch us supper."

I exhale a sigh of relief. "Wonderful. Then he'll be back soon, and we can clear this whole mess up. If everyone puts away their weapons, maybe we could not kill each other before he gets back."

Bruin chuckles beside me. "That's a pretty low bar."

"I know, buddy, but sometimes aiming low gives you the best chance at success."

Both sides of the argument retreat to their corners and I check in with my brothers, Tad, and Sloan. "How much of that did you guys understand?"

Sloan seems to be the only one with me on that. Not surprising. "My Celtic Brittonic isn't as proficient as yers, luv, but I got the gist. We're waitin' on the return of Fionn to settle this."

"Good one, hotness. That's it. Now, we've got to get the rest of you brushed up on the language of the age."

"What's that now?" Emmet says. "You do remember I failed grade nine French three times, right?"

I wave Em's concerns away. "This time you've got magic on your side. Our understanding of the ancient tongue of the day will be important, I'm sure. I can't imagine Fionn drew us back here to hang out in the Fianna fortress learning how to whittle."

"You're sure this Celtic Britton language is what we need?"

Sloan nods. "Celtic Brittonic was spoken in this part of the world from the sixth century BCE to the sixth century CE."

I gesture for us to gather in the back corner of the room. My first instinct is to erect a shield of privacy to have this conversation, but the warriors might take offense to that and think we're up to no good.

Instead, I remind myself they don't speak English, so they won't know what we're doing anyway. "Okay, so let's address the barrier of language, and I'll teach you the spell Fionn taught me. Connect with yer source power and repeat after me."

The six of them draw a deep breath, center their intentions, and when I feel their connection with the earth and ambient magic take hold, I speak the spell.

"Ancient tongues of pasts long gone
Fill the air like Babylon.
Charm my ears and bless my words
To sing their tune like sweet songbirds."

The chorus of them repeating the spell builds in the air and fills me with warmth. "Awesomesauce. Wow. Very harmonic, guys."

"Well done, *a leanbh*." There, in the entrance, stands the blond, weathered warrior I love and admire.

I rush over and hug him tight. "It's about time you got here. We narrowly missed a full-blown Irish donnybrook."

The twists of his braids tickle my cheeks as he squeezes me. "Weel, if I knew ye were droppin' in, I woulda had the welcome ready. What brings ye here, lass?"

I ease back and check his expression to see if he's screwing with me. "You're serious."

"I am. Why wouldn't I be?"

I step back, and the boys close in and grip his extended wrist in greeting. "Because we were portaled back in time and find ourselves in your fortress. If you didn't bring us here, then who did?"

"Aye, who indeed?" Criticism laces the question, and I meet the scowl of the woman stepping into the room.

The hair on the nape of my neck stands on end as I study her. I know her, but I don't. Her features are so familiar. I've seen her…but everything is out of context.

I search my memories and try to call her image to my mind. The picture comes in spits and spurts, and I try to rein it in. The silver hair is what does it. All she needs is a crocheted shawl—it hits me like a bolt of lightning.

"Holy schmoly."

"What's wrong, Fi?" Emmet asks.

"Are ye havin' one of yer moments, luv?"

I cast a studying gaze over the woman, but there's no doubt in my mind. "It's the crazy rocking chair lady."

CHAPTER EIGHT

"The crazy rocking chair lady?" Fionn busts a gut and doubles over laughing. "Aye, ye nailed her there, lass. I've always said she was a bit fer the loons."

Bodhmall flicks her hand at him, sending a spark into the air. It crosses the distance between them and snaps Fionn when he bats it away.

It doesn't seem to faze him. I get the feeling he receives that treatment regularly. "I'll thank ye not to speak about me without cause. I don't know who this lady ye think I am is, but I am not she."

"Of course, you are. You were on the balcony of the house next door, and you spoke to me. You said, *Ní neart go cur le chéile.*"

"Yer sayin' I came to yer time and told ye there is strength in unity."

"Yes. Exactly."

She shrugs. "I'm sorry to bust yer buttons, missy, but I don't have the shaman powers Fionn does. I can't span time or enter the astral plane. While the notion of strength in unity is sound, if I came to yer time, I would have a fair bit more to say than that."

I frown. "Then who is the rocking chair lady?"

"I cannot say, but I can tell ye it wasn't me."

"But ye'll always be the crazy rockin' chair lady to me, Auntie."

Bodhmall flicks her hand again. "Off with ye, now. Go clean the meat fer dinner. Royce and the lot of ye, away with ye all."

People might revere the Fianna warriors as brave, but when Bodhmall snaps her fingers, they jump to attention and follow Fionn out of the Grand Hall without argument.

Fionn and his men take the rabbits and fish to clean them for dinner, and Bodhmall gestures for our group to sit at the round, wooden table. Fionn once told me his aunt was the greatest female druid he ever knew.

I admit I'm a little starstruck.

I settle at the table opposite her and press my hands flat on the pitted, wooden surface. "I'm Fiona…which you already know because you came to see me. Wow, this is trippy."

"If trippy means concernin', aye it is. If neither Fionn nor I brought ye here, there's no explanation as to why ye'd be standin' here in our private space."

All righty then…I guess they didn't set out the welcome mat for us. I straighten and lift one shoulder. "I don't know what I don't know. One minute we were chasing down kidnapping witches, and the next we were here."

Her gaze narrows on me.

She doesn't believe me. I don't have to be empathetic to read her body language. The woman is tense, stern, and not at all pleased to have her family drop in.

"When I arrived, ye seemed happy enough to be here. Why? What business have ye here in this time?"

"None, really. It's not that we have business here. It's that we're readying for a monumental battle between the light and dark empowered communities. When I realized where and when we are, I hoped Fionn brought us here to help us prepare."

"Very well, that much makes sense. If yer Time of the Collidin' Realms is upon ye and ye need guidance, ye might have enough power to manifest the need fer guidance and managed to get yerself here."

Me? She thinks *I* portaled us back in time?

Nuh-uh. Nothing within me thinks that's what happened. Still, she's stopped scowling, so I let her think whatever she wants. "Yes, guidance would be great."

Bodhmall links her hands together and purses her lips. "Fine then. Tell me of yer preparations fer the Time of the Collidin' Realms, and I shall do my best to set ye on a path of strength."

"I'm assuming the Time of the Colliding Realms is what we've been calling the Culling?"

Bodhmall frowns. "I've not heard it referred to by that name, but there are many names for many things. It's the Collidin' Realms to us. Once in a great long while, the earthly plane, the fae veil, and the realm of spirits and souls collide. There is a period of a few fraught-filled days when the three realms mix and a great rebalancin' of good and evil occurs."

"Yes. That's what we call the Culling."

"Aye then, at least we know we're talkin' the same tale." She stands at the table, lifts the flap of her overskirt, and proceeds to wipe the rims of the used tankards.

When she comes to one that still has liquid in it, she gulps back the ale before wiping it with her skirt and handing it to one of us.

When all seven of us have a tankard in front of us, she grips the pitcher's handle and pours us all a healthy slosh.

Thankfully, Dillan and Emmet refrain from voicing an opinion about drinking warm ale from used tankards and everyone accepts their libation with thanks.

"So, out with it. I asked ye a question."

She did? Oh right…our preparations.

I run a finger down the metal band on my tankard. "Well, we aren't sure how to prepare, exactly. No one we've spoken to has any knowledge of the event, so we don't know what to expect."

"Then start with how ye came to have the information ye do have."

"We're good friends with one of the Greek gods—Dionysus. When I noticed the dark sects were becoming increasingly brazen and seemed desperate to gain power, I described what was happening to him. He knew about the Culling and has told us what he could."

"I can't imagine one of the gods carin' one way or the other. At least, they never have in all the years good people have been prayin' fer aid."

I'm not about to get into a theological argument with a woman more than a thousand years my senior. "Dionysus is a different sort of god. He told us what he could, but we'd love to hear what you know."

She lifts her tankard to her lips and swallows. "Well, if the only man familiar with the Time of the Collidin' Realms in yer time is a god—who no doubt, never involved himself in the battles—I expect there's a great deal I can tell ye about what is comin'."

A rushing sense of relief hits me. I've been so twisted up about not knowing what we don't know. The idea of finally getting answers is amazing. "Thank you. We'd love to go home more well-informed."

Bodhmall smiles over the rim of the tankard, the dancing flames of the torches highlighting the mass of freckles on her weathered cheeks. "Och, now that ye mention gettin' home. If yer not sure how ye got yerselves here, there stands the problem of how ye expect to get yerselves back."

Aiden tenses and sits higher in his seat. "No disrespect intended, ma'am, but I have a wife and four kids at home waiting for me. We *all* have people waiting for us. We have to get back. If not through Fi…can't you or Fionn send us home?"

She tilts her head and sighs. "That I don't know, lad. When Fionn went, he sent an astral projection of himself to observe.

When he took her to the past, it was only a spiritual projection made manifest. Her body remained in yer time."

Calum frowns. "Yeah, it scared the hell outta me. It was like she went vacant."

Bodhmall clinks the silver band of her ring against the handle of her tankard and shrugs. "Let's not worry about that yet, children. If ye came to learn about the Collidin' Realms, give me yer full focus fer the time yer here, and we'll train ye up. Perhaps when the universe feels yer ready, ye'll return without difficulty."

"If you build it, they will come," Emmet says.

Calum sets down his ale and swallows. "That's a little too loosey-goosey for my liking. This is our life we're talking about."

"Aye, it is, but I have no other comfort to offer just now. Be patient and Fionn and I will think on it."

I draw a deep breath and focus. "All right. Tell us what we need to know, and we'll hope you're right."

Bodhmall grins and stands to leave. "Och, lass. It won't be a case of me tellin' ye, and it won't be tonight. I'll start showin' ye tomorrow at the rooster's crow. Fer tonight, eat, drink, rest up, and try not to worry. The goddess has a way of steerin' us out of the dark."

With that, she upends her tankard, swallows its contents in several long gulps, and wipes the drips on her chin with the back of her sleeve. "Good evenin'. I take my leave."

Two hours later, the ale pours are slowing, and the boys begin to peel off one by one to claim a straw mat and a bedroll on the floor. The idea of being stuck here still has me wound up, and despite Sloan looking like he's about to drop, he's sitting up with me like the champ he is.

"Do ye fancy a walk in the night air before turnin' in, *a leanbh?*" Fionn holds out his hand and bends at the waist as if he's formally asking for a dance. "I promise I'll return ye in time fer any bed-chamber duties."

I laugh and take his hand. "If it's a duty, you're not doing it right, oul man."

He chuckles. "I assure ye, I am."

Before we leave, I kiss Sloan good night. "Don't wait up for me. You look like you're about to slip into unconsciousness and I have Fionn and Bruin with me. Consider yourself off-duty for the night."

"Wake me when ye get in anyway so I don't worry."

I chuckle. "Worry while you're sound asleep and lost to the world, you mean?"

"Somethin' like that." He winks. "Have fun, luv."

I squeeze his shoulder and slide my arm through the crook of Fionn's elbow, and the two of us meander the corridors of the fortress heading for the world above.

The air "up top" as they call it, is more than crisp after many hours beneath the hill. It's downright nippy. I tug the collar of my jacket closer to my neck and wish I brought Sloan's scarf up with me.

At first, we say nothing and simply enjoy each other's company, but then, he starts us off with catching up. "I didn't miss the matchin' rings." He lifts my hand. "I see ye took my advice and settled down. I'm ever so pleased fer ye."

I tip my left hand in the silver-white light of the half-moon, and my Claddagh band glistens. "Me too. He's a wonderful man and an incredibly skilled druid. Although, I'm not sure we've settled down. The empowered world keeps us very busy."

Fionn nods. "Then it's good ye have a partner fer yer adventures. I can tell by the way ye look at him that he treats ye well and fills yer heart."

I draw a deep breath. "He's amazing. I wouldn't have gotten as far as I have without him. When my shield first activated, it threw me into the deep end of the pool without the security of a life vest."

"I am sorry about that. If I could've been with ye fer it all, I would have."

I hug his arm. "I know. Maybe it's better that I floundered. It made me seek out others for help. When this all started, Da told me I was a danger to myself because I didn't know how to ask for help. When the empowered world started coming at me from all sides, I learned."

He chuckles and pats my hand. "I'm sure ye did. And quickly, I would bet."

We walk some more until he stops and grows very still. It's not a tense kind of stillness. It's about not scaring the doe and fawn foraging close by.

I reach out with my senses and find the two of them. They're aware of our presence but not nervous in the slightest. "The animals here trust you."

"As they should. Other than feeding the circle of life, I'd never cause them harm or allow anyone else to either. Nature is the lifeblood of our heritage. My lands are theirs to roam without fear."

There is peace in his voice and softness in his eyes as he expresses his truth. When he moves his glance to me, that seems to suffer.

"Whatever it is, my girl, ye can tell me. I might not have all the answers, but there are times when simply sharin' yer worries eases the mind."

"What do you mean? I'm good."

He chuckles and resumes our lazy pace through the trees. "Yer bothered by somethin'. It'll do ye no good to deny it. Every time ye look at me, there's a sadness in yer beautiful blue eyes."

I didn't realize he could read me so well.

How do I tell the man who chose me to be his successor I'm not sure I can live up to the faith he puts in me? Just over a month from now, the world's alignment will hang in the balance, and *I* am supposed to lead the way through the darkness.

I've been a druid for eighteen months.

Sloan, Granda, and Merlin are so much more qualified than I am, yet even they look to me for our plan of attack. It's crazy. They respect Fionn's placement of me at the helm but...

What if I let everyone down?

Fionn pats my hand. "This is the part where ye tell me what weighs on ye, *a leanbh*. Whatever it is, ye need to let it out. I see it in the moments ye forget to guard yerself. I recognize it because I walk the same path. I know how the chains of leadership bind and chafe."

I draw a deep breath. "I don't want to disappoint you. I mean…there's so much hanging in the balance. It's all so important and… I watch Merlin fight, and Garnet lead, and Granda and Sloan pore over scrolls of forgotten knowledge, and I think any one of them is better suited to take on the Culling than me."

He leans sideways and kisses the side of my head. "I thought it might be somethin' like that."

"I'm sorry. I want to be everything you need me to be—everything they *all* need me to be—but it's so much. The lives of my family and friends. The future of both human and empowered communities. The gatekeeper against evil taking hold of our world. That shit is cray-cray."

My voice cracks and I pull an unsteady breath through tight lungs. There's no use denying the truth. It'll become apparent in a few weeks. I turn to meet him face-to-face and blink past the tears blocking my vision. "I'm sorry, Fionn. I'm not ready. I've let you down."

Fionn clucks his tongue and reaches into his pocket to pull out an embroidered cloth handkerchief. "Don't worry. It's clean."

He winks as he lifts my chin and gently sweeps away my tears. "Ye'll never let me down, *a leanbh*. Between yer passion, focus, and good intention, yer exactly the right person to lead the charge. Aye, ye may be new to things, but yer also not bent by the winds of life. There's flexibility in a young tree that is lost over time as it grows."

"I like the sound of that, but it doesn't make me feel any more prepared for what's coming at us."

He sighs and takes my elbow again, turning me to walk through the forested hilltop. "Well, yer here now. Bodhmall, the boys, and I will prepare ye the best we can. It'll work out. Ye'll see."

"I hope so."

"With hope and hard work, most things turn out all right. It wouldn't hurt to add a little faith too."

I wish I had more faith to add. "Heavy is the head that wears the crown."

"Och, that's very true. Well said."

I chuckle. "I can't take the credit, I'm afraid. The actual quote is a little different, but that's the common version. It will be part of a very famous play written in about twelve hundred years by a man named William Shakespeare."

"It seems the man knows something of the pressures of leadership. If ye ask me, if ye wear the crown and yer not fraught with conflict and worry, then yer not doin' yer job as a leader of men."

I picture the iron crown hooked on the headboard post of King Henry. "I wanted to ask you about that."

"About what?"

"About the iron crown you left me. My shield has saved me and mine more times than I can count, my bracers are from the tree of life and are an incredible armor, and Birga is a remarkable weapon to bond with. I've never been able to figure out the iron crown. What does it do? Is it enchanted? Does it represent something I've missed?"

Fionn pulls a wine sack from the pocket of his heavy cloak and waggles his brows at me. "Well, if ye have to ask, then ye've missed a great deal. That crown is as important and powerful as the other gifts I gave ye."

I consider the comparison…as powerful as my bracers and shield? Seriously? "I find that hard to believe."

He pulls the cork from the wineskin, takes a long drink, and passes it to me. "I shall prove it to ye in the mornin' then. Yer in fer a treat, luv. Hell, learnin' to use the crown will increase yer power in battle tenfold."

"Tenfold? Are you kidding?" I drink and pass it back.

"Och, I never joke about battle." He grins, lifting the wineskin in toast, and strikes off to continue our walk. "Come. We'll talk battles tomorrow. Tonight, we drink and celebrate ye bein' here."

I wake the next morning to the smell of frying meat and the laughter of men. I suppose it doesn't matter what century you're in. Filling a man's belly in the morning is the surefire way to start the day off right.

"Blessed morn, sister mine." Emmet places his arm across his front and bows when I arrive. "I trust sleep treated you with grace and kept you in good company through the night."

I meet the snickers of my brothers. "What did I miss? Is Em running away to join the Renaissance Faire? Can you even juggle?"

Dillan snorts. "No, but he can rock a leotard."

Emmet straightens and flips Dillan off with a theatrical flourish. "Spew venom if you must, Sir Douche-a-lot. It is known far and wide across the kingdom you covet my form and physique."

Calum snorts, rises from the table, and points at his now vacant seat. "Take a load off, baby girl. I'll grab you a plate."

I sit next to Sloan and reach for his juice. Lifting it under my nose, I see if it passes the sniff test. "Apple?"

"Freshly pressed and quite tasty."

Calum reaches over my shoulder and sets a plate down in front of me. Last night for dinner, we ate rabbit soup, so we left the fish for this morning.

"Thanks." I smile at him and notice the dark rings under his eyes. "Did you sleep last night?"

He scrunches his nose and tilts his head side to side. "Not much. I'm used to Kevin being there beside me."

"What? I'm not good enough?" Dillan asks. "I don't remember you complaining when you hogged the blanket at two a.m."

The two of them sound off, and I turn my attention to more pressing matters...like digging into my fish. The meat is oily but hot, and the bread is heavy but soaks up the grease and fills my tummy.

"How was yer night, luv?" Sloan refills his juice for me. "It was late when ye finally came to bed. Is all well?"

"Yeah, as good as it can be for where we are and what's coming at us."

"I suppose that's good enough."

I finish chewing and sip from the metal cup. "Fionn and I shared some wine under the stars." When we shared a room in the castle, we found we genuinely enjoyed one another's company. "It was fun to catch up."

"Well, I'm glad ye had the chance. I'm glad we're here too. Hopefully, with their help, we'll improve our footing in the uprising to come."

"What did he say about getting us home?" Aiden asks, finishing his breakfast. "I assume you brought it up with him."

"I did. He said much the same thing Bodhmall did. A visitation from the astral plane they can manage. Carrying one shaman back, that's doable too. But portaling seven people through time isn't something they're capable of."

Aiden curses and I reach out and squeeze his hands. "He also said the same thing that Bodhmall did about us learning what we can. Maybe we'll satisfy whatever criteria we're here for and return home. He just doesn't know."

"That's not comforting, Fi."

"No. I know it isn't, but the good news is that when Fionn brought me back, I returned at the same moment I left. No time lost. Nobody worried or freaking out because I disappeared."

"But not so when ye were sucked back into ancient Greece with Nikon, Calum, and Kevin," Sloan says. "When Hecate took ye, I was left to pack up Daisy and our things to get home to worry about ye and try to figure out where she'd taken ye and when."

I glance down at my Claddagh and smile. "Thankfully, Sloan chipped me like a prized cat so he would stop losing me."

"Yer not my cat. And I wouldn't have gone to such lengths if ye didn't disappear every few months."

I laugh and take another sip of my apple juice. "It's not something I plan."

"There's my pet." Fionn enters the room, pats the top of my head, and sits heavily in the seat opposite Sloan and me. "It's nice to see ye again, young man. It's also nice to see ye put a ring on my girl's finger."

Sloan winks at me. "We were just discussin' that very thing. She's a tough one to corral, but we got there in the end."

I snort. "See, I'm a prized cat."

Dillan laughs. "The ring is better than color posters on all the neighborhood mailboxes. Lost. Loves treats and answers to the name of Fi."

"Let's avoid that at all cost." I flip my hand, dismissing his comment with a laugh. "No. I love my ring and everything it implies."

Fionn nods. "It's a smart man who sees the value of a treasure and keeps it close."

I finish my plate and wipe my mouth. "Sloan is a very smart man."

"Ye slept well, the two of ye?"

Fionn gave Sloan and me his straw bed, and I must admit, we were quite comfortable. "No complaints at all. Thank you."

"My pleasure, lass. Ye need a good night's sleep to be in top form fer trainin'. The boys are skeptical of my decision to give ye the crown over yer brothers, but I told them ye'll do our clan proud when the time comes, I have no doubt."

"Good to know. What's their objection? Who do they think should be in charge?"

Fionn tilts his head toward Emmet. "Och, I don't think they have any objection. It's simply the power they feel comin' off Emmet here. He's got quite a connection to the Source power."

Dillan chuckles. "Yeah, it's like he bathed in it."

Fionn doesn't get the joke, so I fill him in. "Last fall, we discovered a couple of covens of dark witches were siphoning from the Cistern of The Source. There was a battle where Emmet was knocked through a wall and thrown into a river of raw prana."

Fionn's face blanches. "Ye could've been killed. Och, by all rights, ye should've been killed. I've heard tales of men who died from a sip or a drop."

"Emmet didn't swallow," Dillan says.

Emmet flashes him a middle finger. "We didn't know what it would mean, but so far I haven't grown any extra arms or started emanating fire or anything, so I think I'm a dud."

"Yer not a dud," Sloan says. "As I've told ye…it takes time for a magical metamorphosis. We must wait and see what the goddess has in store."

Fionn nods. "We'll test ye and train ye up. Maybe we can break yer shell and see what lies beneath."

"Sounds good to me. Looking forward to it."

"Well, nobody will be trainin' if things aren't ready." Bodhmall hands Fionn a plate and points toward the door. "Off ye go. Don't leave the fate of the future to Royce and those eejits. Ye best make sure they do things right."

Fionn takes his plate and hustles off to check on things up top with Bodhmall on his heels. Emmet, Tad, and Calum follow them out. Aiden and Dillan pick up their dirty dishes and leave Sloan and me to enjoy the moment.

"Alone at last." I finish off the last of my breakfast with a couple of chunks of apple. "What do you think they have in store for us?"

Sloan twists beside me and rests his arm on the back of my chair. "Whatever it is, I'm game. Whether they're trainin' us or teachin' us or simply runnin' over a strategy to give us an edge, I'm eager to accept the help."

"Another time adventure to share." I pop in the last of my apple and smile at him. "I think we got the better end of the deal this time, though."

"How so?"

"Because Emmet, Dillan, Calum, and Aiden are all missing their mates and their focus is split. I've been thrown back in time enough to know there's always part of you yearning to get back to the one you love."

Sloan sends me a coy grin. "Was it me ye yearned to get back to even in the early days?"

"Is this you fishing for compliments?"

"Maybe."

I grin. "Well, if the great and talented Sloan Mackenzie needs ego-stroking, who am I to deny him?"

His grin grows wider. "I wouldn't say *need*, but I'll never turn down a little strokin'."

I snort and almost spit out my apple. "No. I don't suppose you would. But we were talking about ego-stroking. That's different."

"Right. Yes, it's nice occasionally to hear I wasn't the only one on the hook. In the early days, I was the one chasin' while ye spouted off about how surly and tightly wound I was."

"True story. That's because you *are* surly and tightly wound. I simply learned to find it endearing. But to answer your question, yes, I yearned to get back to you and am glad we don't have to worry about that this time around. I much prefer having you by my side."

Sloan leans in and presses a soft kiss on my lips. "There's nowhere else I'd rather be. Now, let's go see what's in store."

I rise to join him. "Battles to win. Worlds to save. Busy, busy, busy."

CHAPTER NINE

The Fianna fortress sits buried beneath a seven-hundred-and-eighteen-foot mound of forested earth. Fionn was bequeathed the estate by order of the High King after his grandfather had his father killed and his mother exiled. The two young lovers had run away to be together and were already pregnant when her father hunted them down.

At this time, it's known as the estate of Alum. In our time, it's called the Hill of Allen, and a quarry has eaten into the hill's core.

When Fionn told me to bring my brothers and rescue his trove of treasures, we came in from the north side to find a row of large boulders, and through them, the clearing with the old stone altar.

Only now...the altar stands in perfect condition.

Bodhmall waves to urge us to gather and looks us over. "I know ye didn't get a say in bein' here, but here ye are all the same. We must assume it's important and with what yer facin' it surely is. Fer the time we have, we'll ready ye the best we can. Between Fionn and me, and of course the boys, ye'll not find a better source fer learnin' how to work with the gifts the goddess has given us."

I don't doubt that for a second. "No matter how we got here, we're thankful for the opportunity. When it comes to the Culling, we'll take all the help we can get."

She points at Emmet and Sloan. "Come here to me, boys. I want Arken to test yer strengths. I believe ye met last night at dinner."

Sloan nods. "Aye, we did."

Emmet shifts his stance so he can't see us. Last night Dillan figured out Arken was the nakey guy statue. My brothers and I got a good chuckle from teasing Em about being drawn to touch him. "Yes, we met."

When they've all shaken hands, Bodhmall continues, "Fer the first part of today ye'll train with Arken. Then we'll shuffle things around."

Sloan and my brother nod at him and step up to the altar. "What are we learnin'?" Sloan asks.

"Arken's strengths are of a healin' nature," she says. "I've asked him to see what's what with young Emmet's transition. If he has untapped power, Arken will find it. He's one of the smartest men ye'll ever meet."

Arken is a slight man with a once athletic frame, ebony hair streaked with silver, and deeply tanned skin. He looks a bit like a marauding pirate…but with kind, intelligent eyes that have seen a lot in his long life.

I don't miss the flash of affection that passes between the two when he looks at her. It's true, druids can live centuries depending on their connection to nature and their restoration abilities, but even so, Bodhmall is robbing the cradle.

Good for her.

Arken smiles at her and looks at us. "She's bein' too kind. In truth, I know a little about a lot of things, and it sometimes fools folks into thinkin' I'm smarter than I am."

She rolls her eyes. "Pfft. Fine, I'll leave ye to talk foolishness. Calum and Dillan, yer learnin' stealth with Koen. Aiden, yer on combat with Royce and Tad, yer with Dahir. Fiona, yer with Fionn and me, lass."

I follow Bodhmall and Fionn away from the altar clearing and further into the trees. It's winter here too, and the air is crisp. It doesn't hold the same bite as Toronto, and I'm sure once we get moving, it'll be quite pleasant.

"What do ye know about me, lass?"

I duck beneath a low-hanging branch. "Fionn said you are the youngest of six with five older brothers, like me. He also said you are a great and practiced druidess and an incredible woman to model myself after."

She tilts her head toward her nephew and smiles. "That's kinder than I thought."

He lowers his head, a blush of color rising on his cheeks. "Well, it's the truth. I don't say it often enough, but ye know I think yer a wonder, Auntie."

Her expression softens a little. "The truth is, Fionn was a natural from the time he could hold a stick or press his hands to the soil. I merely taught him the power of his connection, and that's where I'll start today too."

I shake my right arm out.

"Is yer arm still troublin' ye, lass?" Fionn asks.

"It's better than it was yesterday, but it's still not responding normally. I don't know whether it was a witch warding or if I got a shock from the portal magic that brought us all here, but I got quite a jolt."

Fionn gently takes my wrist and raises my arm to test my range of motion. "Does it pain ye when I move it so, *a leanbh?*"

"It's just a bit stiff. The feeling came back to my fingers last night. I'm fine. In the past year, I've been poisoned, stabbed, beaten, and possessed. This is an annoyance and nothing more."

Bodhmall accepts that as the last word on the matter, but Fionn looks concerned. Either way, it seems to be her driving the train, so we move on.

We walk up the slope of the Hill of Allen and switch back on a narrow path. I'm not sure where we're going, but it feels like our direction is purposeful.

Still, the two of them are content to climb the slope without speaking, so I do the same. The three of us spend the next ten minutes with our boots *crunching* against the frozen grass and the sound of our breathing growing louder the higher we climb.

"What do ye know of a general's role in great battles, child?" Bodhmall asks as we stop short of a plateau overlooking the hill below.

I shrug. "In movies, the general is the guy on the horse looking on from the hill."

She frowns. "I'm not familiar with where movies is, but yer only partly right."

Right...*in* movies is confusing. I try again. "From what I've seen, the general is the man standing above the forces assessing how to approach the upcoming battle."

"Largely, that is so. Though, no general worth his salt would remain at the back to watch his troops battle on without him."

"No. I couldn't imagine so."

Bodhmall leads us to the plateau's edge, and we walk forward. Below us is the altar clearing where Tad, Sloan, and my brothers practice with the other Fianna warriors. From up here, we're close enough to see everything but far enough to look at things as a whole.

"A good general is the commander of the fight who sees not only the strengths of his forces and weaknesses of his opponents but also the reverse."

I nod. "That makes sense."

"Fionn says ye've fought with each of them?"

"Yes, quite a lot."

She reaches around my shoulders and turns me to face the forest we walked through. "Then ye'll be able to tell me about the most dramatic weaknesses in each member of your team."

Dramatic weaknesses? In my mind, everyone rocks. "Um…I'm not sure. I've never really thought about it."

"Och, ye must," Fionn says. "It's not about finding fault with the others. It's about understanding the limitations of the folks on yer team."

Bodhmall turns me around again to face the clearing below. "Let's start with yer man, Sloan. What do ye consider his biggest weakness in battle?"

I think for a moment and shrug. "I'm not sure. Magically, he's much more learned and competent than my brothers and me. His understanding of herbology and biology in nature is exceptional. His weapons training and hand-to-hand is honed after decades of training. He's logical and quick-thinking under pressure."

Bodhmall grins. "Ye admire him as a warrior as much as a man, do ye?"

"I do, but it's all true."

"Och, I'm not implying yer wrong. I'm sure he's all those things. Still, ye didn't answer my question. What's his biggest weakness in battle?"

I stare down at him, running through the highlight reel of the adventures we've had. "He really doesn't like ghosts."

"All right. I was thinkin' about somethin' that comes into play more often than ghosts."

I study the two of them looking at me, and it dawns on me where she's going with this. "*I* am."

She winks. "Ye are. It's not a criticism, mind. The man is clearly lost in love. Whenever warriors wed, they become the greatest weakness for one another. That's the way of things. It means ye must take that into account so both of ye can focus."

"That makes sense."

"Now, I'm quite sure not all yer team are equally trained and ready fer battle. Fionn says yer brothers came into their powers last autumn. Is that correct?"

"It is. After I returned home from Ireland, I gave them each the spark of magic they should've received at birth. We're late to the game, but with the Fianna weaponry and knowledge downloaded by the spell you left for us, we've progressed a lot."

"Let's start with the brawny russet one."

"Aiden." I stare down at my oldest brother.

"Tell me where his weaknesses lay."

I don't like this game at all. "This is very hard."

Fionn steps in behind me and presses a hand on my back. "There is no judgment here, *a leanbh*. We're simply takin' inventory of what's available to ye in a battle. Fer this moment, they are not yer brothers. They are simply the men fightin' under yer leadership."

Bodhmall meets my gaze with a stern look. "Take yer emotions out of it."

I study Aiden in action, watching him spar against Royce. Whether or not I say it, he can improve upon some things. If I see them, no doubt Fionn and his aunt can too.

"Aiden is the oldest of us, so he worries. Since the death of our brother Brendan, he's been even more protective."

"A good thing to be aware of. Go on."

"He has almost fifteen years of training and working as a cop. He's a policeman through and through—"

"What does that mean…cop and policeman?" Bodhmall asks.

"He's a King's Sheriff in their time," Fionn explains. "All four of Fiona's brothers are."

She nods and gestures for me to continue.

"Aiden moves like a cop…he thinks like a cop…and with his young family being the priority in his life, he practices his druid abilities the least of all of us."

Bodhmall nods. "What are his strengths? What does he offer to yer party no one else does?"

"Well, him being an active policeman for years has given him the most experience in dangerous situations. He's quicker to assess critical moments and opponents than the rest of us, and he's confident enough to take the initiative or follow orders without question."

Bodhmall nods. "So, the weakness we'll work on with him while he's here is being unprepared as a druid. Good. Pick another. Tell me about Dillan. Strengths and weaknesses."

I scan the clearing and find Dillan is working with Calum and Koen. They seem to be assessing foes from a distance and discussing stealth techniques when approaching from behind.

"Dillan is brave and sacrificing. Da thinks he's reckless at times, but he's not...not really. He won't hesitate to put himself at risk to save another, but he knows what's at stake and accepts the consequences. For weaknesses, I'd have to say...he's a stubborn pain in the ass and quick to temper. He reacts with hostility when offended and has gotten into more than his share of fights."

"A scrapper, then," Fionn says.

"Definitely...but never out of malice. That can be a strength too because even if someone outmatches him, he'll never let us down and will never stop fighting."

"He's the one who inherited Dahir's cloak?"

I nod. "Yeah. He loves that thing."

Fionn smiles. "It's an incredible gift."

Bodhmall nods. "Next we have the southpaw with the ranger's bow."

"Calum," I say.

It goes like that for the next twenty minutes. By the end of our conversation, I've listed each of my brothers and Sloan, and now we're working on Tad.

"Despite him saying he's perfectly fine going into this, I worry. It has to upset him. His father volunteered to be possessed by darkness and tried to kill him. I want to take him at his word, but I don't think even he understands what he's going through."

Bodhmall frowns. "I agree with ye, lass. A betrayal like that could sway any man one way or the other. He might be entirely focused and intent on gettin' through the hell he's been in, or he might be hungry fer answers and determined to prove he's nothin' like the man who sired him. I feel fer the lad."

"Yeah, me too."

She's quiet for a moment as she watches them. "All right. I have what I need to plan a trainin' schedule that'll strengthen yer team. I'll leave ye to focus on what Fionn wants to teach ye next."

When she steps back from the edge and leaves us to ourselves, I smile at Fionn. "So, what do I have to look forward to? What druid mysteries will you reveal?"

He reaches into the pocket of his heavy woolen cloak and pulls out the iron crown I inherited from him. "I promised I would teach you how this works."

A surge of curiosity ignites in me.

When I first inherited the crown, I tried it on a dozen times and never figured out what it did or how it worked.

In the end, I figured it was symbolic.

According to Fionn, it's as important to a leader of the Fianna warriors as my shield, my armor, and Birga. I can't imagine how that's possible, but I'm willing to give him the benefit of the doubt.

At least until I know more.

"There she be." Fionn grins at the iron laurel as he holds it up for us to admire. "Go ahead, try it on. Let's see if ye can get her to work with a little help from the master."

I accept the crown, set it over my forehead, and adjust it. "I'm not sure what I was doing wrong. Maybe it just doesn't like me."

Fionn chuckles. "What's not to like? Yer a breath of fresh air. Patient. Courteous. Soft-spoken."

Now it's my turn to laugh. "Have Emmet and Dillan been teaching you sarcasm?"

He grins. "Perhaps a little."

I let that go. Sarcasm is a necessary skill when dealing with Clan Cumhaill. "Okay, let's focus on the crown. What am I supposed to be feeling, doing, learning? I've got nothing here...again."

He scratches his fingers along the scruff of his beard. "There's that patience we were talkin' about."

"Har-har."

"Aye, har-har. I find it funny ye never figured out what the crown was for. What did ye do, stand in yer wee bed chamber with it on while starin' in yer mirror?"

Yes. "No...okay, maybe." When he laughs, a flush of heat warms my cheeks. "I didn't *only* stare in the mirror. I wore it around the house for a few days."

He laughs harder. "Did it not occur to ye that a warrior's crown might need more stimulation than that?"

"Obviously not or I would've tried something else. When nothing happened after days, and nothing happened any of the times I tried to activate it in front of the mirror, I figured it was a showpiece because you were the Fianna leader."

"Wrong."

"No shit. Now, stop laughing at me and let me in on the joke."

Fionn's eyes glimmer when he's amused by me and by the look of him now, he's truly enjoying this. "All right, I suppose I'll share the secret of the crown with ye. Are ye ready?"

I roll my eyes. "Yes. I'm ready."

He steps in beside me, wraps an arm around my shoulders, and turns me to face the warriors training below. *Hubba-wha?* "Holy crapamoly. Mind blown."

Fionn chuckles behind me. "As it should be."

CHAPTER TEN

Standing fifty feet above our family and friends, I take in the data uploading into my mind. The crown acts like a scanner of some kind, making it possible to see not only how much stamina and strength each of them has but also areas of weakness.

"What do the colors mean?" I hold my hand out, pointing at the colored auras around each fighter.

"The lighter and brighter the color, the better they fare...or at least that's how it is fer me."

"Holy crapamoly, look at Emmet." My jaw drops, my gaze locked on my brother.

While the others give off an aura of pale pink that extends beyond their bodies six inches like a backlit glow...Emmet is radiating Barbie pink power like he's prana radioactive. "That's incredible."

"Ye mentioned he took a dip in waters of The Source. I think it's fair to say it's affected him."

"Yeah. I just...when nothing really happened after weeks and months, I assumed nothing had changed."

"Magic can be mysterious. Sometimes ye feel its effects right away, and sometimes it builds until it bursts free."

"If he bursts, we'll all have to take cover."

Fionn grins. "See the importance of the crown? More than a pretty trinket."

It is. I scan the others, getting a feel for what I'm looking at, pleased everyone is doing well. "What's wrong with Royce's right shoulder?"

"Och, that's an old injury. One night, when we were sleeping under the stars to avoid a convoy of the king's men, we were set upon by a pack of boar that didn't take kindly to us invadin' their lands."

"Territorial, are they?"

"Nasty bastards. Anyway, in the shuffle to clear out of their way, Royce got a tusk lodged into his shoulder. The man bellowed, and the boar did the same and started runnin'. The hole it left bled fer days and took months to heal proper."

"Beware the tusks of wild pigs."

"Truer words were never spoken."

I go back to scanning the men and learning what things mean. "This is cool. I see what you mean about it helping in battle. I can see who's getting tired and who's still going strong."

"Aye, but I've only shown ye half of it."

I turn and meet his gaze. "What? Really? What else can it do?"

"Focus on yer man there. It's not his turn, so ye won't distract him to injury. Ye know how ye can speak with yer bear without usin' yer words?"

"Telepathically, yeah."

"Well, the crown will connect ye with the minds of those in yer party. Ye'll be able to warn them when an enemy is on their flank or guide them to a man down or coordinate an attack or a retreat."

"Seriously?"

He chuckles. "I told ye last night I never joke about battle. Now, go ahead."

"When is it private and when can the whole group hear what I say?"

"It responds to yer thoughts, *a leanbh*. Yer the one to make the connection. Go ahead, make yer man blush. No one but the two of ye will know what's said."

I giggle. "Okay, but turn your back. I don't want to be lewd with my grandfather watching me."

"Yer not actin' things out, ye loon. Yer only talkin' to him. What will I see?"

I raise my hand and circle my finger until he turns. "Nothing, that's the point."

"Yer ridiculous, ye know that?"

"I've been told." When I'm sure he's minding his own and surveying the beauty of the forest behind us, I reach out with my mind the same way I do with Bruin and Nikon. *Hey, hotness. Looking good down there. So good, in fact, I was thinking...*

I go on to describe in dirty detail what I'd like to be doing with him right now.

He glances around the clearing, chuckling. *Where are ye, luv? When shall we make that happen?*

I'm up fifty feet and to your right.

His gaze lifts and I wave when he sees me. *I take it Fionn's teachin' ye a few new tricks?*

Yep. I like this one.

I'm sure the skill is supposed to be more than ye makin' ribald remarks to yer lover.

Probably, but this was fun too.

Aye, it was. Okay, my turn with Koen. Back to work, my red-headed sex fiend.

All work and no play makes Fi a bore.

How do I turn this thing off?

I chuckle. *Fine. Back to work.*

When I return my attention to Fionn, he's already turned and grinning.

"No fair. You cheated."

He laughs. "One thing ye'll soon learn in this century, *a leanbh*. There is no privacy. Everyone knows yer business, so there's no use tryin' to hide it. Besides, it does my heart good to see the two of ye so happy."

When he turns to go back the way we came, I link my arm through his and grin. "Mine too."

We finish the morning with me joining the hand-to-hand drills and working off some energy. I find wearing the crown during battle drills distracting, so I hand it back to Fionn for a while.

He's right, though. Wearing the crown during the battles of the Culling will be a huge advantage. I'll be able to not only assess and communicate with my peeps but also assess the weaknesses of the opposing forces. Since the crown responds to my thoughts, I bet it'll let the others talk to each other too.

"Does the crown work on other species?" I ask as we sit in the Grand Hall and eat our lunch.

"Aye, it does. Although, I think ye deal with species in yer city we've never met up with. Around here, there are fae creatures, a few lake monsters, and the odd demi-god bored with life."

"Yeah, we have lots of different sects and pantheons and races of beings. I'll have to try it out around town."

Dillan chuckles. "You're going to look like quite the fashionista walking Queen Street with your crown on, baby girl."

"Maybe I'll bedazzle it and make it look more like a tiara." Fionn looks horrified, and I bust up laughing. "I was kidding, oul man. I would never defile my ancestral treasure with rhinestones and glitter."

"Thank the goddess," he says.

"Speaking of thankin' the goddess." Bodhmall hands Koen an empty ale jug and points for him to take care of things. "What have ye done to earn her favor with the event comin' on?"

I look from her to Fionn and back again. "What do you mean?"

"I mean yer interactions with the goddess. When did ye last speak with her about the way of the world?"

"We saved the Cistern of The Source from having fae prana siphoned and caught those responsible. She was happy about that."

"What about her favor for the Time of the Collidin' Realms?"

I check in with my brothers and Sloan, and they all look as blank as I feel. "I've got nothing. I'm not sure what you mean."

Fionn grunts and sits back in his chair. "How long have ye got until Alban Arthan, my girl?"

Alban Arthan is the old-fashioned druid term for the winter solstice. "Six weeks," I say.

"Then there might still be time."

Bodhmall frowns. "Aye, but not much."

The look that passes between Fionn and his aunt makes the butterflies in my stomach flutter more than usual. When I see the reaction of Arken, Royce, and the other Fianna, it's even worse.

"What?" I say, my heart rate picking up its pace. "What don't we know?"

Fionn exhales heavily. "Maybe it's nothin'. Yer experience won't be the same as ours. Yer from a different time with different evils and different foes."

"But if it were the same?" Sloan asks.

Fionn takes a long pull from his tankard, sets it down, and wipes the froth from his beard. "Like all things, there is a balance to be recognized. A balance in nature. A balance in alignment. And a balance in power. We've spent the better part of the last year evaluating our strongest foes. I assume ye know the worst of who ye'll be facin' too, aye?"

I swallow and set down my tankard. "We do. We've got Mingin and Melanippe, the Barghest, vampires, witches, nixies, and possibly the Morrigan if she escaped her banishment before I fried her son."

"Do ye also know who backs them?" he asks.

I shrug. "What does that mean?"

"Exactly what it sounds like." He pulls the basket of bread closer and tears off a chunk. "There are people in the hierarchy of power who wish to sway the outcome one way or the other, and they grace their chosen victors with favors."

Dillan sits back and curses. "You mean we need corporate sponsorship?"

Calum grins. "Do you think Nike will back us?"

Emmet chuckles. "That depends if you're talking about the sports company or the Greek god? We have more pull with the latter. At least then, Dionysus could invite him to one of his orgies so we could ask."

I wave that away, trying to make sense of this. "So, you're saying, not only do we need to worry about the evildoers trying to kill innocent people to get a foothold, but we also have to worry about evil backers too?"

Bodhmall shakes her head. "Not in the sense that they will be participating, no. For us, it's simply a force to be acknowledged. We pled our case to Lady Divinity and explained who and what we are up against, and she graced us with favors to strengthen the outcome of the just and righteous."

Emmet sits up straighter. "If it's any benefit, I think she likes us. The last time we spoke with her, she was grateful for our help and said she'd support the rebuilding of the white witches."

Right, she did. "She invited Sarah to keep in touch with her while they work on setting things right with their coven."

Fionn nods. "That's very good. Do ye think ye could get an audience with her and ask fer her support?"

I meet the gazes of my brothers, and they look as lost as me.

"Maybe. I'm not sure how to get an audience with her, but Sarah might know. Em? Can you call her and see when we get back?"

Emmet makes a face. "Um, yeah, looking forward to it. That should go over very well."

"What do you mean? I thought you and Sarah parted as friends and everything was cool."

"It was. Then she found out I hooked up with Ciara and we handfasted right after. Sarah was hurt and said some things. Ciara overheard, took the phone, and she said some things back…it's a catfight clusterfuck."

Calum and Dillan are both trying not to laugh.

I point at them. "Not the time, you two."

Dillan holds up his hands. "Can I just say…it can't be that bad. The woman is so benevolent her getting worked up would be like a kitten batting you with her fuzzy little paws." He turns to Calum and pats at his shoulder. "Emmet Cumhaill, you're a cad. Take my beating and feel my furry wrath."

"Stop. Stop. Please," Calum says, chuckling. "You're tickling me with your fury."

Emmet doesn't find that funny.

I give them a look of warning. "Stifle the role play." When they sober, I give Emmet my complete focus. "I'm sorry things didn't end as well as they could have, Em, but Sarah is lovely and dedicated. She'll understand what's at stake. We'll work it out."

Sloan leans forward and raps his knuckles against the table. "I'll talk to her if ye like, *sham*. She was a friend of mine first. We can leave ye out of it altogether if that's better fer yer marital harmony."

"Yeah, that would be good, Irish. Thanks."

I smile at Sloan. "Breakup drama averted. Now, at least we have a task to do to help us prepare."

Sloan nods. "Fionn, ye mentioned ye know who's supportin' the forces yer up against. What are the odds we might be up against the same power? Was it a man, an immortal, or a god?"

"Good question, hotness." I get back on track. "Point to you for that one."

Fionn shrugs. "I can't say if it would be the same man, but he has the longevity to be a problem still."

"Who is it?" I ask. "We can check him out and see if he's still a problem in our time. If he's going up against Mother Nature and her wishes, he must be powerful."

"Or stupid," Dillan says. "Never discount stupid."

Fionn frowns. "No. Death isn't stupid. He is invested in the turmoil because he will reap the most from the chaos, the killings, and the battles to follow."

"Death?" I repeat, my voice cracking. "Like the head of the reapers and Evangeline's boss?"

Fionn shakes his head. "Who is Evangeline?"

"My girlfriend," Dillan says.

Fionn's expression tightens, and the look of horror is mirrored around the room by all the Fianna. "Yer involved with a reaper? Lad, have ye got rocks fer brains?"

Dillan stiffens. "She *was* a reaper. Now, she's in the process of changing her designation in the Choir of Angels. Even if she wasn't, that wouldn't change how I feel about her. She's amazing."

"Changin' her designation?" Bodhmall says. "Can that even be done?"

Dillan nods. "It can. Death reassigned her to our family as a guardian angel."

My mind is buzzing. "Except…do you remember what she said to us after the nasty vampire business when she was gone for all those days?"

Dillan scowls. "She said a lot of things. What are you thinking?"

"She said considering the dangers we face and the level of violence against us, a family like ours should have several guardians watching over us, not one."

"True story," Emmet says.

"She also said our protectors should be experienced warriors who can keep us safe. Not a novice trainee. Eva thought he was setting her up to fail."

Sloan looks more surly than usual. "And we wondered if it was *us* being set up to fail."

"Because we were," Dillan says in a rush. "If Death knows who we are and what we represent, he wouldn't want to give us full guardian support."

"Do ye think yer woman is part of it?" Koen asks.

Dillan's head cranks around, and he pegs the guy with a glare. "What did you just say?"

Koen stiffens but doesn't back down. "Come now. Ye have to wonder if maybe yer woman is more with her people than yers."

The legs of Dillan's chair scrape the stone floor before the thing tips back and crashes. He rises to his feet at an alarming speed. "Are you calling my angel a traitor, because if you are…"

"He's not!" I stand and press a hand against Dillan's chest. "Koen doesn't know Eva. It was a simple question looking at things from a different perspective."

Koen doesn't look alarmed…if anything he looks amused that he riled Dillan up as much as he did.

"There's no way Eva is duplicitous." I pass a sweeping gaze over the Fianna group. "She is an angel in the truest sense of the word. Genuine. Honest. She is pure joy to be around."

Dillan flashes me a look of thanks and settles down a notch. "Eva *couldn't* be duplicitous if she tried."

"Agreed." Calum is standing on the other side of Dillan, coaxing him back toward the chair Emmet has picked up and returned.

"She is the sweetest, most easy-going woman we've ever met," Emmet adds.

Calum grins. "The only question we've ever had about her is why she settled for this loser."

Dillan pushes back from Calum, but his outrage seems to have dissipated. "I'll have you know that she thinks I'm amazing."

Aiden chuckles. "That's because she only knows like what... five humans?"

The tension eases, and my brothers sit.

Sloan waits until everyone is settled and brings the conversation back to what's important. "If we assume Death is once again rooting fer the dark side to gain strength, his manipulations began months ago."

"And we never realized it," I say.

"Aye, unknowingly, Eva has likely reported back to him about our strengths and weaknesses and how we've faced the trials we've come up against."

"That dirty, cheating asshole," Dillan says.

I wave that away. "That's fine. I hope he got an earful. We might be late to the game, but we've caught up. Now that we're on the same page, we'll crush the asshole, and he won't even see it coming."

Dillan nods. "I'm looking forward to it."

CHAPTER ELEVEN

The training goes late into the afternoon on the third day. By the time we call it quits, the sun is glowing orange against the horizon, and our stomachs are rumbling. Druids of the past don't seem to consider three squares a necessity.

I am more of the hobbit frame of mind: breakfast, second breakfast, elevenses, luncheon, afternoon tea, dinner, and supper.

We're following their lead, so when Bodhmall says there's no time to worry about full bellies when the world is going to hell, who are we to argue?

"How were your training sessions?" I ask Sloan.

Everyone has wandered off in one direction or another, and the two of us are standing on a ridge of the hill, absorbing a moment alone.

"It was illuminating," he says. "Arken possesses a wealth of knowledge, and although I was familiar with much of it, he approaches healing from a different perspective than I ever considered. Once I have a chance to digest what that could mean, I think it will give me a greater efficiency of healing reserves going forward."

By the excitement in his tone, that is great news.

I don't have to understand what that means. Sloan is excited about something, and I'm jazzed for him.

"What about your tactical training with Dahir and Tad? I didn't catch much of it, but from where I was working out with Royce, it looked like you were *poofing* in and out in every direction in rapid-fire."

"Aye, the idea is to use our wayfarer gift as an offensive attack. Dahir was teaching us how to make short bursts of travel from one side of an opponent to another to keep them off-balance."

"Cool. It looked wild."

"Honestly, it got a bit dizzying, but Dahir says it'll become second nature with practice and a wicked effective way to fight."

"Awesome. It makes sense though. Your gift should be useful for more than convenient travel."

"It should. It took a bit of effort to teach us how to tap into less power more often to get a handle on the process, but once we got that, we were on our way."

"Is Dahir a wayfarer?"

"No. He had kin who was and knew a great deal about it, but not him, no."

I lean sideways and bump his shoulder. "Well, I'm glad our time here is turning out to be productive."

He lays his arm across my shoulders and hugs me to his side. "What did ye work on today?"

"More work with the crown. I'm getting better at assessing the strengths of our team and our opponents, but I'm not great with the weaknesses of our group. I get the importance of acknowledging we all have weaknesses, but I don't like doing it."

"I suppose ye must separate emotion from assessment when war is on the horizon."

"It doesn't come naturally to me."

"No. It wouldn't. Yer need to support others would conflict with analyzing shortcomings."

"It does. In my mind, we're better to compensate for weaknesses by focusing on strengths."

"Aye, I pay attention." I expect him to ask what I think his weaknesses are, but he doesn't. "Well, it's good to know the iron crown is more than a heavy accessory."

"Or bedpost décor."

He chuckles. "Honestly, I think the look suits King Henry. Very regal."

"Right. It's amazingly powerful when you know how to use it."

"Which ye do now."

"Yeah. It's super cool. It was also a bit dizzying, but Fionn says with practice, I'll get the hang of it."

Sloan steps back from the ledge. The sun is dropping toward the horizon, and the light will fade soon after. "It'll be interesting to see what else we learn and how we can apply that when we get home."

"*If* we get home."

Sloan gives me a side hug and kisses my temple. "We'll get home, luv. There's a reason fer all of this. I feel it. Bodhmall's right. When we've satisfied the universe, it'll send us back."

"I hope so. I miss Manx and our house and Liam and the monkeys. And what about Nikon? Did they get Andromeda back?"

"I'm sure it'll all work out."

We're halfway back to the entrance to the underground bunker when Fionn finds us and waves us to follow him. "Come, lovebirds. There's trouble involving the Emhain Abhlach. If we leave now, we can be there by tomorrow night."

"We can be there right now," Sloan says. "I've been to the island more than once and can take us there straight away."

Fionn blinks as if that hadn't occurred to him. "Aye, of course, ye can. Come. We'll gather the others. There's no time to waste."

Thirteen of us *poof* from Fionn's land in Kildare, east past Dublin, onto an island in the Irish Sea. The moment we materialize, the ambient magic bombards, and my cells ignite. My fatigue and hunger evaporate, and my muscles sing with newfound energy.

"Holy schmoly, what is this place? It's like this island is a battery charger and I just got plugged in."

I take in the ropes of white waters cascading down a sheer, black rock face. The waterfalls don't descend in a straight line but instead zigzag this way and that around the rocks and the thick green moss clinging to it.

"Yeah...uh, me too. Am I glowing? I feel like I'm glowing." I glance over at Em and gasp.

The aura I've seen over the past three days of training with the crown has been supercharged, and yeah, Emmet is lit up like a hot pink night light. "What the serious hell, Em? Are you all right?"

"Other than being a living Barbie Dreamhouse lighthouse edition, yeah, I'm good. Great actually. It's hard to explain, but I feel like...I'm in sync with this place."

Aiden is studying Emmet and looks as freaked out as I feel. "What is Emhain Abhlach? Should we have heard about it before now?"

Sloan shakes his head. "Unless yer a person who studies Celtic lore, ye won't know of it. Emhain Abhlach is a mythical island paradise of old. Many scholars have tried to guess whether it was a land of the dead, home to the gods, a gate to an Irish Valhalla, or a portal mouth to a mythical realm."

"They don't know?"

He shakes his head. "Whatever Emhain Abhlach was in a time gone by, in our timeline, it's an island abandoned by the gods and empowered members alike. There are tales of a great city, but no one has ever found any evidence of ruins or where it might have stood. It's the druid equivalent to our great white whale."

Well, that sucks.

I glance around, and though it's a beautiful island covered in lush vegetation and pulsing with raw power, it doesn't seem to be any of the things Sloan suggested. "It's nice but not Valhalla nice…and there's no city. Are you sure we're on the right island, hotness?"

"As sure as I can be about a mythical island no one is sure of."

"Touché."

"It's the right island." Bodhmall points at the forest opposite the waterfall. "The city isn't out where everyone can see it. Come. The time we saved on travel gives us a fortunate edge. Whoever is here disturbing our connection to The Source power, they won't expect us to respond so soon."

Excellent. I always enjoy the element of surprise.

I scan the surroundings as we hurry away from the water's edge and overland toward the forest and waterfalls. Dusk is upon us. In another twenty minutes, it'll be dark. Even so, I can see a great deal of the landscape in both directions.

No city. No sign of anyone needing saving.

"This place feels like it's already abandoned."

"It's not," Bodhmall says.

I hustle to keep up. The woman might be a few centuries old, but she's fast. "What did you mean when you said someone is disturbing your connection with The Source?"

"Just that," she says.

That's where the explanation ends.

"Not a big talker in a crisis, I take it."

"Pay her no mind, *a leanbh*." Fionn trudges across the frosted terrain beside me. "The island of Emhain Abhlach is a special place in our time. It's sacred and important to a great many fae civilizations. It's a direct conduit of raw fae prana."

"Like ley lines?"

"The same concept but with much more power."

Yeah, I feel that…and poor Emmet. He looks like a nightlight for a four-year-old girl.

Being the shortest of the bunch, I'm jogging now to keep up. "If it's an emergency, it would be faster for Tad and Sloan to *poof* us over to the forest."

"Oh, that he could, lass," Fionn says. "No magic will take hold between the shoreline and the hidden city, I'm afraid. It helps to keep out the unwanted."

Sloan nods. "I remember the tales of capsized ships and mysterious deaths connected to people tryin' to find the island."

"Is it a warding thing or a Bermuda Triangle thing?" I ask.

"It's a vengeful god thing," Sloan says.

Fionn sweeps an arm, pointing at the Irish Sea all along the coastline. "Emhain Abhlach falls within the realm of the sea god Manannan mac Lir. He's quite strict about who may approach his island. Only those who are pure of heart and in need of respite gain access to these lands. Those who try with false intentions are sunk at sea and never heard from again."

"A bouncer on a power trip," Calum says.

Emmet snorts. "With the power to suck you to the bottom of the sea."

I wonder where that puts us. "So, since Sloan bypassed the entry requirements of a sea voyage, what are the odds he smites us for being here?"

Fionn shakes his head. "Not to worry, lass. We fall in the pure of heart category. If evil forces wish to destroy the isle as a place of strength, Manannan won't begrudge us comin' to put a stop to it."

I hop over a wide rut in the ground and hustle to keep up with Fionn's long, powerful strides. "Do you have any idea who's attacking the power of the island?"

"Ye ask too many questions," Bodhmall snaps, casting me a stern look over her shoulder. "Perhaps ye might hush yer curiosity and learn by observation."

Calum blinks at me and straightens.

I shrug and push on unaffected. "We came to help you protect somebody from something. Telling us what you know allows us to prepare better. It's not like we're Joe Schmoes and you have to keep us at arm's length."

Bodhmall surveys the landscape, scowling at the dusky sky when her attention falls on Fionn. "Ye said she was strong-minded, but ye neglected to mention annoyingly tenacious."

Fionn grins. "Just like her Great Auntie."

Bodhmall flicks her fingers. Sparks fly and snap at him like exploding fireworks.

As before, he pays little attention.

"Pay her no mind, lass. Ye see, Emhain Abhlach isn't solely an island paradise. It's also the home fer those mythical and magical beings who live outside of society. We were here not long ago to strengthen our bond to The Source before the Collidin' Realms and made a great many friends."

See…*that* I understand.

I get majorly cranky pants when my friends are in trouble, and I need to get to them.

We follow Bodhmall and the others toward the forest, and I draw a deep breath of the ambient magic. It's incredible. When I first became a druid and felt the ambient magic in Ireland, it was like being offered a refreshing glass of pink lemonade on a hot summer day. I drank it down in gulps.

This is like diving into a massive swimming pool of it… assuming it's refreshing and not sticky and gross.

Cray-cray. After eighteen months of training, study, and being thrown into the fire, I thought I had a handle on the kind of power available around me.

The untapped energy of this island blows the doors off that theory. And it's getting stronger the closer we get to the trees.

"If Emhain Abhlach is abandoned and in ruins in our time, why have you been here, hotness? Another one of your childhood field trips?"

Sloan grins. "I ventured here a time or two with my parents.

They had their faults as caregivers, no argument, but were exceptional as druid instructors."

Yes. They made sure their only child was chipped and chiseled into the best druid soldier evah.

"This is creepy cool." Calum is scanning the ebony cliffs rising two hundred feet in the distance and the dense forest between them and us. "Is it an optical illusion or have the trees grown that tightly together?"

"A bit of both," Fionn says.

"To keep out unwanted visitors, the forest of Emhain Abhlach shifts to block entry," Sloan explains. "It's one of only three such forests on the planet."

"Wicked cool," Emmet says.

"It is," Fionn says. "Unless ye want to gain admittance into the private realm of the island. Then it becomes a bit of a bite in the arse."

I can see how that would make things difficult.

"Everyone needs to focus on wanting to protect the sanctity of the island," Bodhmall says. "There are a great many sentient creatures in this forest—including the trees themselves. Our success will depend on them allowing us to gain entry."

We fall in behind Bodhmall and the Fianna warriors.

When we get to the edge of the tree line, however, the trees do nothing to block our path. Bodhmall and Fionn hesitate for a moment at the first line of trees, then frown and step into the shadows of the forest.

"That was a little anticlimactic," I whisper.

Emmet looks at me and nods. "I wanted to do the deciduous dodge."

"And the willow weave," Calum says.

"And the spruce spin," Dillan adds, looking at me.

"And the walnut waltz," I add, glancing at Aiden.

He rolls his eyes. "And the elm evade."

The Fianna look at us like they don't know what to say. "It's best to ignore them when they get like that," Sloan says.

I laugh. "It means we wanted to see what the trees could do when protecting the hidden city."

Koen frowns over at us. "No, ye don't. They don't just block intruders…they crush them to a pulp."

"Well, that's less intriguing. Let's not get trunk-pressed if we can avoid it."

Calum chuckles. "I prefer to remain three-dimensional myself."

"Agreed," Aiden says.

Fionn and Bodhmall raise their hands, and a surge of magic circulates in the air. It triggers the hair on the nape of my neck to stand on end, and I draw a deep breath.

I study the roots and ground. Squatting, I press my palm against the rich soil of the forest floor. The energy that comes back to me isn't natural at all.

It's pained.

"Someone has bound the trees in place. There's an immobilization spell holding them prisoner."

Fionn presses a hand against the bark of a large deciduous tree I've never seen before. Its bark looks dark blue in the shadows of early nightfall. "Fi's right. It's dark sorcery."

Bodhmall reaches toward the tree she's next to and touches its trunk. "What sorcerer has the power to bind the enchanted trees of Emhain Abhlach?"

The two of them stare at one another and whatever conclusion they come to doesn't seem to bode well for the people of Emhain Abhlach.

They turn and run.

We launch into a high-speed chase after them.

"Should I release Bruin to check things out?"

Fionn glances back at me, his expression tight. "Aye. A good idea. Tell him not to engage until we join him. Somethin' isn't right, and we shouldn't act until we know what it is."

Did you catch that, Bear? The forest of shifting trees is bound, and we need you to see what's gone wrong. Intel gathering only for now.

On it. Call yer armor, Red. I sense ye'll need it.

I release Bruin to go check things out and do as he suggested and activate my body armor.

As the inkwork of branches stretches along the surface of my skin, Sloan glances over at me, and his gaze narrows. "Has yer shield weighed in?"

"No. Bruin requested I activate my armor. He has an uneasy feeling."

That statement carries a lot of weight. Bruin isn't an alarmist, so if he wants my armor activated, there's a good chance things are going to swirl the shitter.

We continue, our party separated only when we weave our path around trees. Even without them actively moving to squish us or keep us away from the hidden realm beyond, it's a feat to make our way forward at the speed we need.

The ground heaves unevenly around the wide trunks, further rutted and pitted by the roots of hundreds of trees pressing close together.

A gentle tremor under my boots has me checking my footing and scanning the mossy groundcover and scrub. "Did everyone feel that?"

One look at my brothers answers my question.

Dillan has called his twin daggers, Calum his bow and quiver, Aiden his curved sword and buckler, and Emmet has unsheathed the knife Kevin bought him so he wouldn't be unarmed.

"The city is our priority," Bodhmall says. "Don't be distracted. It's likely the trees breakin' their hold."

I can't decide if that's good or not. Will they try to pulp us, or do they understand we're here to help? The scowl on Sloan's face makes me think he's wondering the same thing.

Whatever is happening, the tension building in the air is palpable.

Bruin roars up ahead.

Bodhmall curses and glares at me. "Ye were told he wasn't to act without us."

"He knew that. There must be a damned good reason he didn't listen." I don't wait for her to respond.

Launching forward, I overtake them and gun it.

Fionn curses. Bodhmall calls after me. It doesn't change my decision to break from the group. If my boy is in battle, my place is at his side, not back-seating it so they can ream me out.

Another vicious bellow rings through the night, and I push forward with even more power. Bruin is battling, and he's angry about it.

It's really dark now. The trees are so tight together no moonlight is making it through the canopy above. With Emmet behind me, I can't take advantage of his Barbie nightlight abilities.

I release the glamor of my fae sight and the darkness of the forest flips to the bizarre night vision Mother Nature gave me in the Cistern of The Source.

The closer I get, the more fae prana feeds my cells. I rush through the trees, drawing the magically rich, cool, night air into my lungs as I run.

Being able to see speeds me up considerably.

In a different situation, this would be fun. With Bruin's angry roar ringing in the distance, it's not.

Where are you, buddy? I send out my question, staring forward into the depths of an endless forest. Even if we ran until morning, we'd never reach the end of trees.

So, where is my bear?

I'm in the magical realm beyond the trees. Yer close. I feel yer approach.

His words and my reality don't align, but I believe what he

tells me. The empowered world is all about glamors and deceptions.

Bruin is pure truth.

Somehow, as I run straight into the massive forest, the ebony stone of the cliff face appears ahead. *Did you go through the rock face? Is there a crevice or a door?*

There's not. He grunts and takes a hit. *Focus on helping the creatures, and the rock face will let ye pass through it.*

Through the rock? That doesn't sound crazy or dangerous at all. There's not enough time to stop running even if I wanted to chicken out. At least with my body armor on, the worst thing will be bouncing face-first off a rock wall with my family and friends watching.

I've lived through worse ridicule.

Five feet…two…*yikes!*

I close my eyes and keep running, needing to get to Bruin, and whoever he's helping. Breaking through to the other side, my mental hamster tumbles in his wheel, and I'm momentarily at a loss.

I stumble to a jog and glance around to get my bearings. "Holy shitballs."

CHAPTER TWELVE

Passing through the ebony stone takes me from the darkness of night to the golden brilliance of day, from a dense forest to a waterside clearing reaching along the shore of brilliant pink waters. Yep, a fae prana river flows freely through this entire secret valley and wow…it's lush and fragrant and puts any utopic Garden of Eden imagery I've seen in movies to shame.

Fi, when yer done sight-seein' I could use yer help.

Right. As incredible as it is, it's also under serious attack. I gather my thoughts and resume my run toward Bruin. He's taking on three beasts with tusks and horns.

The things are hairy, massively muscled, and wielding spiked clubs. Miniature dragons are swooping at their heads but must retreat each time any of the beasts swing.

Sadly, the dragons are getting swished away like flies flicked by a horse's tail.

At Bruin's feet lies an unconscious female leprechaun. She's battered and bloody, and I know in an instant why he jumped the gun and engaged before he was supposed to.

Orders or no orders, he would never stand by while someone killed an innocent. Nor should he.

The attackers haven't noticed my approach yet.

Bestial Strength. Once the infusion of power strengthens my cells, I draw back my arm and launch Birga through the air. True to form, she sails with such accuracy and vigor that she lodges deep in the throat of the biggest oxen beast. "Good girl."

The beast lets out a horrendous cry that draws the attention of a dozen friends. It's too late for them to do anything for him. He's clamped his hands around Birga's spear tip, but there's no stopping the blood-fountain spewing from between his furry fingers.

I arrive at Bruin's side and take position over the dying beast. The stench of him and his friends burns my nostrils. It's like cat diarrhea and dead fish spawned a new scent.

"Gah...what do you guys roll in that makes you smell so bad?" I flex my hand and call Birga back to her resting place, then back to my palm.

As the fugly oxen backup fighters get closer, the one I nailed goes down for the count.

"The bigger they are, the harder they fall," I say.

"Ye've got a poetic soul, Red."

When the hairy mofo hits the ground, the thundering *thud* echoes all around. His buddies take it poorly and rush us in a wave of stinky violence.

Bruin is better matched against two than three and is back in his groove. He takes care of the original fighters so we can turn and face the incoming horde.

I lower my stance, lock into position, and scan our surroundings.

Because I rushed straight to Bruin's aid, I didn't assess the other players on the field. There are several dozen oxen beasts, a squad of warriors in forest green fighting gear and wide gold weapons belts, and an ebony-haired, red-skinned sorceress with protruding eyebrows that extend past the sides of her face and look more like horns. She's wearing golden armor, kickass black boots, and is brandishing a gold whip.

She's the big boss of the situation.

"There are so many things I could say about the dominatrix, but I'm trying to stay focused."

"Well done." Bruin's amusement is thick in the gravel of his voice. "I award ye a point for it."

"Thanks. See how mature I'm getting?"

Stepping in beside Bruin, I windmill Birga and smile as she sings on the wind. As a necromancer blade, there's nothing she enjoys more than drawing blood and drinking the powerful essence of her kill.

Bruin isn't much different.

When my bear flips the switch to his Killer Clawbearer persona, he likes nothing more than to cull through a line of bad guys. How I ended up with two such aggressive sidekicks, I'll never know.

Or maybe it's the universe's way of ensuring I have enough of the killer instinct on hand to do what I need to do without wavering.

Not that I would...

Or maybe I don't know shit about the universe, and I'm lucky to have such wicked cool friends at my side.

Yeah...that's likely it.

Bruin and I keep our backs together and manage to take down the fourth and fifth oxen beast by the time the others are in place and joining the fray.

"Oh-oh, here comes trouble."

The whistle of Calum's arrows sounds, and I follow the flight path back to where my brother has taken the high ground. He's crouched on the thatched roof of a massive palapa by the river and looks every bit the part of Robin of Locksley.

If only Kevin were here to see it.

Aiden and Sloan rush to join our fight while Fionn, Dillan,

Tad, and Emmet take on several fancy green coat fighters, and Bodhmall and the Fianna five are going after the sorceress.

"By the look on the sorceress' face, she wasn't anticipating company," Bruin says.

"She's not too pleased about having her murder and mayhem interrupted."

"That's a sad, sad story." Bruin sweeps his claws through the air and fells another beast onto the blood-soaked ground.

"Yeah, sucks to be her."

"Fi! On yer six!"

The urgency of Sloan's warning has me spinning to block the downward strike of an oxen beast...which, now that I've spent time looking at them up close, could be the demon lovechild of a water buffalo and a bigfoot.

"Damn, you guys really are ugly, aren't you?"

He doesn't answer. Then again, it was rhetorical.

With a grunt, I push back against his attack. He might be ugly and smell like ass, but he's a brute. *Bestial Strength* will only get me so far. I'd say we're well-matched for strength.

Thankfully, I've got brains and brawn.

"Confusion. Giant Insects. Hallucinations." As my intention takes hold, the three spells activate. Our opponents lose focus on their offensive objectives and back away, swiping at themselves and growling.

The massive scorpions, wasps, and fire ants are real enough to do damage, but I have no idea what kind of monsters their minds are barfing up.

"Hallucinations are a bitch." I remember how panicked and confused I was when Discord first started messing with me.

He made me kill Nikon. I'll never forget the horror of that moment as long as I live.

The number of attackers thins and when I drop my next opponent, I leave Birga lodged in the body so she can drink her fill. I'm not fond of necromancy as a source of magic, but Birga is a friend, and the power of death is what keeps her healthy and happy.

With my weapon of choice otherwise occupied, I bring out some other weapons to stretch my boundaries. *"Flaming Sphere."*

I draw the power needed to create fire orbs and send them streaming through the air at the furry beasts still standing. When my fireballs crash into my opponents, the flame takes hold of their matted fur like a brushfire, and they turn screaming for the water.

Dropping to my knees, I press my palms to the spongy ground and connect with the surface growth and the soil beneath. *"Mold Earth."*

Creating a fissure in the ground is the work of a moment and the effort of thought. The crack in the earth widens and swallows up the bodies of the fallen and two more beasts rushing us.

The panic in their eyes moves me, and I change tactics mid-spell. Instead of swallowing these raiders alive, I reform the soil around them so they're buried up to their armpits and secured by the ground.

"Earth to Stone." With that, they're trapped and no longer a threat.

Straightening, I dislodge Birga and rush to join the battle against the primary sorceress. Experience dictates that when the leader falls, the raiders fold.

Whoever she is...she's got her claws out and isn't about to back down. If I'm getting this right, people like Bodhmall and the Fianna come here, get a direct line to the power of The Source, and that empowers them to be better warriors.

No wonder Team Evil wants to take this place down. If Team Good has no direct line to The Source, Team Evil has no infused strength to contend with.

If I were an evil bad guy, it's what I would do.

"Look at Emmet go." Aiden raises his buckler and swings the curved blade of his sword. "Should we be worried?"

I find Em in the thick of things. He's got his hands up, and it looks like he's doing some kind of gymnastic ribbon dance. As he spins and lunges out of the fighters' reach, long streams of pink power twist and turn in his path.

"I didn't know he could do that."

"I don't think he did either." Sloan joins us.

I try to focus on the guy I'm up against, but Emmet's display is very distracting. Still, after my opponent gets a lucky crack to the side of my head, I figure I better focus. Enemies have only breached my armor a couple of times, but they *have* breached it.

"On your back, hotness." I strike hard and spin to work my way toward him. I grunt as I'm hit from the side and kick that guy right into Bruin's clutches.

Free to move again, I focus on the feet of the incoming force. *"Reverse Gravity."*

Their forward advance abruptly ends as they flip in the air and their rising feet keep them dangling above the ground. Twisting in fury does them no good, but it's huge fun for me.

Then, Aiden rushes in and knocks them out.

"Yay team!"

The sorceress sees her efforts are getting sucked down the shitter and lets out a banshee wail. I don't know what kinda evil juju she has behind her, but the hair on my arms stands on end.

A moment later, I feel what's coming next. "Eyes wide, boys. A portal is opening somewhere."

With that...it does.

Beside the thatched gazebo, the air fluctuates in a withershins swirl of black energy and a horde of oxen beasts vomits out at us.

Just like that, it ruins my good mood.

Thanks to the sorceress' tantrum, we're heavily outnumbered, and now it's *us* in deep manure.

"Well, crappers." I brace my stance and ready for the onslaught.

Fionn and the Fianna are already struggling to take down the sorceress, and now she has enough muscle power coming to her aid that we're likely outnumbered seven to one.

We're good at what we do, but that's stupid.

"Where's Dart when we need him?" My dragon boy could fry these beasts in one giant bonfire and give us a fighting chance.

"He won't be born for a thousand years," Aiden says. "So, I think it's safe to count him out on this one."

We fight against the undulating wall of hair and horns. It's a futile effort.

Sloan, Aiden, and I are back-to-back, defending against the massive force. It's exhausting.

As quickly as we cut an opponent down, three more push in to take its place.

I glance toward the prana river in time to see Dillan and Tad disappear behind a screen of matted monster hair. I scan the area wildly, hoping McNiff was able to *poof* them out of there before they got mauled. "Dillan! Roll call!"

Nothing comes back to me, or if it does, I can't hear it over the sounds of battle.

Calum shouts, and I watch in horror as the attackers overrun the palapa. Four hairy beasts scramble onto the thatched roof, grab him, and shove him down into the reaching grasps of the sorceress's minions.

"No!" There are too many. He'll never be able to defend, and there's no one there to help him escape.

"Bruin, help Calum by the gazebo!" Bruin is on his hind legs, swiping his claws through the air and snarling so loudly he doesn't hear me. "Bruin! Help Calum!"

My focus is shit, and I'm not paying attention to my battle. The high hit comes in hard and fast from my left while another furry fucker goes low and takes out my feet from my right.

I go down hard.

Sloan curses. I don't know if he saw me go down or if he's distracted by me and takes a hit of his own.

Either way, I can't fix it.

Three beasts are holding me down and pummeling me. Even with my armor up, the thundering punches are rattling my cage.

Maybe it doesn't matter that we're not ready for the Culling? Maybe we won't have to worry about it.

"ENOUGH!"

The beating stops, and it takes a moment for my cranium to stop sloshing around.

"Fi? Are ye all right, *a ghra*?"

Sloan crawls across the grass the short distance to grasp my arm and make a connection.

"What happened?" I scan the empty battleground. "Where did they go?"

Aiden's there a moment later, and he extends a hand. "I think Emmet did it."

I accept the hand up and take a moment when I get to my feet to make sure I'm not going to take another header. "Em did it?"

Searching the clearing, I find Emmet standing alone with his fists clenched at his side and a look of fury on his face I've rarely seen.

Sloan's sitting up. Calum waves at me. Tad and Dillan are over by a building near the river. Fionn and the Fianna look okay too. With the attendance taken, Aiden and I head over to check on our brother.

"Em? Are you okay?" I ask.

His expression is locked in a mask of fury, but there are streaks of clean skin where his tears have fallen and washed away the grime of our day.

Tracking the heavy rise and fall of his chest, I'm more than a little freaked. "Em...are you hurt?"

I step right in front of him and cup his jaw with both hands to get him focused on me. "Hey, there. It's me. Anybody home?"

He blinks, and his pupils adjust. His focus locks when he sees me. "What happened?"

"That's what we're trying to figure out. We were getting our asses handed to us, and you yelled, and the opposition was gone. Did you do that?"

He swallows and lets out a long exhale. "Yeah. I think so. We were getting pulverized, and everyone was going down…I couldn't help. I tried to use those ropes to fight, which worked for a bit, but it wasn't enough. There were so many of them."

"Yeah. A fuck ton," Aiden says.

Emmet shifts his gaze to our oldest brother and some of the tension in him eases. "Yeah. It bothers me, you know? I hate seeing all of you fighting with your powers and taking on the enemy, and I'm the asshole with basic spells and a knife."

I scoff at that. "You're more than that, Em. You have incredible power. You boost us. Your healing is getting stronger all the time…"

He shakes his head and steps back. "Yeah, I know all that, but I was so angry and scared, and all of a sudden, the ropes of power I found disappeared, then everything inside me was building until I couldn't take it. I just wanted it to stop. I wanted them all to be gone."

"So ye willed them away?" Sloan joins the family huddle.

"Yeah. I wanted them gone. I'd had enough, and it all kinda exploded out of me."

I swallow and meet Fionn's wide eyes.

"Where do ye think ye sent them, lad?"

Emmet shakes his head. "I honestly don't know, but I wanted it to be really far."

"It doesn't matter where." I brush the last of the moisture from his cheeks. "You saved the day, Em. You did great."

"He did," a feminine voice coos behind Fionn.

Stepping back, I stare at the place where someone should be standing. There's no one. "Who's there?"

The air ripples and my vision wavers. It's like trying to focus on seeing someone right in front of you through the distortion of heat coming off hot pavement. Like a mirage in the distance—only it's six feet away.

I take inventory of my instincts and my shield. Neither one is ringing warning bells.

Well, that's something.

As the distortion eases, an oddly tall woman with glistening silver skin and a teal feather mohawk steps into view. All she's wearing is a loose sheath of linked gold netting and a smile as radiant as the sun above.

I push back the wild compulsion to point out her delicate mesh doesn't cover any of her girl parts...or any of her parts for that matter.

She's nakey in front of two dozen strangers but doesn't seem to notice. In fact, she doesn't seem to notice anything or anyone except Emmet.

"Welcome, warrior." She lowers her chin. "We, the keepers of Emhain Abhlach, have long awaited your arrival. Finally, you are here, and the prophecy can be fulfilled. Praise the Light."

Emmet forces a smile. "Uh...sure, praise the Light."

CHAPTER THIRTEEN

Of all the crazy moments in our druid lives thus far, Emmet being the destined warrior of prophecy is one of the craziest. It's also one of my favs. Too often I'm the one with the cray-cray spotlight blinding me. Having this one on Emmet is fun for me.

"I am Kyna, of the Light," the naked silver lady says, addressing all of us. "I am one of the Ladies of Light, the protectors of this great city."

I'm still not sure what she considers a great city.

I scan the palapa Calum used for a perch and half a dozen wooden huts by the water where Dillan and Tad were fighting. Whatevs. Maybe where she comes from, this is a great city...or maybe city means something completely different in nakey Ladies of Light-landia.

"You and your people fought well today, friend," she says to Bodhmall. "Our deepest gratitude for your intervention in aiding us."

Bodhmall lowers her chin and bends forward in a subtle bow. "We were happy to be of aid...and happier still when the battle ended in our favor."

When Kyna faces me, a rush of raw prana power washes me, and the butterflies in my stomach flutter wildly.

"Are you and yours all well?"

I scan the group and other than filth, blood, and a hefty dose of post-battle exhaustion, everyone seems fine. "We are well, thank you."

"Thank the Light." Kyna raises her hands. "It's all right, everyone. All is well. You can come out now."

As she addresses the vast space between us and the huts on the shore, another rush of raw power hits and I brace myself against Bruin's round rump to keep from ass-planting on the spongy ground.

As before, the air ripples and waves before my eyes but when the distortion clears this time, four more oddly tall silver women step out of nothingness.

Then the city arrives…

I suppose it doesn't arrive so much as reveal itself, but it takes a moment to grasp. We're down at the water's edge. Then rising in tiers, a bustling city of multicolored buildings climbs toward a great golden tower. It's like those iconic images of a Greek island but with mauve, gold, seafoam, and fuchsia buildings.

"You hid the whole city?" I say, awed.

"Not me alone," Kyna says. "Me and my sisters."

"Kyna and her sisters are Light Weavers," Fionn says. "I take it from yer faces ye don't have their kind in yer time and place?"

I glance at Sloan. If anyone knows about the rare, mythological races of our time, it's him. He shakes his head. "No. It's believed we lost the last of them durin' the great wars a century ago."

"That is sad news indeed," Kyna says. "But today is not about sadness. It's about joy. Come, we will prepare a great meal in celebration of the day's victory and the arrival of our warrior."

"What about yer dead?" Fionn gestures at the fallen. "We can take care of that if ye wish."

Kyna scans the bodies of her citizens, her expression filled with sorrow. "If you could gather our fallen and return them to the earth, we have a sacred spot near the river. Syma will show you where."

"I can help," Tad says. "Once I see where, I can transport them, so you can set them to rest."

"Happy fer the help, lad," Fionn says.

Tad strikes off with the Fianna crew, and Syma and my brothers gather. Thankfully, with the excitement of Emmet taking out close to sixty raiders at once, he seems to have upstaged the nakedness of the Ladies of Light.

"Emmet, we should tend to the triage." Sloan gestures at the two dozen citizens injured during the battle.

"Oh, good call, Mackenzie." I shuffle off to check on Bruin and the lady leprechaun he was protecting when I first arrived.

I jog over to check on the Man o' Green—wait, nope, that's wrong. "Is *Woman* o' Green a thing?"

Bruin lifts his snout and snuffs at me. "How do ye think they procreate if it's not?"

"I hadn't really thought about it." Squatting, I press two fingers against the vein in her neck and meet with a strong pulse and warmth. Yay. "Just unconscious then. Come on, miss. Let's get you off the ground."

With my *Bestial Strength* still activated, I pick up the lady leprechaun, ready to carry her to wherever she needs to go.

"Put her down," a hostile wee man shouts, rushing over to join us. "Ye'll not have any gold, ye fiend. She hasn't any even if ye wanted it."

Sloan jogs over to intercede. "Fiona has no interest in gold. She's merely keeping the lass off the bloody ground to take her somewhere more comfortable."

"Why? Has she met her end?"

I frown. "Why would she need to be more comfortable if she's dead?"

Sloan throws me a look, but the words are out of my mouth before my brain kicks in.

"Sorry. I'm tired."

Kyna hears the ruckus and comes over. "All is well, Anghus. Your mate simply needs time to recover."

Dillan joins us, cradling one of the baby dragons in his arms. She's a beautiful little thing, long and lean, dark purple with gold webbing for her wings. The webbing is really cool. It's more like the spined membrane of a bat's wing than the thick scales of the dragons I know.

He stops in front of Kyna, looking bereft. "I'm sorry. I fought to get to her as quickly as I could, but I wasn't quick enough. One of those furry warthog beasts got to her first."

"Nyrora…" Kyna rushes to my brother and bends to examine the dragon. The Lady of Light stands a good six inches taller than any of my brothers and is as willowy as a twig. "Oh, thank the Light."

"Is she okay?" Dillan asks.

"She will thrive and soar the skies again."

"That's a relief." Dillan exhales, smiling down at the little she-dragon in his arms. "I was scared for her. She's such a beautiful little thing."

"She is." Kyna smiles and glances at where her sisters are standing outside our group. Something unspoken passes between them, then Kyna gestures at the city. "Come. The citizens will want to celebrate your victory, and there is much to discuss. Would you mind a banquet in your honor, warrior?"

Emmet grins and stands a little straighter. "Well, I'm not much for fussing but if the citizens want to honor me, who am I to say no and disappoint them? Sure. S'all good. Let the festivities commence."

Kyna leads our procession away from the waterfront and through two massive golden gates set into an ebony stone wall. The city streets lay beyond that and slope uphill toward the palace. She and her sisters wave at the citizens coming out of their homes as we pass. I get the impression the Ladies of Light are the rock stars of Emhain Abhlach.

It makes perfect sense since they weave light to keep the people who want to remain unseen hidden from their enemies.

As we make our way, I scan the curious faces of the citizens. Most have come out to the street or onto balconies to watch the procession. Others watch from behind the shield of draperies and window shutters.

Bruin is attracting a lot of attention.

I'm not surprised. During normal moments, he's awe-inspiring simply because of the massive grizzly he is. Right now, he's more. Evidence of the threat he poses to an enemy is still dripping from his fur. He's a bloody battle bear, and people can't help but stare.

Cheers of celebration follow us, and citizens tap their hands over their hearts. It's all a bit surreal.

We've never really received praise for what we do.

Usually, Garnet gives us a nod and a "well done," and we move on to the next crisis. This is...

"It's crazy that this is our life, don't you think?" Emmet takes the thought right out of my head. He gestures at our hostess on parade. "Do you ever look around and wonder, how can this be real? Secret cities. Sorceresses. Tusked beasts and miniature dragons...it's crazy, don't you think?"

"I was thinking the same thing. When Fionn first took me for a fireside chat, it was bizarre, but I could grasp it. We were alone, and my mind pretended we were at a normal bonfire. Going back to King Arthur's court was what first blew my mind."

"Going back to Merlin's cave first blew mine." Sloan smiles.

"This is totally blowing mine," Emmet adds.

I draw a deep breath, smiling at the creatures and people paying their respects.

"This is a nice change, eh?"

"A nice change from what, baby girl?" Aiden asks.

"Most times when the world goes to hell, I feel so guilty for foisting this whole druid can of worms on you guys. *I* love it, but you didn't choose it. Then there are moments when I wonder what in ordinary life could ever make us feel as alive as these moments."

"Don't ever feel guilty on my account." Dillan smiles at the purple dragon in his arms. She's revived enough to open her bright, teal eyes and has grasped Dillan's finger with both of her talons. "This life is the bomb. I wouldn't trade the work we do, meeting the Greeks, or loving Eva for anything. Whether it's good or bad coming at us, being a druid is everything to me."

Emmet smiles at the blonde lady leprechaun Sloan's now carrying and her auburn-haired, foul-dispositioned hubby. "Same. Between the friends we've made, the powers we've gained, and Ciara, I'm all in. Don't feel bad about the chaos that comes with it."

Calum chuckles. "Who are we kidding? There was chaos in our lives long before now. Between us raising ourselves with Da working to keep a roof over our heads, and being cops, and being us…becoming empowered is only a different kind of chaos."

Aiden doesn't volunteer an opinion, and I feel bad.

"I know you don't share the same zeal for the lifestyle we do, Aiden. I'm sorry. I hope you don't regret it too much."

He shakes his head. "I don't. I worry for my kids and wish they could've had a normal childhood like ours, but I'm good."

Calum snorts. "Can you honestly say, 'normal like ours' and keep a straight face?"

He chuckles. "Yeah no, maybe not."

"Other than the kids...what do *you* think?"

He considers that for a moment and shrugs. "I'm happy to have the druid heritage, but I'm more grateful to have Gran and Granda."

There's a shared mumble of agreement about that.

We might've been able to have them and not be druids. Da kept us away, but I always wanted to do an AncestryDNA test to find long-lost relatives. If I had, maybe Aiden wouldn't be stuck with this life.

That hurts my heart.

"Look, Fi," he says. "You chose to save Granda's life and take this on. I'd never judge you for that or wish you had chosen differently. You gave us your love and support for years while we found our purpose and now, you've found yours. Being a druid lights you up like nothing else ever has. All is right in the world, baby girl. Don't worry."

I draw a deep breath. He's being honest. He's there for us, he enjoys being a druid, but it doesn't feed his soul as it does for the rest of us.

It's nothing I didn't know.

"Aw, don't cry." He takes my hand and squeezes it. "I'm good. There's nothing to cry about."

I swipe at the tears and draw a deep breath. "I just want you to be happy. I want all of you to be happy."

"I *am* happy. Sure, I'd be happier if we knew how we were getting home, but that's not on you. Don't cry."

I draw another long, deep breath and push down the disappointment. "Sorry. I'm not usually such a sap."

Calum chuckles. "Who are you trying to snow? You're the biggest sap there is."

I swallow and force a smile for the people watching. "S'all good. Like Kyna said. This isn't a day for sadness. It's a day for celebration."

Aiden pulls me to his side as we walk. "I'm happy to walk this path with you four. My problem is when I'm here, I worry about my family back home, and when I get left back home, I worry about my family out living magical adventures. There's no right answer, so there's no need to stress about it."

I understand that. Still…it hurts.

"This is us." Anghus points at a mauve home facing the palace.

"Would ye like me to take her inside or upstairs?"

"No. I wouldn't like that," Anghus snaps. "Padraig, come help with Betrys. She took hurt in the battle."

I'm pulled out of my mood the instant I hear the name. No. It couldn't be…

I turn and my heart hammers in my chest. The Man o' Green struggling to hold himself upright in the doorway is the spitting image of my dear friend…except his snowy white hair is still russet red…and he isn't wearing spectacles…and he's fall-down drunk.

Well, that's not totally out of character for Patty, but he doesn't look like he's partying so much as drowning his sorrows. Still, there's no mistaking him.

It's Patty all right.

"Patty, ohmygod, look at you!" I move to hug him but get shoved back by a pulse of magic and freeze as my shield flares.

He's staring up at me, and his eyes hold none of the warmth I'm used to. In fact, he has a dagger drawn and aimed at me. "I'll thank ye to keep yer distance, female."

I take a step back.

It shouldn't sting as much as it does, but I'm still a little emotional from my talk with Aiden. "Sorry. Right. You don't know me yet, but I assure you, in my time we're close friends. Me hugging you wasn't anything out of the ordinary."

He arches a brow and gives me a skeptical look. "I doubt that very much, lass. I'd never trust a greedy human enough to be friends, let alone allow one to touch me without puttin' up a fight."

"Yeah, well, your attitude on that will change."

"I doubt it."

"I can prove it." I pull out my phone and turn it on.

"Maybe ye should let it be, luv." Sloan is in the process of handing Betrys over to them when she rouses.

A sharp elbow to his gut has his breath escaping in a rush. He bends over, setting her on her feet as quickly as he can. "Be calm, miss. I'm merely deliverin' ye back to yer—*Fuuuuck!*"

A solid punch to the groin has Sloan doubled over and going red in the face.

Patty's sister looks so much like him when she's pissed it's hilarious. Well, it would be hilarious if Sloan's testicles weren't under attack.

"Are you okay, hotness?"

Sloan has his hands braced on his knees and is trying to breathe. "I'll be fine," he wheezes. "Talk amongst yerselves."

Poor hotness. He's going to need a minute.

That reminds me of the pictures.

"Here. This is us last month at the birthday party we gave to the young dragons. This is you and me getting drunk at the pub after Calum's wedding. Here's one of you passed out on my couch, sleeping off a night of drinking last summer. That's Daisy, my brother's companion skunk."

He scowls. "I don't know what kind of witchcraft this is, but last summer I wasn't drinkin' with humans or goin' to birthday parties or sleepin' with skunks."

Right. "Sorry. We're from the future…about a thousand years from what we can tell."

He's frowning at the pictures. "That's supposed to be me?"

"It's not supposed to be you. It *is* you. Look, here's angry Patty. I took this one when we went up against a bitch of a witch that kidnapped Sloan last year."

Emmet laughs. "Oh! That was an awesome night for you, Patty. We couldn't get through the warding, so you connected with all the valuables in the house and threw your arms left to right and back and again. You trashed the place, and we could hear the witches screaming out on the street."

Dillan's laughing now too. "It was classic."

Sloan clears his throat. "I think that's quite enough sharin' folks. It's never a good idea to muddy the waters of the timeline. Less is more in this instance."

"Maybe yer right, hotness." I don't find an ounce of my friend in this version of Patty. "Whether you believe me or not, we *are* friends, so I'll tell you this because I love you. When you hit your darkest time, and humans have taken your treasure trove, make an alliance with the Dragon Queen of Wyrms. She'll chomp anyone who comes to collect, and you'll rebuild it all—"

"Enough, Fi." Sloan grips my elbow and gives me the bum's rush back into motion. He seems to have recovered from the attack on his knackers, but his mood hasn't improved. "What part of not talking about decisions yet to be made don't ye understand?"

I shrug, glancing back at Patty standing in the street outside his little mauve house. "It was a very hard time for him. He almost gave up hope. Look at him…this could be it. If I can point him in the right direction, I have to try."

Sloan *harrumphs* and turns us toward the palace. "I know ye think ye do, but ye *don't*. He made the right choice last time, hopefully, despite yer interference, he will again."

"Or maybe he made the right choice because we met up, and I helped him find the path that will lead him back to me. That's possible too, isn't it?"

Sloan scowls at me and rolls his eyes. "Whether it is or it isn't, is not fer us to toy with. Ye mustn't meddle in such things, luv."

I hold up my hands and surrender. "Fine. I said what I wanted to say. I'll drop it and won't say another word."

He lets out a long breath. "I'll believe that when I see it. And if we're lucky, ye haven't set off a cataclysmic event."

I flutter my lashes at him and feign innocence. "Who? Little ole me?"

CHAPTER FOURTEEN

Kyna leads us through the winding streets of the hidden city and straight into the golden tower. If I'm honest, it looks like a tall, golden dildo with a lot of inset balconies. I glance at my brothers to see if they've noticed and yep. Of course, they have. They're all biting their lips and about to bust up—which would be bad form as guests.

I focus straight ahead as quickly as I can.

What lovely stairs. Yes, let's all look at the stairs leading up to the golden tower. Oh, and the double doors are opening as we approach. I smile at the doorkeepers as we pass, and my mind flips from golden dildos to trying not to react to the cat men smiling back at me.

Seriously, they are cat men—not even kidding.

Standing on two feet in guard uniforms, they have cat heads, paws, and tails.

"Thank you," I say as we pass.

I'm half waiting for them to meow or purr or something, but they don't acknowledge us. Maybe they didn't understand me, or perhaps they're like the Queen's Foot Guards at Buckingham Palace and are trained to remain stoic and silent.

We continue inside, walk beneath the swaying incense chandelier, and Kyna leads us up the curved stone staircase to the second floor. The stone is smooth and a light, golden beige. The subtle curve of the walls makes it feel like we're inside a cylinder.

It's weird. The other times I've spent in the past were in castles too, but those felt strangely familiar. This palace doesn't. Everything about it feels odd and sets my awareness on edge. It's like someone is blowing on the hair of my arms and making it rise.

Maybe it's the sensation of so much raw power all around us. Or maybe I'm feeling wacked and punchy because I'm so tired.

Likely the latter.

"Here we are," Kyna says.

The room she leads us into is a large, open rectangle with four framed beds placed in the corners. A long table with twelve chairs runs across the center of the room. Beyond that, there is an open portico with a balcony overlooking the city we walked through.

"Swanky." Emmet whistles through his teeth. "This is one of those, 'fit for a king' moments, eh?"

"True dat." Calum pulls out his phone to turn it on. "Kev will die when he sees this."

As we disperse deeper into the room, a cat lady arrives with a trolley and sets it inside the door. It has two basins of water with a stack of cloths.

"If it pleases you," Kyna says, "Take time to rest and wash while I tend to the preparations. I will send for you all shortly."

I run a finger through the hot water in one of the washbasins and smile. "It pleases us. Thank you."

Kyna moves to step out into the hall and Dillan follows. "What about Nyrora?" he asks. "Do you want to take her? Does she need medical attention?"

Kyna looks down at the wee thing and grins. "She looks perfectly content where she is. Koinonos dragons have incredible regeneration abilities. Given a chance to rest in a safe environment, they can heal themselves. Continue what you're doing, and she'll have fully recovered in time for the celebration feast. Unless you've grown tired of comforting her?"

"Oh, no," Dillan says. "It's nothing like that. I wanted to make sure her needs were met."

Kyna cups Dillan's cheek in her silvery palm. "A wonderful start to a bonding of friends."

A shiver runs up my spine, and I can't shake the feeling there's more to her words than we know.

Another cat woman stops outside the door, and Kyna turns to leave. "I'm off to prepare a fitting celebration for our brave warrior and his company. Be well, friends. The palace of Emhain Abhlach welcomes you."

Kyna leaves us to ourselves, and Emmet walks her out. When he closes the door, he's all puffed up and grinning. "Well, who woulda thunk it? I'm the warrior of an ancient prophecy. Pretty cool, huh?"

I shake my head. "I'm not sure what to think about that, honestly. What is the prophecy? She didn't say. I'm hoping it's not one of those things where they feed you a feast to fatten you up, then feed you to the hideous beast who lives in the volcano."

Emmet frowns. "Harsh."

"Are your Spidey-senses tingling?" Aiden asks.

"My whole body is tingling...and not the good way. This prana-powered island is hell on my equilibrium. I'm all jittery and jazzed."

"Well, that's never good," Calum says. "What about your shield?"

"Nope. Nothing there either."

Emmet frowns. "Why can't it be a good thing? Maybe I really

am a wonder and meant to do great things. Have you ever considered that?"

I meet his gaze and sober. "Of course, I have. You are a wonder in a dozen ways that would dazzle the world. Emhain Abhlach would be lucky to have you as their champion. I simply want to make sure that the 'preparations for the warrior' don't involve anything you don't walk away from."

Emmet nods. "Okay, yeah. I'll give you that. Honestly, I don't think it is. I feel at home here, like seriously in sync with this place. I don't think the universe would be so cruel as to give me such a warm fuzzy then try to sacrifice me."

"At home? What does that mean? Em, we're the farthest from home that you've ever been."

"Yeah, I get that, but I can't explain it."

"Maybe it's yer connection with the prana energy," Sloan says. "The rivers run pink with it, and the air is full of power. I bet it's yer connection that makes ye feel that way, Em."

"Maybe."

"So, we'll wash up, rest, and regroup. Everyone to their corners for a bit and we'll reconvene once we can come at it with fresh minds."

Sloan frowns. "Do ye think Bruin has time to go fer a swim before the next catastrophe strikes?"

I laugh. "Oh, yes, please. We'll make time for that."

Bruin chuckles. "What are ye gettin' at? I feel ganged up on."

Sloan chuckles. "Ye stink, Bear. Ye traipsed blood and death through the halls of the sacred palace and ye smell like the insides of a rotting corpse."

I jump on this train and back Sloan up. "There's not enough water basins in the palace to clean all the blood from your fur, buddy."

Bruin raises his black nose and grins. "A job worth doing is worth doing well."

"Aye, it is."

I giggle and point at the open balcony. "You know where we are now. Go find a freshwater pond or a pool or something."

"Don't swim in the pink water," Emmet says. "You'll end up glowing, and I don't think pink is your color."

Calum snorts. "News flash, Em. It's not doing much for you either."

Emmet waves that away. Thankfully, once he detonated half an hour ago, the glow was gone. Whether it comes back or is gone for good is yet to be seen.

"All right." I cut off the banter about to break loose between my brothers. "Bruin, go get cleaned up and come straight back. If there's something brewing with the warrior prophecy, we might need you here. If not, you don't want to miss dinner."

Bruin lumbers toward the balcony and ghosts out, chuckling. *As if that would ever happen.*

Chuckling, I wet one of the towels, wring it out, and hold the steamy fabric over my face. My skin tingles and I drag in a deep breath. "Man, this feels good."

After I finish wiping down, I take off my boots and jacket and lay on one of the beds. "Wake me up when it's time for food. This is me tapping out. Peace."

"Power nap for the win." I hop off the bed, stuff my feet back into my boots, and bend to latch the chrome buckles. "How long was I out?"

"Forty minutes or so." Sloan is sitting at the long table in the middle of the room, scanning through a book.

"What have you got there?"

He holds up the leather-bound tome for me to see the cover and sets it back onto the table. "There's a library at the end of the corridor. I might have helped myself to a few books to tide me over while everyone is quiet and we wait for dinner.

I chuckle silently. He's the only person I know who needs more than one book to tide him over during a forty-minute break in the action.

Well, maybe Myra would too.

Either way, I'm in love with a word nerd.

Who would've seen that coming?

My chair makes a soft scrape against the stone floor as I pull it out to sit next to him. "I don't read whatever that language is. What does it say?"

"It's a journal of natural remedies written by a green witch who lived in ancient Turkey. Some of her thoughts are based on a lack of understanding of science. Still, others are quite interesting…particularly her experimentation with mixing certain herbs with spells to bolster their efficacy."

"Cool. Did you take notes?"

He grins and holds up his phone. "I took pictures to go over more closely later."

"What's this?" I tap my finger on a rolled piece of parchment.

"That's a demon trap spell. I thought it might come in handy. We've accounted for many of the species of power we'll be coming up against in the next weeks, but there's always a chance others will surprise us."

"That's my Boy Scout—always prepared."

He winks at me. "How was yer nap?"

"Awesome. All I needed was a chance to catch my breath and adjust to this power level."

"And saw some major-ass logs." Emmet comes in off the balcony with Calum and Tad.

Tad glances at me and laughs. "Ye've got quite a trumpet on ye, Fi. It must be why Mackenzie is always so surly. The guy never gets any sleep."

I roll my eyes. "I only snore when I'm worn out. Otherwise, I'm as quiet as a little kitten curled up in her bed. Right, hotness?"

He laughs. "Whatever ye say, luv. I'll not out ye in front of our friends."

Calum laughs. "You don't have to. We grew up with her. We know how loud the trumpets blare."

"Rude. I bet you haven't heard me snore since I moved in with Sloan."

"Because you spell your bedroom for silence at night. Thank you for that. Big brothers should never hear their sister in the throes of anything."

"I prefer to tell myself Sloan's a eunuch and nothing ever happens," Emmet says.

My jaw drops. "You do not."

Emmet snorts. "No, I don't. Sorry, Irish. I wanted to see her face."

Sloan stares at us with the same blank expression he often gets when he's ignoring us.

I shrug. "Back to the point at hand, even exhausted, I don't snore as badly as Drunk Dillan."

My brothers nod. "True story."

I glance around the room, past Bruin curled up on the rug, and find Dillan's feet hanging off the side of one of the other beds. "He's still out?"

"Like a light," Calum says. "He took the baby dragon with him to have a snuggle sleep."

"Noice." I pull out my phone and call up my camera. "I gotta get a picture of that."

"She's not a baby dragon," Sloan says. "I was speaking to one of the castle attendants while I was in the corridor. The Koinonos dragons are a species of pseudo dragons."

"Pseudo, as in not real? She looked real."

"No, luv. It's a term fer a miniature dragon race. She's not tiny because she's a baby. She's tiny because that's the size she's supposed to be."

"Aww…that's awesome." Rising from the table, I make sure

not to scrape the chair legs. Getting secret photos of each other for teasing and blackmail purposes is what we do.

Rounding the footboard of the bed, I sneak into position and get ready to snap my shot. "Where'd the little dragon go?"

Sloan looks up from the table and frowns. "Nowhere that I noticed. Not unless she flew off while I went to the library."

Emmet shakes his head. "No. I've taken a picture of them since you were back. That's when we went out onto the balcony to let you read. No little dragon came out our way."

Dillan must sense me standing over him because his eyes flutter open. He draws a deep breath and blinks awake. "Hey. Is it chow time?"

"Not yet. Where did your little dragon friend go?"

Dillan snaps more awake and sits up, glancing around on the bed. "She's not here? Where did she go? How long was I out?"

"A half an hour," Emmet says. "We can't figure out where the dragon could've gone. Irish was reading at the table, and we were out on the balcony, and none of us saw her leave."

"Did she get scared and go under the bed?" Calum heads over.

I tuck my phone into my pocket and get down on my hands and knees. Peering into the shadowed space under the bed, I scan the empty stone floor. "Nope. She's not here."

"Are you sure?" Dillan slides off the straw mattress to check for himself.

"I'm sure. It's not dark enough under there for me to miss a dragon."

Dillan straightens, looking frustrated. "I hope she's okay."

The genuine concern in his expression makes me smile. Dillan comes off like a grumpy hardass, but he's a huge softy. He leans across the bed to check behind the pillows, and his shirt rucks up.

I stare at the purple ink across his lower back and chuckle. "When did you get a tramp stamp? More importantly, what is it? A purple butterfly? Please let it be a purple butterfly."

Calum busts up and jogs around the bed. "This I gotta see. How drunk would Drunk Dillan have to be to get a purple butterfly?"

Dillan pushes Calum back. "Fuck off. Like I'd ever get a tramp stamp." He straightens, searching the room, thoroughly distracted.

"I know what I saw." I step in behind him. "Stand still for a sec."

Despite him not standing still, getting annoyed with me lifting the tail of his shirt, and trying to shake me off his ass, I get the job done. My reward for the struggle is the answer we've been seeking.

"Okay, I found Nyrora."

"Where?" Dillan is still glancing around the room.

I hook my fingers through the belt loops of his jeans and turn his hips so he's facing away from the others. Grabbing the hem of his shirt, I shove it up his back.

"Holy fuck." Emmet jogs over to get a better look. "How the hell did she do that?"

"Do what?" Dillan snaps as Sloan, Calum, and Tad rush over. "Someone, use your words."

"Nyrora's not missing." I smile at her bright seafoam eyes staring out at me. "Somehow, she bonded with you like Bruin does with me. Only we can see her. You have a purple dragon tattoo looking out at me from your left shoulder blade and her tail curls down your right ribs and across the small of your back."

"Are you sure?"

"Do you think we're having a group hallucination?"

"Do I think you wouldn't gaslight me for a laugh?"

I snort. "I totes would, but I'm not. Em, hold his shirt so I can take a picture." Emmet does as I ask, and I snap the image. "See."

He takes the phone and blows up the image. "That's fucking spank, but what does it mean? Why is she there?"

"Ask her."

He chuffs. "Oh, right. Why didn't I think of that?"

"No, seriously, dumbass. Close your eyes, clear your mind, and speak to her internally. Bruin and I were able to do that from the moment we bonded. There's no language barrier when you've bonded. Give it a try."

He makes a snarky noise but says nothing.

I point at the edge of the bed, and he leans his butt against the mattress. "Okay, deep breath, clear intention, reach out and say hello."

Eyes closed, he draws a deep breath and exhales, tilting his head from one side to another.

I glance at Sloan, Tad, and my brothers. They look as baffled and excited as I feel.

Physically bonding with a dragon seems crazy. I can't imagine having a beast as massive as a supersized Dart bursting out of me during battle. Well, not that there's room inside me anyway.

Bruin already laid his claim on that territory.

Maybe it's a good thing Nyrora's a tiny dragon. She'd take up less space.

Dillan's intake of breath brings me back to the situation at hand. By the arched brows, I assume he's having at least some success.

I hope the smile softening his expression indicates that things are going well. Between his love for Eva and having a little dragon to love, I can see Dillan finally being truly happy.

I'm getting ahead of myself, I know, but he was the one of us who never truly recovered from losing Mam. We all still miss her and think about her all the time, but Dillan's the one who's still angry and hurt.

I have no idea why the little dragon bonded with him or what it will mean.

The logistics alone are boggling.

Are her family here? Can she live in Toronto? Is there room in the grove dragon lair for a third dragon?

I think about Merlin's warning last summer. He said a dragon needs his kind to be truly happy. Maybe establishing a dragon brood in our backyard is the answer.

Okay…I'm getting ahead of myself again.

"She's mine," Dillan says, his voice laced with equal parts confusion and surprise. "According to the customs of her species, a life saved is a life owed. She bonded with me because she's mine now."

"That's honorable," Sloan says, his brows tight, "but is it what she wants? A life owed isn't the same as a choice made."

"She does. She's super excited." He pushes off the bed and meets our gazes and—

"Holy hell!" I gasp.

"Houston, we have a problem," Emmet says.

"What now?" Dillan asks.

"Your eyes. They're the same teal as Nyrora's." I open the camera on my phone and flip the view so he can see himself. I've never seen any human's eyes this color, but it's hella striking with his black hair.

"Well, that's new."

"Yep. It kinda gives me the feeling that this bonding has taken hold." I tuck my phone back into my pocket and glance at Sloan. "Any insights on this, hotness?"

"None that would prove to be anything beyond a guess. I think yer right. He spoke with her, they came to an agreement, and his eyes changed. I'd say that's a sign that the bonding has taken hold."

The soft *swish* of the door swinging open brings the Fianna in to join the party.

"I hear ye have water to clean up," Fionn says, leading the way, followed by Royce, Arken, and the other men. "Goddess knows we could use some."

By the looks on our faces, he must realize we're in the middle of something. He stiffens and changes course from the wash station to us. "What's happened?"

"Look at Dillan's eyes." I point at my brother before turning him around to show them his back. "It seems the little dragon Dillan rescued has taken a liking to him and decided they make a good team."

"Blessed be. To have a Koinonos dragon bond with ye is a rare honor." Arken rushes forward. "Look at that. Yer system accepted her without issue. The goddess must approve of the match."

"Without issue?" I ask. "What does that mean? Do some people's bodies reject the bonding?"

"Of course. Not everyone is a good match. If they were, everyone would be trying to bond with them."

I'm about to ask what would've happened if they were *not* a good match when Sloan shakes his head. "We don't need to know, *a ghra*. The point is they matched well, and yer brother is no worse fer wear."

"Except the eyes," I say.

"Honestly, I think they're cool," Emmet says. "We've all got green. His are unique."

"Aiden and I have blue."

"Yeah, but you two are freaks. You're the A-F bookends to the clan. Everyone knows it's better in the center: Oreos, bulls-eyes, hurricanes—"

"And three-ways," Calum adds.

I roll my eyes. "I'm not saying they aren't cool. I'm saying that when your eyes change, it's not easy to get used to looking at yourself in the mirror."

"It wasn't easy for you," Calum says. "Sorry, Fi, but these are way better than your freaky fae eyes."

I make a face at him. "How did this get turned around on me?"

"It didn't," Dillan says. "It's all about my dragon and me. Everyone, focus. What do I do?"

"What do ye do about what, lad?" Fionn asks.

"What do I do about a dragon making me her daddy and merging with me? Is she stuck there? What does it do to me? Does she have family here? Will they think I'm taking their child? I don't know…I'm freaking out here and need someone to tell me what I'm doing."

Royce finishes washing up, and I can't stop thinking about that water being cold and dirty and already used by like six people….

Ew, moving on.

Royce hands Fionn the cloth next and comes over to check out Dillan's dragon tattoo. "Yer fine, lad. The bond between Koinonos and master is stronger than a father and child, a husband and wife, or a lifelong friend. She is a part of ye now and will be whatever ye need."

"But what does *she* need?"

"Only to be of use to ye. Do ye not understand what a gift she's given ye?"

Dillan frowns and sighs. "No. I don't. I don't even know what a Koinonos dragon is. What keeps swirling around in my head is, what happens when I'm at the gym and take off my shirt? What about when I'm working on the streets, and I get into it with a perp? Can she get hurt if I get jumped from behind? There are so many things to worry about."

Fionn finishes washing up and chuckles. "How about ye not worry about them all at once. Let's go find our supper and see how Bodhmall's time here has gone with the Ladies of Light. We can take yer concerns one at a time."

Bruin yawns wide and pushes himself up onto his paws. With a powerful twist, he shakes himself, and his fur rustles and settles in place. "Did someone say supper?" He looks at us and reads the room. "Och, hell. What did I miss now?"

CHAPTER FIFTEEN

The celebration dinner prepared in honor of Emmet's mass evacuation takes place in a great, golden dining hall. Four long tables stretch the room's length with benches already filled with excited locals. Above the tables hang elaborate chandeliers with a glowing plant woven around in an ornate pattern to provide light.

It reminds me of the phosphorescent moss in Gran's and Granda's bathroom. It's quite beautiful—as well as bright.

At the front of the room, there's a head table running perpendicular to the others, and those seats are all vacant. "I guess we're at the front?"

"We're the teachers at Hogwarts," Calum whispers under his breath. "I'm Lupin. Dillan, you're Snape. Emmet, you're Hagrid, and Aiden's Flitwick."

"I'm McGonagall," I say, pleased with my pick.

"I'm not Hagrid," Emmet gripes, casting us a shit-eating grin. "Tonight, I'm freakin' Dumbledore. Behold the warrior of the prophecy. Bow to me, assholes."

Hilarious. "He's not wrong." I hold up a finger and stop Calum's argument before it begins. "He can be Dumbledore for tonight, and Aiden can be Hagrid. He's not a good Flitwick anyway."

"Who am I?" Sloan asks, playing along with our shenanigans for once.

"Definitely Hermione," Calum says, laughing.

"Isn't that the girl?" Sloan asks.

I chuckle. "The incredibly smart girl who's read all the books and knows all the answers that save the others on the daily. I think it was a compliment."

He arches a brow at me, and I can't help but laugh. "No. You don't have to be Hermione. You can be Sirius Black. You're smart, mysterious, and misunderstood."

He gives Calum a suck-it smile and carries on toward the head table, looking pleased with himself.

Calum and I have to stifle our laughter behind our hands because that was honestly the most childish thing I've ever seen Sloan do. "Hilarious."

"We're breaking through his tough exoskeleton one jab at a time," Calum says. "I do think he'd make a great Hermione, though."

I push him ahead of me and try to look professional. "I'm still worried Dumbledore might end up getting fed to the volcano beast as an offering."

Calum nods. "We'll watch for it."

When we arrive at the head table, Kyna and two of her sisters are waiting to greet us. "Blessed evening," Kyna says, welcoming us. "You remember my sister, Syma. This is Lyri."

"Welcome to our city," Lyri says.

"We're honored to be here." I bow my head and try to emanate the appropriate amount of reverence.

"Is that Bodhmall?" Dillan tilts his head toward where our great-great-auntie is chatting with one of the cat women.

"She looks lovely." I admire her pale green dress and how it hangs and clings. I look down at my battle leathers and shrug. Fionn taught us a spell to remove the day's blood, and we all wiped down our clothes, but it is what it is.

We finish with the pleasantries of introductions and take our seats. My instincts are still niggling at me, so I'm relieved my back is against the wall, and I can see both the entrance door as well as the open wall leading out to the balcony.

Sloan is seated to my right and Emmet to my left.

Kyna sits to Emmet's left, and her sisters are beside her. Once everyone settles, Kyna leans forward to speak to us. "I trust you had a chance to rest and recover this afternoon in your chambers?"

I nod. "We did, thank you."

"We did have one unexpected thing happen, though," Dillan says, holding up a finger. "Nyrora bonded to me and is now a tattoo on my back."

Kyna grins unrepentantly. "How wonderful. I had a feeling something like that might happen."

I unfold the linen napkin at my place and set it in my lap. "You didn't think to mention it to us?"

Kyna unfolds her napkin and sets it into her lap. "In truth, I was *hoping* it would happen. Nyrora's siblings have all bonded and found their place. Two chose to bond with feline folk and remain here, while the others found life partners with visitors over the years and have gone to live out in the beyond."

"Nyrora was waiting," Syma says. "It's a long, lonely life for a creature without a match."

"Another reason to celebrate," Kyna says. As she raises her glass, the air sparkles like champagne, and the empty glasses in front of us fill with a pale rose liquid. "To the bonding of new friends."

I scan the expressions of our group, the Fianna, and the Ladies of Light. Everyone seems to agree we're celebrating, so I lift my glass and bring it to my lips.

I don't ingest the drink.

Tipping it back gently, I let the liquid bubble against my lips and set the full glass back on the table. Having worked the bar for years, I'm used to guys buying me drinks. I would be a sloppy mess on a Saturday night if I drank them, so I got really good at faking it.

Unless it's Redbreast. *That* I totally drink.

I'm not about to partake until I know what this prophecy business is about and their plans for Emmet. I scan the room.

My shield is quiet.

There's no reason for my trepidation, but I can't shake the feeling that something isn't jiving. Someone says something uproarious at the table by the window, and the air fills with wild laughter.

Kyna chuckles. "It's wonderful to have a chance to give thanks. The goddess always provides, but—for a brief moment today—I did worry that help might not come quickly enough."

A man in an apron steps inside the door and bows at the head table. The crowd lets out a round of cheering. Then the man swipes a hand, and large serving bowls and platters full of food suddenly cover all the tables.

"I told you," Calum says. "Just like Hogwarts."

Dinner goes off without a hitch, and when we retire to the receiving room for sweets and drinks, I'm beginning to think maybe my need to protect Emmet has colored my instincts. Maybe these Ladies of Light aren't planning on offering my brother up to the volcano beast.

"Do they even have a volcano?" Emmet asks.

"No, they don't." Sloan whispers to me, "Ye need to stop before they hear ye, *a ghra*. They've been nothin' but cordial and gracious."

"Fine, I'll give them the benefit—"

"Hush now." Sloan forces a bright smile and holds up his drink to welcome Bodhmall and Fionn to our conversation. "How has yer night been?"

"Och, I can't complain," Fionn says. "Good food and good friends make fer a good time."

"Aye, it does at that." Sloan gives me a look.

"I spoke to the Ladies of Light this afternoon," Bodhmall says. "About Emmet, I mean. They have some very determined ideas about ye, lad, and I thought ye best hear about them."

"Uh-huh." I nod. "Who saw this coming? Oh, yeah, that would be me."

"You haven't heard what she has to say, Fi. Maybe you could hold off the gloating until the woman's had a chance to speak."

"Fine. Sorry. Go ahead. I give you the floor."

Bodhmall doesn't seem to know what to make of us, but that's nothing new. Fionn is easy-going and good-natured and doesn't take things too seriously. His auntie is quite a bit sterner.

"Aye, well, I was tellin' the ladies about the troubled times on the horizon and about what ye said about this island in yer time. They think there is somethin' to be done about that."

"Oh?" Emmet says. "About what, exactly?"

"About Emhain Abhlach bein' abandoned and in ruins in yer time. Ye see, fer as long as the rivers of The Source have fed the world with raw power, this island has been a direct conduit to The Source. When druids and other nature magic empowered folks need a little extra strength, it's always been there. If what ye said is true, somewhere along the line, that will end."

Kyna and her sisters step over to join us, and they look more than a little apprehensive.

That does nothing to quell my anxiety about what's coming next.

Sloan greets the ladies and includes them in our conversation. "I've been to this island several times, and though I've never been inside its heart like we are now, I've never felt the power of energy like we did today when we arrived on the shoreline. If this island is a conduit now, I'm sorry to say that it won't be forever."

Kyna smiles. "But it could be again."

I'm lost. "How so?"

"There is a prophecy known by my people. It says that a great warrior wielding the power of The Source will come when the hour is dark. He will save us from certain defeat and will stand as the hope for the future."

"You think Emmet is that warrior."

They all nod. "We do. If Emhain Abhlach is abandoned and access to the heart of the island is lost in your time, he is the one to re-establish that link."

"How would I do that?" Emmet asks.

"We could teach you the ways of the Light."

Emmet looks stunned. "You could teach me how to shimmer the air and go invisible like you did by the water today?"

Kyna nods. "Then you would be able to access the hidden city and perhaps mend the break in the conduit of power."

I'm watching Sloan to see if he thinks this is as cray-cray as it sounds. He's got his thinking cap on. "If I'm not mistaken, the Ladies of Light use their connections with one another to bolster the power of the ways of the Light, am I right?"

Kyna nods. "You are very observant."

True story.

"My question would then be, how much could he do on his own? He possesses an incredible tie to The Source because of a physical incident with the raw power. He is unique in that sense."

Emmet is unique in many other senses too, but I keep that tidbit to myself.

"It would be different for our warrior, no question. While we can teach him to command and manipulate light, we *are* light."

"Ye believe we could repair the conduit and reactivate Emhain Abhlach to strengthen our position fer the Cullin' and the battles to come?"

"How does fixing the island strengthen our position for the Culling?" I ask. "I'm not following."

Bodhmall looks at me like I'm daft. "The Collidin' of Realms is a conflict between light and dark, aye?"

I nod. "Right."

"Then adding more light to the side of light is a good thing."

"But the battles aren't going to be fought on the island, and we couldn't feel the impact of The Source from the mainland of Ireland. I agree it would be great and that Emmet is special. I just don't see how it helps us in regard to the Culling."

Sloan sets a hand on my arm and squeezes it. "I think I understand."

I'm glad someone does because I'm lost.

"Bodhmall and the others said they were here to gain strength fer the Collidin' of Realms. They felt the power disturbance here from Fionn's land and knew to come. Yer tied to the city, aren't ye? Ye've made a blood bond or ritual connection to draw on the city's power, right?"

"That's right," Kyna says.

Sloan tilts his head. "It's an intriguing idea. If Emmet can learn the ways of the Light, we are close to a family with strong Source power who could help us. This could work."

Emmet hangs on Sloan's opinion and smiles when he says he thinks it's a good idea. "All righty, then, let's do it. When does my light schooling begin?"

Kyna smiles. "At first light, of course."

The next morning, I wake to the mumbling of male voices in the distance and lay in bed while I let the world catch up with me. It's one of those brain-tangle moments when you rise from the depths of sleep, and you're not sure where you are or what time it is, or who is speaking in your bedroom.

It doesn't take long to remember being on the island of Emhain Abhlach. Yesterday's events were quite memorable and today promises to be even more exciting.

Throwing back the covers, I swing my legs free of the sheets and drop my feet to the stone floor. Grabbing my leathers from the end of the bed, I pull on my pants and jog out to the balcony to see what I've missed.

"Sleeping Beauty awakes." Sloan smiles as he turns away from his view of the city below.

Sloan, Aiden, and Dillan are enjoying the morning view of the colorful and quaint city below and letting me sleep in. "What did I miss?"

"Other than breakfast, you mean?" Aiden says.

"Yeah, other than that. Did Emmet already leave for his training?"

Sloan gives me a good morning kiss and reaches out to flatten some of my morning scaredo. My hair is long enough and curly enough to cause problems when I'm not at home with my normal brush and conditioner.

He fusses for a moment but then chuckles and gives up. "He left a few hours ago with Kyna and her sisters."

"Do we know where they went?"

"Not exactly," Aiden says. "Calum and Tad went along with him, so if anything unexpected happens, they can be back here in a flash."

That's good. I don't like to think poorly of people who have been good to us. Still, one thing I've learned about dealing with other empowered sects is sometimes their intentions and motivations can be very different from what we consider acceptable.

"How's our little dragon this morning?"

Dillan takes off his shirt. While yesterday Nyrora had settled herself on his back, this morning, she is on his chest with her tail wrapped around his waist.

It's both cool and disconcerting to have a sentient creature smiling out at me from my brother's chest. I bend and raise my finger to touch her little snub-nosed snout. "Hello, little girl. How was your first night sleeping with Dillan?"

My brother takes a step back, his bright teal eyes glowing with excitement. "Check it. We've been working on something."

Holding his left arm out into the air between us, he says, "Come on out, Rory. Meet your Auntie Fi."

The little purple dragon pushes out from his body as if she was pushing through a thin veil. First, her head sticks out, then her shoulders and wings, and her taloned feet grasp his arm to prop her up.

When she's fully free, she turns toward his head and climbs up to rest on his shoulder.

"You trained her to be your pet parrot?"

"That was her choice. Koinonos dragons are also called shoulder dragons. Her species link with their bonded person and augment their magic in battle. So, if she's going to stay this small and cute forever, there's no reason why she can't sit on my shoulder."

I don't know why her staying tiny thrills me as much as it does. As much as I love Dart in his adolescent and adult forms, he was such a cutie in his blue boy baby days. The idea of Dillan's dragon never growing out of that is awesome.

"It's lovely to meet you, Rory." Holding my hand up, I give her a moment to sniff my fingers before I attempt to touch her. "I have a dragon too. I can't wait for you to meet him. He's a lot bigger, but I bet he's a distant cousin of yours somehow."

"Actually, not." Sloan gestures for us to step inside our suite. "From what I've learned from this text, the creation of Koinonos dragons stemmed from the magical splicing of species, not evolution. While there are some definite similarities between Rory and Dart, genetically, I would be very surprised if they were related in any way."

I'm not sure how I feel about that. "Her species was genetically created to enhance the magic of empowered people?"

"It seems so."

"Do you know who did it?"

"Dark witches, if what I've read is true."

I gaze into the bright teal eyes of the newest member of our family and try to reconcile myself with her creation being tied to magical servitude. "That's sad, don't you think?"

"We did at first," Dillan says. "After spending time researching and talking with Rory, we decided that however it began hundreds of years ago, as of now, she is free to make her own choices and live her best life."

Rory coos and tilts her head to rub it against his.

He winks at her, and there's no doubt in my mind that he's already fallen in love. "I'm honored she chose me, and I promise to work to fulfill her needs as much as she does mine."

Sloan taps a finger against the leather cover of a thick tome. "The intentions for something in its origin inevitably change over time. Whatever Rory's ancestry was, she is her own being and will be loved and respected on her own merits."

I brush my fingers against the dark spine of her wing. Where Dart is scaled, tough, and rough, Rory is smooth and much more delicate. "Welcome to Clan Cumhaill, baby girl. I think you'll like being one of us."

Rory purrs.

Dillan reaches up, and she pushes her face into his hand. "Come on. Let's go see how Uncle Emmet is doing learning the secret art of light weaving."

CHAPTER SIXTEEN

On our way through the golden palace, we detour to the dining area to grab a few pastries for me to eat on the go. Dillan and Aiden say they can go ahead if I want to eat a full meal, but there's no way I'm getting left behind.

Emmett is learning how to weave light.

How cool is that?

Jogging down the stone steps at the front of the golden palace, I bite off a chunk of oddness. My biscuit is pale blue and glazed with a jammy layer of something that resembles...passionfruit, maybe?

It's hard to describe.

It's not bad. It's just odd. Thankfully, after fending for ourselves over a lifetime, my brothers have created every scary surprise meal you could imagine. We all have iron stomachs and can eat practically anything.

"Do we know where they're training?" I ask.

"We watched them leave this morning," Sloan says. "It seemed like they were headed out the gates toward the meadow beyond."

"That makes sense. There are fewer people out there, and if

they need space to weave light, they have it. Do you think they need space to weave light?"

Sloan shrugs. "Ye know as much as I do, luv."

"Ha! If only that were true. You out-wisdom me five to one, hotness...maybe ten to one."

He chuckles. "Yer the one who out-devours me. It must be twenty to one at least."

I snort. "Are you saying I eat more than you? You think I'm a pig?"

"*No!*" He scowls at me. "I think yer daft, but what I meant was that ye devour life better than I. Perhaps I should've said out-relish...maybe out-delight? I'm trying to say—"

I laugh and raise my hand to stop his tailspin. "I get it. You're the head, and I'm the heart."

"Aye, that's it."

Dillan looks at Aiden, and the amusement that passes between them is something I've become accustomed to over the past year.

"I know. We're lucky we found each other because no one else would get us."

Aiden holds up his hands in surrender. "I never said a thing. Kinu and I have a crazy rhythm that others might not get too. I just think it's nice that the two of you complement each other so well. I'm happy for you both."

"Who are we kidding," Dillan adds. "You're a Cumhaill, so anyone would be lucky to have you. The lucky one here is Irish."

I burst out laughing and smack him. "Be nice. You know that's not true."

Sloan's got his middle finger up. "Never make an enemy outta the smartest man in the room. Ye never know how that'll come back to bite ye in the arse."

I link my arm with Sloan's and lean against his shoulder, pressing my cheek against his arm. "Oh, if you're planning evil revenge, can I help?"

The four of us are chatting and chuckling and making our

way toward the golden gates below when a magical green shamrock sails through the air and hits me in the chest.

It doesn't hurt, but it doesn't exactly tickle either.

"Ow. Dammit. What's that about?"

"It came from over there." Dillan scowls at a sunshine yellow building four times the size of most of the houses.

I scan the front of the building, the windows, and the balcony above. That's when I see her.

"It's Betrys, Patty's sister." I lift my chin in greeting. "What do you think she wants?"

Dillan chuckles. "Likely another shot at Sloan's groin. Hey Irish, why don't you go say hi and find out?"

"Funny not funny," I say. "Okay, I'll go see."

Sloan's got a hold on my arm and is looking dour. "I don't think that's a good idea. Ye've said too much already. We don't know what kind of butterfly effect ye've already caused."

I glance at his grip on my arm, and he has the good sense to let go. Otherwise, I might take a run at his boy parts myself. "I hear what you're saying, and I understand where it's coming from."

"Do ye? Are ye sure?"

"I am. Just like I'm sure I'm going up there to see what she wants."

"Fi, I don't think—"

"—I won't speak about the future. I won't endanger the timeline. *Annnd,* I promise I'll come right back."

"I'll compromise with ye. I'll come up and stand off to the side."

I shake my head. "Nope. You'll go with Aiden and Dillan and trust that I'm an independent, intelligent woman and you don't need to police me."

He meets my gaze, and I know I've won.

Part of my hesitation to date him—or anyone else—is that I

refuse to lose my independence. He's protective, and that's fine, but I won't let him manage me.

Sloan sighs and steps back. "Go ahead without us, boys. Yer sister has someone to meet, and I'm goin' to stand here and keep an eye on her, solely for the peace of mind that she doesn't go missin' in a strange city in a strange time."

I hear the compromise in his tone, and I accept. "Thank you. Don't worry. I'll be right back."

The large yellow building turns out to be a local watering hole. The main floor has a long bar running the length of the back wall with seating on the open floor and a server and a barkeep working the crowd. I suppose it doesn't matter what century you're in. A bar is a bar is a bar.

I locate the stairs to the upper patio area and make my way to the table along the railing where Betrys sits. "Hello again. You wanted to speak to me?"

She looks up at me and tilts her head toward Sloan standing alone in the street below. "Is he afraid to come up?"

I sit opposite her. "No. I simply asked him to wait for me downstairs so we could talk. What can I do for you?"

"Those images ye showed Padraig yesterday…"

"Yes?"

"Were ye sincere about knowin' him in a different time?"

"Absolutely. He's one of my closest friends, and I love him dearly."

"Can I see them again…those images?"

I pull out my phone and call up my gallery. Shifting around the table, I sit next to her so I can scroll through.

"Can ye tell me about him then?"

I glance down at Sloan. "He's worried if I say too much, I'm going to undo the way the future is supposed to unfold. I promised I wouldn't do that."

"Maybe if not specifics, can ye tell me if he's happy?"

I don't see how that would affect the world order, so I go with my gut. "From one sister to another, I assure you, he's very happy. Yes."

"Ye mentioned that when he hits his darkest days and humans stalk him and steal his treasure... How did ye know about that?"

"Because he told me. We've spent many a drunken night sitting up and talking about life. He told me about his losses and his wins. We won't meet for another thousand years, but in my time, he has a good life."

She wipes her stubby fingers across her cheek and sweeps away her tears. "I'm so relieved to hear it. He's had such a hard time since he got robbed. My people pride themselves fer their cleverness. To be caught by humans and have all his gold stolen has been a blow."

"It'll get better, I promise."

"Ye mentioned that he should join up with a dragoness. How does that work?"

I wonder about explaining, but I guess I already let that one out of the bag. "He becomes the companion of the Queen of Wyrm Dragons and builds up his treasures again. The brilliance of his plan is that he lives in her lair. When anyone catches him and demands his gold, she chomps them up, and his treasures are secure."

Betrys laughs, taking another long look at the pictures. "That sounds like Padraig."

"I couldn't help but notice he wasn't himself yesterday. The Patty I know would've been out on the battlefield with his axes flying, giving hell to those oxen beasts. The fact that he was hiding away drinking tells me he's hit his rough patch. Just know that it doesn't last forever."

Betrys sinks back in her chair and nods. "Then from one sister to another, I need to ask a favor."

I'm back down on the street with Sloan in less than five minutes and hold my hand out so we can walk together.

"How'd that go, then?" he asks.

"It went fine. I promise you I didn't say anything future-related, didn't reveal any secrets, didn't even tell them to invest in Apple or Microsoft."

"So, what did she want to talk to ye about then?"

"She's worried about Patty. He's in a low point, and she was looking for reassurance that he would come out of it and find happiness again. I assured her the Patty of our time has a good life and is truly happy. That's all she wanted to hear."

"Well, I don't suppose we'll cause the collapse of society over that."

"I didn't think so either."

He chuckles and gives me a look. "Are we all right, *a ghra*? I know I test yer patience sometimes."

"No more than I test yours. We're fine…always."

I squeeze his hand, and we walk in companionable silence for a few minutes, absorbing the quaintness of the colorful city. I breathe in the power of the ambient energy.

It's a rare and exciting life we live to share these kinds of adventures with one another.

It's a gift.

We nod at the feline folk in uniform at the massive golden gates and step through to the grassy meadow beyond. After only seeing it torn up and littered with bodies, it's nice to see it pristine once again.

"There you are," Calum says as we join everyone in the large, thatched palapa. "Last to the party again."

"Best for last, baby. Don't you forget it." I step past him and hug Fionn. "Good morning. What trouble have you all gotten into so far this morning?"

Fionn chuckles. "Mornin' is it? Why, it feels like half the day has passed already. Have ye forgotten ye've been sent back to ready fer battle?"

I exhale. "Nope. The impending doom of the Culling looms darkly over every waking moment of our lives right now."

Fionn tilts his head toward the open grass. "Then I guess we ought to get to work. Why should Emmet be the only one breakin' a sweat?"

I chuckle and turn back the way we came. "Fine, fine. I suppose if Emmet is working hardest, we're all in trouble."

Aiden, Calum, and Dillan all start laughing.

"No shit."

We spar with the Fianna for the better part of the next two hours. Fionn is annoyed that we got our asses handed to us yesterday. "Despite bein' better fighters and doin' all things right, sometimes ye'll simply be outnumbered."

"Especially when sorceress bitches open a portal to bring in reinforcements." I spin Birga in my hand and duck my head from the swing of his sword.

"Aye, so what can ye do to ensure that doesn't happen in the future?"

"Block portals?" With Birga's staff grasped in both hands, I dive-roll forward, rising to my feet. Fionn's heavy footsteps behind me betray his position, and I release my spear, drop, and spin. Gripping his feet between my legs, I twist at the same time.

"Move Earth." When the ground opens, I command it to...

Fionn laughs, and I scramble not to faceplant.

He counters my spell, and my footing gives way. I might as

well be standing on quicksand for all the traction I have. I stop talking long enough to focus and regain control of my environment.

"Good one, oul man." I pull myself off the ground. "Sloan? Is there such a thing as a portal jammer spell?"

Sloan is overseeing the sparring between Dillan and Arken, observing how he instructs my brother to work with Rory in battle. "Not a spell *per se*, but I'm sure there are ways to keep intruders from joining the fight. I can look into it."

"Yes, please. Put it on your list." I feel bad for the guy. His list is long and demanding of his time. "I love you."

He chuckles. "Not to worry, Cumhaill. I love ye right back."

"Wait. Can it be?" Calum points at where Emmet is approaching. "Is that the mighty warrior of the prophecy?"

"Be still my heart," Aiden says. "I think it is."

Dillan releases his daggers and Rory settles on his shoulder. "Do you think he'll remember us from the days before the sisters discovered him?"

I brush myself off and straighten. "He better or he can forget his ride home."

Dillan laughs harder. "What is his ride home? For that matter…what's ours?"

"TBD," I say. "If we train hard, it will come."

"Thanks for that. You gotta love a good *Field of Dreams* moment."

"It's a classic."

"Would you guys shut up and ask me about my morning?" Emmet snaps. "You're so annoying. Come on. Fawn over me. Bask in my greatness."

I laugh. "Fair. Okay, oh great warrior of the prophecy. Tell us about your morning."

"Well, the actual light weaving techniques are an ancient art, and I'm not allowed to share it with anyone not touched by The Source, but I can show you."

I point at a long cut across the meaty part of his palm. "Did you have an accident?"

"No. It wasn't an accident. I did it with my knife. It was a blood sacrifice to the island and to Manannan mac Lir. I pledged myself as a defender of Emhain Abhlach, and in return, I get a remote connection to The Source."

"Aye," Fionn says, showing us the thin white scar on his palm. "We all took the oath as well. It's part of our preparation fer the Time of the Collidin' Realms."

Emmet nods. "Yeah, it's cool. It's like my cells are humming with potential power. If I need it, all I have to do is call it into action."

His smile is radiant, and his energy has replenished enough that he has a pink aura like the rest of us now. It's not as powerful as it was before he sent the sorceress and her henchmen away, but he's not depleted anymore. "Cool, Em. Then, let's see what you can do."

We gather around and give Emmet our full attention. I'll be the first to admit, as happy as I am for him, I'm also nervous. Emmet needs a druid win. He's been floundering to find his place in the empowered world, and I hope this is it.

Being the man to reboot an arcane knowledge of light weaving seems like a great thing to have on your resume of druid skills.

Not to mention that it's just damn cool.

Kyna and Syma were the ones to escort him back to us, and they don't look at all nervous when he sets himself up and gets started.

"Okay, check it." He pulls off his boots and shirt and undoes his pants.

My gaze flickers to the very naked ladies, and it hits me. "You can't make clothes disappear?"

Calum's look of horror is too funny. "Crikey, do you have to be naked for this demonstration?"

"Not completely," Emmet says, unabashed. "Clothes are hard to disappear, so being in my boxers helps. I stayed dressed when I first tried, and I couldn't hide my pants. It looked stupid to see an empty pair of pants walking around."

I giggle. "I wish I had seen that."

Emmet flashes me a wide grin. "I'll show you another time. Right now, I'm gonna do this right. Ready?"

"Go for it, Em."

Sloan steps in behind me and wraps his arms around my shoulders. "Are ye nervous fer him? I don't know why I want this so bad fer him, but I do."

"I was thinking the same thing. I worried that when he used up his pink glow yesterday when he combusted, he might be low on juice today for his big training."

"The Force is strong in this one," he says in a decent Darth Vader voice.

I chuckle. "Well done, Mackenzie. You get a point for the reference and the delivery on that one."

"Thanks. I thought it worked."

Emmet has finished stripping down and is standing in front of us in his BoJack Horseman boxers. "Okay, now you see me…" He closes his eyes, and I feel the subtle shift in power as the air grows wavy.

As we all stand and watch, he steps back and vanishes from sight.

"You did it! Yay, you, Emmet! Woohoo."

We're all still staring at the spot where he disappeared when a tap on my arm startles me. He reappears and grins. "Thanks, Fi. It was pretty good, wasn't it?"

"It was awesome, Em," Sloan says. "Congrats, *sham*. Ye've got a wonderful new skill in yer toolbox."

He nods. "The ladies showed me how the conduit to The Source works too. I think I have a good shot at repairing the island when we get home and getting us hooked up for a NOS boost when we need it."

"Good on ye, lad. Ye've done well." Fionn smiles at us. "I couldn't be prouder of the lot of ye. Yer true Fianna. Make no mistake about it."

I'm about to respond when my stomach lurches and the world spins. I'm not sure what's happening, but then I'm rushing down a set of stairs. Sloan is in front of me, and Emmet is at my back.

"What the… Holy schmoly… We made it back." Garnet's lion roars somewhere in the distance, and my mental hamster catches up. I look around and laugh. "And Em's still nakey."

CHAPTER SEVENTEEN

We race down the stairs, and it takes a moment for my memory to catch up. We're back. What were we doing? Right...Yorkville Library...Andromeda and Maxwell kidnapped...and we're chasing Nikon, Garnet, and Anyx into the lair of the witch bitches.

"Well, that's not disorienting at all," Tad says from up ahead. He's searching the glossy marble catacombs we've portaled into looking like his brain centrifuge is stuck on spin.

I can relate. The first few times my time slip reinsertion occurred, it boggled me too. "Forget the mind-tripping for the moment. Right now, we're focusing on getting Andromeda and Maxwell back from the witches, remember?"

Another roar from Garnet's lion draws us forward like a violent beacon.

"Bruin, find Garnet and help secure Andy and Maxwell." I release my bear on the fly. There's a brief flutter in my chest, then he bursts free and is gone.

With our boots drumming out a heavy rhythm on the marble floor, we follow the sounds of magic bolts striking and lions roaring.

Aiden grips the long handle of a floor-to-ceiling door and yanks it open. Dillan, Tad, and the rest of us race through ahead of him.

The disorientation gets shelved fast once we see what we're up against. We surprised the witches because they're obviously fighting on the defensive. The lions have torn through two women already, and there's an empty chair with bindings where I assume Andromeda sat a short time ago.

I rush to Maxwell and reach for his bindings. Around each wrist is a strong band of magic tying him to the arm of the chair. "Are you all right?"

"Furious but fine."

I check him over and take his word for it. He has a few bloody knuckles and a wicked bruise on his right cheekbone, but he looks whole. "Did Nikon get Andy?"

"Yes. Just," he says.

"Good." I scowl at his restraints.

I don't have the juice to break the magic bond, so I go for the chair's wooden arm. Reshaping the wood, I slide the binding rings off it, and voila, Maxwell stands wearing two magical new bracelets.

"What do I do with these?" He frowns at the glowing orange bands sliding up and down his forearms. Now that his hands are free from the wood of the chair arms, they aren't bound to him.

"Just fling them over toward that discard pile of mangled witches."

He glances over at where someone threw five witches against the wall in varying degrees of wounded, unconscious, and dead. If I were in a more charitable mood, I might feel bad for them. They followed their coven leader, and she led them very much astray.

Maxwell does what I suggest and flings the two orange rings at the witches. He has amazing accuracy, and I make a mental note not to bet against him at the summer horseshoe competition.

"Sloan. You're on evac."

"Fuck that," Maxwell says, getting up. "I want my moment with these bitches."

I'm about to argue, but Sloan shakes his head. "He deserves that much."

I glance at where Bruin, Garnet, Anyx, and several more Moon Called from his pride are taking apart the witches too stupid to flee.

"Leave one alive," I say. "If High Priestess Drippy Face is behind this, we need confirmation."

Garnet snarls at me, but he knows I'm right. With the swipe of his mighty paw, he flicks one of the badly beaten witches my way. She's a heap of crumpled and rumpled, but she's still breathing.

"I guess that makes you the lucky winner." I grab her and pull her to her feet. "Can I get a lift to the Batcave?"

"Got ye, Fi," Tad says.

"Me too." Emmet jogs over to join us. "This is well in hand, and I have too much of me on display for a battle with witches."

I laugh. "You have too much of you on display for anything beyond your front door."

I duck as Rory swoops past and catch sight of Dillan chuckling as he backs up Anyx. It's a good chance for them to solidify their bond without the risk factor being too high.

"Meet you back at the clubhouse, boys."

When I nod at Tad, he *poofs* us out.

Nikon and Andromeda are inside the main room of the SITFU home base when we arrive. Located on the tenth floor of the Acropolis building Nikon bought for us, it's our home away from home. Once we get inside the security doors, I hand our witch prisoner to Tad and rush to check on Andy.

"Are you all right?"

She has her butt perched on the edge of the conference table, and Nikon is disinfecting some cuts with supplies from the first aid kit.

"I'm so sorry, Andy. When I secured you in that sphere and left, I never imagined you were the target."

Andromeda shakes her head but gets a scolding from Nikon. Instead, she reaches to the side, and I take her hand. "You couldn't have known. Who in their right mind would want me?"

"Anyone who knows the power you hide from the world," Nikon hisses. "Which, apparently, they now do."

"How anyone found out where your family's immortality comes from is the next mystery on the list." I meet Nikon's gaze. "For now, let's take the win and be thankful she's home safe."

Nikon frowns and eases back from his ministrations. "You look like hell, Red... And why the hell are you in your boxers, Em? Did the witches steal your clothes?"

I stride over to the water cooler and get Andy a cup. "That's a long story involving a backward time jump, a mythical island, and a project we need the Tsambikos family for to strengthen Team Light."

Nikon scowls. "What does that mean?"

"Don't get defensive yet, Greek." I offer him a reassuring gaze. "It'll be a covert project, and seeing how the cat might be out of the bag about your family's tie to The Source, it will strengthen your tie and give you a few extra offensive and defensive skills."

Andromeda has had enough of her older brother fussing over her and takes away the bloody antiseptic wipes. "I'm in. Whatever you need, Fi. I'm sick of sitting on the sidelines. If we can take the offensive and strengthen our position for the Culling, we're all in."

Nikon chuffs. "Don't the rest of us get a say?"

She looks at him and smiles. "No."

Ten minutes later, Sloan *poofs* into the elevator area of the Batcave with Maxwell, Calum, Aiden, and Dillan. Dionysus comes on his own. Garnet and Anyx arrive then too. Once everyone is in the office, and the adrenaline is easing off, the questions start flying.

"Why do you all look like you've been living out of your car for a month?" Anyx asks. "I swear Dillan and Aiden were pressed and dressed to impress in their uniforms an hour ago."

"Was I hallucinating, or did Emmet lose his pants somewhere between the library and the battle?" Garnet looks around.

"What's with your hair, Jane? Frazzled Einstein is not a good look for you…at all."

I chuckle. "We've been living in the same clothes for five days, no brush or showers, and yes, Emmet was only wearing his boxers when our *Back to the Future* moment occurred."

Garnet arches an autocratic brow and studies me. "Tripping through time again?"

"Through no fault of our own, yes."

"Who pulled you back this time?" Dionysus asks. "And why didn't I get to come?"

"Sorry, Tarzan. It was a druids-only excursion. I'm not sure who engineered it, but I have a sneaking suspicion it might have been Lady Divinity herself."

Calum looks at me. "You think?"

"It's only a hunch, but yeah. If she's the anchorwoman for Team Light and knows what Death is up to, giving us an opportunity to regroup with our mentors and level up is a great way to support our team without outwardly influencing the outcome."

Tad *poofs* back and he and Emmet—now fully clothed—come in from the elevators. They've gathered Ciara and Kevin along the way.

"You didn't tell them about me and my news, did you?" Emmet sends me a pleading gaze.

"No, Em. It's your news to tell. Have at it."

While Emmet weaves the tale and fills them in on the excitement of the past few days, I meander over to Sloan and lean into him for a hug.

Emmet skims over our time in the Fianna camp training and gains momentum as he gets to the mythical island of Emhain Abhlach.

When it's time to explain the small dragon perched on Dillan's shoulder, Emmet lets Dillan take over the story. Then he takes back the narration for the big finish.

"The Ladies of Light recognized me as the great warrior of their prophecy and trained me in the incredibly secretive art of light weaving. It takes a person with a direct connection with The Source, and that's where you guys come in."

Nikon looks from Emmet to me. "You want us to learn to weave light and resurrect an abandoned island?"

"Hells yeah," I say. "Emhain Abhlach provides a direct conduit to raw prana, and anyone who shares a bond to it can draw on it when they need to."

Nikon doesn't look convinced.

"We're in," Andromeda says. "Tell us where and when and we'll be there. How many of us do you need?"

Emmet shrugs. "As soon as possible. There were five Ladies of Light, so maybe us and two more?"

"Pick me!" Dionysus says. "Oh, please pick me. I want to play too."

Emmet chuckles. "Have you come in contact with The Source power before?"

The grin he flashes is too funny. "It's a rather wild and inappropriate story involving me, a group of nymphs, a Celtic maiden, and a very territorial swan."

I burst out laughing and end that convo right there. "Nope. We don't need the details. We take your word for it. Of course, you can join the fun, Tarzan. If you've got the fae prana juice flowing, you're in."

"Welcome aboard," Emmet says. "Now, who should be our fifth?"

Nikon looks at his sister. "Politimi?"

Andy chuckles. "Good luck with that. No offense, Fi, but Timi is *not* your biggest fan."

"No offense taken. I'm aware."

"What about Papu?" Nikon suggests. "I bet he'd want to do it. He has FOMO and loves anything to do with Fi."

I curl my fingers into a heart and touch my chest. "I heart Papu. He'll be great because he's ground zero on your family's immortality."

Andromeda agrees. "All right, leave it with me. By tomorrow afternoon you'll have your team, Emmet. I'll round us up a Tsambikos light weaving crew and text you when things are a go."

"Noice," Emmet says. "Thanks, Andy. I'm glad you're on board with this."

"It's going to be awesome. Go, Ladies of Light!"

I burst out laughing.

Nikon rolls his eyes. "If four of us are men, I don't think we should still be called the Ladies of Light? I vote for a new name."

Andromeda laughs. "I don't know. I think it's cute."

Nikon shakes his head. "Three Tsambikos' in one endeavor might get a little crazy. I hope you know what you're in for."

I raise a hand to my brothers. "Can you honestly say that? I'm not worried. Our family can handle all the crazy your family can dish out."

Nikon laughs. "Challenge accepted."

It takes another twenty minutes for Garnet and Anyx to get things sorted out in the holding cells before Garnet comes back to the main room so we can catch up. "So, what happened after we left?" I ask. "Do we have enough on Drippy Face and Malachi to cite them with starting a mutiny?"

Garnet pegs me with a gaze. "The last time I checked, we weren't sailing the high seas, and I wasn't the captain of a ship. I don't know that a charge of mutiny would stand. Do I have enough evidence to take down Janeera and her coven? No. Will I let it go? No."

"Hells no. Whether or not we can prove it, she manipulated an exposure event, ambushed us, and targeted one of our inner circle. That chick be bad news. That chick be going down."

Garnet chuckles. "Yes, well, we still have a governing body to answer to and laws to enforce. Don't worry, though. Janeera and Malachi might think they got away with something today, but they most certainly did not."

"Glad to hear it. Now, if you'll excuse me, I stink and desperately need a bath."

"No argument."

I laugh at his immediate response. "Sorry. It was five days of training and living in an underground bunker. I can't help that I got transported back to before a time when indoor plumbing existed."

"No, you can't. Might I say, I'm relieved, as always, it was a round trip ticket. It would crush both my girls if you were suddenly sucked into the past and taken from them."

I chuckle. "Just them, eh? Nice try, puss. I know you love me too. You can play the surly brute all you like. I've seen your gooey center."

The growl of his lion vibrates in the air between us and my chest. "I assure you, I don't have a gooey center, Lady Druid."

"If you say so." I wink and blow him a kiss goodbye as I hustle my ass out of the back room. "Happy torture and interrogation. Call me later if you need me. Who are we kidding? You always need me."

"Good night, Lady Druid."

Sloan *poofs* us into the back hall, and it feels like ages since we left. Bruin, thankfully, is back from washing up after the battle and lounging in the living room with Dillan, Eva, Rory, and Manx.

"You made it back all right, I see."

Bruin grumbles. "Yer not supposed to leave without me, Red. It's one of our agreements."

"Sorry, buddy. I wanted to get back to the Batcave to check on Nikon and Andromeda, and you were having a good time attacking bad people. I had no intention of going anywhere else, and we came straight home."

He lumbers over to me and drops his head, so his face is in front of mine. "I choose to be yer companion over fightin' every time, Red. Don't think it's a sacrifice. I want to be with ye when trouble strikes."

I lean forward and rub my face into the long fur of his forehead. His fur is soft against my face, and I breathe in his scent. He's had a bath in the river. He smells wintery clean and of evergreen trees. "I love you too, buddy. Thanks. You rock."

He slaps my face with a wet, sloppy tongue and grins. "That was yer punishment fer leavin' without me."

I swipe my hand over my face and chuckle. "Fair enough. I'll take my punishment without objection."

Bruin swings his head toward the group in the living room. "Rory. Do ye want to come with Manx and me and see our cave wall? Now that Doc and Daisy moved out, there's room to share."

The little dragon looks at Dillan, and he smiles. "Go ahead, sweet girl. I'm not going anywhere. When you finish with the boys, I'll take you outside and introduce you to the dragons and our fae friends."

Rory leaps off the back of the couch where she was sitting

with Dillan and flies the short distance to land on Bruin's back. It startles him for a moment, but he doesn't seem to mind.

"She's a shoulder dragon," I say. "You've got nice big shoulders, Bear."

Bruin raises his black nose and grins. "I do at that. We'll be downstairs if ye need us or if ye plan to go out."

I chuckle at the not-so-subtle hint not to leave him behind. "I'm in for the night, buddy. I'm looking at a long, hot bath, an hour with my anti-tangle spray and brush, then to bed early. Tomorrow I'd like to visit Patty before we go to Emhain Abhlach, so I'd like to go a bit earlier than the rest."

"I think Em wanted to invite Gran and Granda to the island," Dillan says. "Maybe we all go early, and we'll visit there while you visit Patty."

Sloan twists the cap off a beer and offers Dillan and Eva one too. "Oh, if Lugh and Lara are comin', do ye think Emmet would mind if I invited my da? He's had it a bit rough as of late, and I bet an adventure on Emhain Abhlach would make him delira and excira."

I chuckle at the face Eva makes at the phrase. "It's an Irish way of saying he'll be delighted and excited."

"Only it sounds better the way I say it," Sloan tips back his beer and hands the bottle to me.

"It definitely does."

"Make yerselves at home." Sloan tilts his head at the stairs. "I'm off to peel off these clothes and burn them."

"Yeah, I'll join you in a sec." I know my brother, and there's a reason he's hanging out in our living room instead of the one next door. "What's up with you two? What are your plans?"

Dillan flashes me a grin. "You know those empty rooms upstairs?"

I chuckle. "Yeah. Do you want to crash?"

He shrugs. "Aiden was pretty freaked about being away from

Kinu and the kids for the past few days. I said I'd give them some family time."

"You're welcome to stay here. You know that."

He nods. "Actually...with Kev and Calum moving next door and Emmet moving across the road with Ciara and Tad, I was wondering if we could stay here for more than tonight?"

I blink. "Oh...yeah, it's fine with me. I'll mention it to Sloan, but I don't think he'll object to you claiming one of the spare bedrooms."

"Thanks, Fi. We thought if Death is keeping tabs on Eva, it's better if she's not in the apartment he arranged for her through the Choir of Angels."

"You've gotten into that already, have you?"

"It was a majorly important point to cover."

"True story. We'll need to put our heads together to decide how to handle it."

Eva looks at me, and for once, she's not her sunshiny self. "I never imagined he could be using me against your family, Fi. I need you to believe me."

"I do. Don't worry about that. We never doubted you for a moment. We just need to figure out what to do about it. Yeah, now that I'm thinking about it, you guys moving in here is probably the best idea."

Dillan nods. "I gotta admit, it wasn't my only motivation. It's hard to start my adult life with babies screaming all night and toddlers deciding to snuggle into my bed in the middle of the night."

I giggle. "Stay tonight, and we'll have a family meeting in the morning. I don't see a problem, though. Just don't stay up too late. We have a big day tomorrow."

CHAPTER EIGHTEEN

"You're sure you don't mind?" I toss a spare outfit into my backpack and add my favorite hoodie and the kerchief-wrapped package I need to deliver. "You don't have to agree because I spoke for you. This is your house. If you want it to be just us, you can veto me, and I won't be mad or anything."

Sloan exits the shower and wraps a towel around his hips. With a second swatch of terry, he gathers the last persistent drips clinging to his sixpack.

He grabs his toothbrush from the base and gets things lined up. "It's fine. If we'd had the room when we got the place last December, I would've invited Dillan then. With Eva's situation, it makes perfect sense they stay here. Yer brother is welcome to claim a room."

I wrap my arms around him and kiss his freshly shaved jaw. "Thank you, hotness. The fact that you put up with my family as well as you do makes me love you even more."

He looks down at me, and his smile dims. "Thanks, luv. That's nice to hear."

I ease back and take in the shift in his mood. "Why don't I feel like it *was* nice to hear? I've upset you. How? What did I say?"

He shakes his head and tries to snow me with a fresh smile. "It's nothin'. Ye didn't upset me."

"I did, and now you're making me more nervous because you're lying and pretending I didn't. Stop that. Be straight with me. If I'm screwing up, tell me."

He closes his eyes and draws a deep breath. "Ye haven't screwed anythin' up."

"But?"

"But, if we're bein' totally honest—"

"—which we always should be—"

"Then I wish ye'd stop referrin' to them as yer family and me puttin' up with them. It makes me feel like I'm on the outside. I've lived with ye full-time fer a year now. I'd like to think they've become my family too. At least I hope they feel that way."

I see the hurt in his eyes, and I don't know why I hadn't realized it. Sloan never had siblings or family or anything like we have.

This relationship is about more than him and me. He's part of this because he's part of this family.

"I'm so sorry. I never thought of it like that, but I should have. In my mind, you're a good sport and putting up with the chaos of my crazy family, but you're right—they're your family too. Gran and Granda always were, and now you've been assimilated by the rest of us."

"Resistance is futile."

I love that he makes comments like that now. "Forgive me. I was dumb not to make the connection."

"There's nothin' to forgive. I'm a little sensitive to bein' on the outside of relationships. I don't want that here with ye…or with them."

I wrap my arms around him and squeeze. "Then you're in luck because you're very much in the inner circle of this family. I love you. They love you. You're stuck with us now."

"Good. That's right where I want to be."

I step back, press my hand against his bare chest, and take comfort at the strong and steady rhythm under my palm. "Finish getting ready, and I'll meet you downstairs. And hotness, thanks again for loving me."

He winks and puts the toothbrush in his mouth. "There's no choice in the matter. I was a goner from the beginnin'."

As the hum of his electric toothbrush starts, I snag my backpack and head downstairs. When I get to the kitchen, we already have a full house.

Calum and Kev, Emmet and Ciara, Dillan and Eva, and all the companion animals have gathered and are laughing and eating our food.

"Good morning, all." I open the dishwasher and grab two mugs. "Glad you all could make it to breakfast at Sloan's and Fi's house."

Calum laughs. "I figure there's a grandfather clause. Anyone who's lived here within the past six months is still an honorary housemate."

"That counts us all in." Emmet pours himself more juice. "Although, when we lived here, I remember there being more sugar cereal options."

I laugh. "That's because you and Kevin bought it. I don't know if you guys have noticed, but Sloan's more of an Oscar Benedict on ancient grain toast than a Count Chocula kinda guy."

"No accounting for taste," Kevin says.

Sloan chuckles, coming down the stairs behind me. "Don't judge me for valuing taste and nutrition over the prize inside."

I laugh and pour us both a cup of flavored coffee. "This is a judgment-free zone, hotness. You do you."

He joins us, and we spend the next twenty minutes pulling together our breakfast and catching up with the boys and their significant others.

"You're okay with Eva and I inviting ourselves to move in?" Dillan asks.

Sloan waves that away. "Without a doubt. There's nothing I hated more about growing up in my house than having nothing happening and no one to shoot the shit with day after day."

Dillan comes over and meets him chest-to-chest. "Much appreciated. I think it'll be good for Aiden and Kinu too. They have their rhythm as a family, and the twins are on a bit of a schedule."

Emmet laughs. "I think that's a stretch."

"I said a *bit* of a schedule. Anyway, once Da moved out, I started feeling like the odd man out. Aiden would never have said anything, but they were accustomed to living on their own."

"And we're not." I finish my fried egg sandwich, slot my plate into the dishwasher, and rinse out my mug. "So, who's coming when?"

Emmet brings over his empty bowl and rinses it out before putting it into the dishwasher. "I have to run back and get Doc. I'm not sure how long we'll be at the island, so I want him to come with us."

"Good point, Em," Calum says. "Maybe we should bring the camping gear."

"Sure, a great idea." I stride down the hall to the back door, step into my boots, and grab my coat. Leaning over the railing to the basement, I call to my bear. "Bruin, I'm ready to roll, buddy."

"Comin' right up, Red."

I shrug on my winter coat as I walk, pull my ponytail free, and twist my scarf so it covers my neck as I zip things up. When I get back to the kitchen, I sling on my backpack and buckle the waist strap.

"You in a rush, Fi?" Dillan asks.

"I made Betrys a promise back at the city and need to stop in to see Patty before the island. If I leave now with Dart and Saxa, I'll have time to visit and meet up with all of you at the island."

"Is Nikon takin' care of yer transport?" Sloan asks my brothers.

Calum shakes his head. "He left for the vineyard in Rhodes this morning with his sisters. He's picking up his grandfather and meeting us at Gran's in a few hours."

"So ye'll need me fer transport then."

"No, we're good, Irish," Calum says. "Dionysus is our tour guide today. He said he's going to—"

"—knock your socks off," Dionysus interrupts. He appears out of thin air and winks at me. "As if there were any doubt."

"Not an ounce of doubt." I step over to kiss his cheek. "Thank you for joining the Emhain Abhlach team. It means a lot."

"Of course. That's what family does, isn't it?"

"It sure is."

His grin is innocent, and I can tell he's pleased with himself. He might be thousands of years old, a badass supercharged Greek god, and as knowledgeable as any scholar, but he's just getting a handle on family and what it means to be part of a support structure like ours.

But he's right...he's knocking our socks off.

Bruin lumbers up to join us, and I scrub my fingers through the fur on his shoulders. "Ready when you are."

"Awesome. Come aboard." Bruin ghosts out and bonds with me. As always, his presence is a comforting flutter in my chest and gentle pressure to let me know I'm no longer alone in my body.

"Am I late?" Dionysus looks surprised. "You're ready to leave, and I thought I was early."

"You're fine. I'm stopping at the dragon lair to see Patty before going to the island. With the way time travels in the lair, I thought I'd go as early as possible."

"I'd like to go too, *a ghra*." Sloan returns from the back hall with his jacket on and boots in his hand. "Not to the lair, of course, but through the stones."

"Oh, sure. How come?"

"If I portal to Ireland, I'll use up my wayfarer energy and won't be able to pick up my father or get us home if we need to return quickly. If I ride with you, I can *poof* to Stonecrest Castle once Dart passes through the stones."

"Sure. That works. What about Manx?"

"I've got Manxy." Dionysus pats Manx's head. "You kids go have fun. We'll leave for Gran's in a little while."

How cute is it that he's adopted Gran as his own?

Or maybe she's adopted him…

I check in with everyone else, and it seems like the plan is good. "Okey-dokey, we'll see you guys in a bit."

Sloan and I head out to the sacred grove, and I make it a point to check in with Nilm before we leave. Brownies are about the size of a toddler with cherubic faces, round eyes, and antennae that bob over their heads. "I brought the proud parents a few extras." I set the gift bag down. "How are mother and baby doing?"

Nilm gives me a thumbs-up and a gleaming smile.

"Awesome. Do you need anything?"

He shakes his head, and his antennae bounce.

"We're going away for a few days, so if you do and we're not here, climb through the doggy door and get the attention of Kinu or Aiden. Okay?"

Another thumbs-up.

I can't wait for them to introduce us to the wee baby but brownies nest with their young for a few weeks before they come out to show them around.

We're patiently waiting.

Emmet is the only one of us who can converse with the brownies, so we get by with charades and hand gestures. It's fine. S'all good. We get the job done.

"Excellent. Well, here are a few things they might enjoy. Kinu sent out some of the little blankets and sleepers she had for the twins, and there are quite a few snacks and treats for the three of you too."

Flopsy and Mopsy, our Ostara rabbits, flutter down from their nest in the tree and plop their furry butts in the mossy scrub.

I stroke their velvety ears and start unpacking the second bag. "Don't worry, guys. We didn't forget you. We've got sweet and salty, veggie treats, a new salt lick for the deer, and all the usual delights. Did you hear me tell Nilm that we're going away for a few days? If you need anything, Kinu and Aiden are here with the kids."

I don't need to tell them that.

Jackson and the rabbits have established quite a bond. He spends almost as much time out here as I do.

I set out the smorgasbord on the ground between the two hanging chairs and leave them to investigate.

Even though it's a chilly mid-December day, our sacred grove is toasty warm. Last winter, we established extensive warding and the hot springs to regulate the temperature. Our fae friends now are cozy with their thermal heating.

Leaving them to fend for themselves, we continue to the new dragon lair. It's incredible.

Even knowing the magic a dragon possesses, the vastness of the lair Saxa created is astonishing. It's disorienting at first because the depth and breadth of the space defy logic.

The stone archway into the lair isn't any bigger than the door to my house. Seeing it, you'd wonder how a dragon could possibly get through. As we approach, the open space expands to accommodate our size. It does the same thing for Saxa and Dart. It just has to expand a great deal more.

"Is everybody ready?" I ask the darkness as my vision adjusts to the lack of light.

Dart and Saxa round the corner from their private nesting area and join us in the main cavern. "Dragons are always ready," Saxa says with a little sass.

I chuckle, appreciating the added swish in her tail. Girlfriend is feeling good about herself today. I hope their little romance is budding and it's my blue boy who put that razzle in her dazzle.

"Sloan will come with us through the rings and *poof* off to collect Wallace at Stonecrest Castle while we visit Patty and the other dragons."

"Then we're off," Dart says.

The four of us exit the lair and assemble in the back yard. Dart is growing rapidly but still isn't half as large as Saxa. Until he supersizes, of course.

Because he's a male Western, his adult size is noticeably larger than his golden girlfriend. Once he's up-sized, Sloan and I mount his shoulder and jog over to the saddle handles wrapped around his spikes.

As Dart's bonded dragon rider, I take the first spike, and Sloan gets settled at the spike right behind me. He's had a few voyages now, so I don't worry about him as much as I did in the beginning.

Honestly, when Nikon mentioned that he'd like to have a dragon of his own, it got me thinking. How cool would it be to have some of the other dragons form attachments to our family?

I was hoping at the birthday party something might spark between Dart's family and ours, but so far, no such luck. Saxa has lived her entire existence as a free dragon, so I'm not expecting anything will change there, but with the size of the lair she made, it's possible we could provide a home for another one or two.

Is everything all right, Fi? Dart asks directly into my mind.

Right. I'm standing at my saddle but haven't taken hold or engaged with him to get us into the air. *Sorry, buddy. Just daydreaming. Go ahead and glamor us and get us going.*

With that, I create a streamlined bubble around me and the

spike. It's cold in the air at this time of year. Snug as a bug, I engage after checking that Sloan did as well, and away we go.

CHAPTER NINETEEN

"Hello the lair!" I say twenty minutes later. At the beginning of my druid adventures, it was time-consuming and annoying to arrange a flight to get back and forth to the Emerald Isle every time there was a crisis.

Now it's the work of minutes.

Whether it's Sloan, Tad, or Nikon portaling us, or the dragons flying us, with a little organization, we can be there at the drop of a hat.

"There ye are." Patty comes out of his treasure room to greet us. "Och, and ye brought company fer a visit as well. Hello again, fair Saxa. It's a pleasure to have ye in our home."

Saxa spreads her wings to the side and lowers her head in an elegant bow. "The pleasure is mine."

"We've come to say hello to the others while you visit," Dart says. "Where is everyone?"

"Most of them are flying in the caverns. They've made themselves a bit of an obstacle course and are testing their speed and dexterity."

"Fun," Saxa says.

Patty chuckles. "Aye, it is, until one of them misjudges and crashes into things. I'd swear the entire lair has nearly crumbled a couple of times."

I chuckle. "Away you go, you two. Shall we say, half an hour?"

As the two of them tromp off for some dragon fun, I hug Patty and take his hand. "Can we go sit?"

He looks up at me and adjusts his spectacles, concern bright in his blue eyes. "Are ye all right, Red? Should I be worried?"

I shake my head. "I don't think so, but I ran into someone on my last adventure, and I want to tell you about it."

He leads me back to his treasure room, and I smile at all the shiny, jeweled objects. From magical artifacts that would make Sloan swoon to coins and crowns and goblets and gems. Patty has amassed it all.

He's also moved in our recliners and our *Animal Crossing* setup. "Do ye have time to play?"

I take my seat and wait for him to pull himself up into his recliner. "Not today, I'm afraid."

While he settles, I adjust my backpack on my lap and think about how best to do this.

"Why do ye look like ye've got my dead cat in yer bag, Red? Goddess knows I've always wanted a wee kitty of my own, but I don't have one, so it's not that."

"No, it's not that." He's waiting for an answer. There's no good way to say it other than to speak the words. "I was pulled back in time this week and met up with you and Betrys. She gave me something to give to you the next time I saw you."

He blinks at me, and I pull the handkerchief-wrapped heirloom out of my bag. "Do you remember meeting me on the isle of Emhain Abhlach back about a thousand years ago?"

He looks at me like he's searching his memory but coming up blank. "No. I'm sorry, I don't."

"I'm not surprised. You weren't yourself, and from what you told me of your dark years, you didn't find yourself for quite a long while after."

His normal lighthearted cheer seems to dim. I'm having that effect on people I love today. I'm not a fan.

"Anyway, I promised her I'd bring this to you when you were in a better frame of mind."

"Och, my Bets. She always was a thoughtful wee lass. I miss her deep to the core of my bones."

I think about Brenny, and I draw a long breath through tight lungs. "Does the ache for a lost sibling ever get any easier?"

Patty lifts a shoulder. "It dulls a little and the time that passes between moments of achin' stretches out so it's not so constant, but it's always there."

Not really the answer I was hoping for.

"What I think improves is the funny memories strengthen and grow. Betrys and I used to fight like enraged devils at times, but I don't remember those moments now. When I think of my older sister, I remember how we used to get ourselves into trouble and take care of one another when things went sideways."

"Well, she wanted you to have this." I reach forward and give him the bundle. "Don't feel you have to open it now. I'm heading to Emhain Abhlach next and wanted to give it to you to fulfill my promise."

"Do ye know what it is?"

"No. She'd already wrapped it when she gave it to me, and she didn't say. It was between the two of you, so I didn't ask. I can say she was worried about you and seemed genuinely relieved that we would become friends and that you would find happiness again."

He smiles. "I never would've survived without her. Did ye know it was Betrys who thought of me pairin' up with Her Graciousness? Aye, after a long time of me despairin' that I'd be a man with no gold and no treasure ever again, she convinced me to rebuild once more. She told me that a pairing like this was what I needed. That Her Mighty Fierceness would help defend my trove and I need never have anyone steal from me again."

I smile inwardly, happy to leave that one alone.

"I'm glad you pulled it together and gave it another try, Patty. Not having you in my life would've made my world a great deal less interesting."

He turns his hand over and squeezes my fingers. "I can say the same, lass. I believe it was our destiny to meet and become family."

"Me too."

With that, he pats my hand and pulls the twine holding his bundle closed. When he opens it, he stops, and his eyes glass over with tears. "Och, Bets. Ye always were a sly one."

I look at the shamrock carved out of Connemara marble. It's the same green stone as Birga's spear tip. As he tilts the palm of his hand, the four-leafed clover catches the light this way and that.

"What is it?" I ask.

"It's a family piece—a source of great pain and comfort at the same time." He touches it, gently stroking over the petals of the carving before turning it over and smiling at the worn family crest and script engraved on the back.

"As the oldest born, it was Betrys' duty to guard it and give it to the oldest of those who might carry on our family line. Our father was harsh and thought less of Betrys because his firstborn wasn't a male. He gave it to me instead. It hurt her a great deal and caused a rift between her and Da evermore."

"How did she end up with it?"

He looks up at me and wipes his sleeve under his eyes. "I don't know. I thought I gambled it or sold it or did something equally stupid. Ye see, it's a great source of shame fer my people to be caught and relieved of our gold. Once it happened to me, I lost myself, and it happened again and again. I didn't think much of myself after that, and a great deal of time passed where I drowned my sorrows and hid from the world."

That lines up with the Patty I met a few days ago.

"Well, you're here now, and who you were then helped to make you who you are now. Betrys might not have wanted you to be in charge of your family treasure then, but you're not that man anymore, and she believed in you enough to want you to have it back."

He clutches the shamrock between his stubby hands and nods. "Aye, yer right. It's a rare gift this, Red. I'll never be able to thank ye properly fer givin' me a second chance as ye have."

I kneel on the cave floor and open my arms. Patty's hug is tight and squeezes the breath from my lungs, but I don't complain. This is the stuff I live for.

"Don't thank me. Just live your best life, be happy, and be my friend."

"Consider it done."

Dart, Saxa, and I say goodbye and fly off to our next destination. If Emmet is right and reinstating the sacred island is part of our success plan during the Culling, getting it done sooner rather than later is a good idea. I could've used a few days to recover from our time slip, but he's anxious to follow his path.

Closing my eyes, I hold onto the upper and lower handles of my saddle and let my body sway with the motion of Dart's flight.

Life is too busy. Sometimes I have to remind myself to slow down and be present in the moment. Like now.

Are you all right, Fi? Dart asks. *You've seemed distracted since you arrived home yesterday.*

Lots to think about, buddy. The potential importance of the island of Emhain Abhlach. Connecting with Mother Nature for favors. Whether or not the Morrigan escaped her banishment. How Mingin and Melanippe are regrouping. The growing unrest of the empowered to live in the open. Where we'll fight the battles. How Death plays into all that. How the outcome will change the world going forward...

I see your point. Perhaps work on one thing at a time. It might seem more manageable.

With just over a month until the Culling, I need to consider all those things, but Dart's right. It doesn't help me to get overwhelmed. *I'll try, buddy. Thanks.*

When Dart's trajectory dips sharply, I open my eyes and smile at the little island below. Sloan said the island's warding is much like Myra's bookshop. Only those who know about it and need to be there will find it. Otherwise, it will remain invisible to them.

We definitely need to find it.

It might be a key factor in our preparations for the battles to come.

Dart and Saxa land on the sandy beach next to where our family and friends have gathered. I release my saddle and jog over to Dart's shoulder to dismount and join the others.

By Papu's eyes, wild and wide with wonder, either he didn't know I was arriving by dragon, or he wasn't prepared for what that would look like.

"Welcome to the mythical island of Emhain Abhlach, everyone." I gesture over the long grass at the waterfalls flowing down the black stone cliffs and the forest beyond. "Other than needing a lawnmower in the worst way, it looks the same as it did a thousand years ago."

"And the same as when we visited over the past decades," Wallace says. "I must say, kids, the idea that the legends of the hidden city are real, and we might make it into the internal sanctum is incredibly exciting."

"Agreed." Gran holds out her arm. "Ye can't see it, but under my coat, I've got goosebumps."

Granda chuckles and takes her hand. "Then away we go, my sweet. Let's start our adventure."

The two of them strike off with Da and my brothers close behind them. I catch Calum's arm and lean in. "No Aiden today?"

"No. He opted out to stay home with Kinu and the kids. I

think the throwback in time rattled him more than the rest of us. He's tagging out for now and sticking close to home."

I can't say I'm not disappointed, but on the other hand, I understand where he's coming from.

Letting that go, I adjust the strap of my backpack, hike it higher on my shoulder, and fall in with Sloan, Wallace, Nikon, Andromeda, and their grandfather. "It's wonderful to see you, Papu. I'm glad you're joining us."

Nikon Tsambikos senior is a wonderful man who I would adore even if he wasn't the sweet grandfather of one of my closest friends and hadn't saved my life and offered me a home when I was trapped back in time.

"It's always a pleasure, Fi. And it's I who should thank you. After a lifetime of one day looking much the same as the last, having a new adventure is exhilarating."

I breathe in deep and fill my lungs. "Hopefully, it will be. The difference in ambient magic between now and the first time we arrived on the island is staggering. The conduit to connect the island with The Source prana is definitely broken."

"Then our task is set."

I nod. "That it is."

Lifting our feet high as we walk, our cross-island trek through the overgrowth is like a high school science class field trip. Between Gran pointing out the plant species and commenting on the birdsong and Granda, Wallace, and Sloan rhyming off legendary tales about the island, it's a lesson on several fronts.

"Why did your brothers insist on bringing camping equipment?" Dionysus drops back to walk with the Greek contingent. "You said there was a city and a palace. Won't we stay there?"

"There *was* a city and a palace a thousand years ago. At some point between then and now, the island broke. We're not sure what we'll find. If something destroyed the city, we're camping. If the city is intact, we'll find a place to hunker down while we work on island restoration."

Dionysus chuffs. "If something destroyed the city, I'll portal us home to sleep in beds and bring us back in the morning."

"Don't be so sure about that," Emmet says. "When we were here last time, Sloan and Tad weren't able to *poof* into the island's interior. The shoreline was as close as they could get."

Dionysus frowns and by the look on his face he's trying to snap forward to the trees. "Why can't I portal? I don't like that one bit."

"The island falls within the domain of a Celtic sea god, Manannan mac Lir. He's quite strict about using magic to access the island's center. Only those who are pure of heart gain entry to the hidden city."

Nikon snorts. "Then I'm surprised he hasn't struck down Dionysus already."

"Rude." Dionysus flicks a hand at Nikon. "I might not be pure of body, but I think my heart and intention will surely pass the test."

"They absolutely will," I say.

We arrive at the edge of the forest, and an eerie sense of *déjà vu* strikes me. "The trees aren't moving in this time either."

"No, I don't suppose they would," Sloan says. "If the link to fae power is corrupted, they won't have the power to shift."

"So, no deciduous dodge again," Emmet says. "Disappointing."

"Definitely disappointing," I say.

Sloan chuckles. "Once we right whatever is wrong with their connection to the prana river, I'm sure they'll shift and try to crush ye into pulp. That is what yer hoping for, isn't it?"

"Maybe."

"Yer ridiculous."

I roll my eyes, but he's not wrong. "Tell me you don't think trees that try to squash people is cool. Let's take a vote. Who thinks homicidal hardwood is cool?"

Me, my brothers, Dionysus, Gran, Da, and Nikon put our hands up. That's fewer than I thought. Well, to each their own.

I suppose there must be some risk-averse people in the world to balance out the rest of us.

Stepping into the spackled light streaming through the canopy above I press a hand against the bark of a tall elm tree. The energy coming back at me is too familiar.

It's still pained.

"The trees don't like being bound in place. It's not an immobilization spell this time, though. Sloan's right. They don't have the power they used to."

Gran presses a hand against the bark of a tall willow and sighs. "Oh, my dear, I'm so sorry ye suffer. We'll do what we can to rectify that fer ye. Don't worry."

We plod on, and I try to remember the way. Except last time, it was dark and I was running, and following Bruin's call.

"Bruin? Wanna come out and help retrace our steps? You were the one who led us to the entrance last time."

I release my bear, and he materializes between two evergreens up ahead. "I'd never turn down a romp and tromp in the forest."

"Who in their right mind would?"

We continue through the trees, and like the last time, the forest seems to stretch in front of us endlessly. It's an illusion. I learned that the first time.

The only question is, how do we get through the hard outer shell to the gooey center?

"How are we doing, Bruin?"

"Fine. I found the spot where we went through before, but something is blocking me."

"What is it? A ward? A spell?"

"I'd say a spell, and if I'm not crazy, the signature of the power behind it feels a lot like the dark power that sorceress possessed the last time we were here."

"Seriously? That was over a thousand years ago. Trace magic

from her spell couldn't still be here, and I can't see how it could be the same sorceress. She'd be long ago dead."

"Unless she time-slipped like we did," Sloan says. "Because technically, druids don't live long enough to see two Culling periods either, but here we are."

"And Merlin too," Dillan adds. "His longevity from being dragon bound made that possible."

"Okay, it's possible...however unlikely."

"What makes you so sure, *a ghra*?"

"Well, why would a sorceress come here to destroy the city of Emhain Abhlach then and come back a thousand years later once she'd already destroyed it?"

"Maybe the city's not destroyed, and she came to finish it off," Ciara says. "Or maybe it was never about the city. Ye said the sorceress was in the open grasslands by the prana river."

"She was. Kyna and the others thought she was trying to take out the city's defenses."

"What if she wasn't?"

"It's certainly a possibility," Emmet says. "Once they were gone, we never gave it much thought. Maybe the attack was about the prana river and the connection to The Source all along."

Maybe. "If at first, you don't succeed, try and try again? Is there something about the period of the Culling that makes it particularly optimum for trying to access the prana conduit to The Source?"

Emmet shrugs a shoulder. "I have no idea."

The more I think about it, the more uneasy it makes me. "Okay, we need to get inside. Everyone get your thinking caps on. If the sorceress is back, it's no coincidence she's here right before the Culling like last time. Whatever her reason, I doubt it will benefit Team Light."

Da meets my gaze and frowns. "No, *mo chroi*, I don't suppose it will."

CHAPTER TWENTY

Sloan and I work with Wallace and Granda, running our hands over the ebony rockface as we try to bring down the spell holding us out. "Any luck?" I ask, hoping I've missed something.

"Nothing here," Dillan says. He's got his hood up and is searching for a hidden entrance or seam to the spell or something we can use.

Sloan holds his hands up. "All right. Fi, take a step back. I'm not sure this will work."

I do as he asks and ensure Gran and Papu are back as well. Dionysus is currently entertaining them and they're out of the fallout zone.

It's futile to hope he's keeping his stories clean, but I send out a wish for it anyway.

Energy builds in the air a moment before—*Snap!*

I twist my face away from the sparks of electricity and Sloan jumps back, cursing and shaking his hand.

"Hurts, doesn't it? I know exactly how that feels."

Sloan sticks the tips of his fingers into his mouth before

shaking them out again and examining them. "Aye, I suppose ye do. I think my fingers will be numb fer the rest of the day, the same way yer arm was."

It's too bad, but it still doesn't get us inside.

"So, taking it down isn't working. What about a counterspell of some kind? Could we modify the spell to something we can manage easier?"

"We tried that." Da stands with Calum.

"Dionysus and I tried portaling in," Nikon says. "We're still being blocked."

"What about burrowing?" Doc says.

Emmet's pine marten stands on his back legs and looks at us. He's been sniffing along the bottom edge of the rockface, and maybe he found something we missed.

"Burrowing where, dude?" Emmet asks. "You mean under the massive rock face?"

He nods. "Yes."

"Is the stone really there or is it an illusion?" I ask. "Last week when I ran at it, the stone seemed real, but I was able to pass right through it."

"I was thinking about the nursery rhyme Kinu tells Jackson and Meg about the bear hunt," Doc says. "Can't go over it. Can't go through it. Have to go under it."

He hasn't got it right, but the idea is the same.

"Well, we can give it a try."

The druids step forward, and we make a collective effort to *Move Earth* and gain access to the area on the other side of the stone rocks.

Nothing happens.

"Okay, now what?" I ask. "It's hard to stop whatever is happening and restore the island to its former state of power when we can't get in the door. You'd think the island would want us to help."

"The trees do, luv," Gran says.

"That's it," Sloan says. "Maybe we're goin' at this the wrong way. Instead of our efforts focusin' on the sorceress and her spell to keep us out. Maybe we could entice the god of the island to let us in another way. Our intention is pure, and we're here to restore his beloved Emhain Abhlach."

Granda nods. "That's a fine idea, lad, but how do ye suggest we get his attention?"

Sloan shakes his head. "I don't think we can, but if I'm right, Emmet can. He has the most prana power, and he took the blood oath to bind himself as a defender of the island. If Manannan mac Lir is as devoted to Emhain Abhlach as legend says, I'm sure he'll hear Emmet's call for help."

Granda thinks it over and winks at Em. "Aye, it could work. Give it a try, lad."

I squeeze Emmet's arm. "It's a big day in the life of you, oh great warrior of the prophecy. Go, Em, go!"

Meditation isn't Emmet's strong suit, so I worry about his focus and whether or not he'll have the oomph to reach a Celtic god. If Manannan mac Lir isn't interested or nearby or tuned into Emmet's frequency, this whole operation goes belly up.

True, I don't really know how contacting a god works, but I still worry.

"Can you help him?" I ask Dionysus. "You're a god. You know how to get the man's attention, don't you?"

Dionysus chuckles. "Not all gods are the same, Jane. Different pantheons. Different powers. Different people. You can't lump us all in together."

"I'm not trying to stereotype you. I know you're unique. I thought maybe you could guide his message or amplify it or something."

He lifts a shoulder and winks. "It's not my pantheon, but I

suppose I could give the message extra power and amplify his call a little."

I squeeze his hand and pull him toward Emmet. "Thank you, Tarzan. I appreciate all you do."

We leave the two of them at the rockface and the rest of us back away several yards to give Emmet enough quiet to filter out distractions.

"Do you think he can do it?" Andromeda whispers.

I nod. "Em's got this."

Between one moment and the next, a rush of fae energy bombards me. It's nauseating and sets my head spinning. Closing my eyes, I lean forward and wait for the ride to come to a complete stop.

When the fog clears enough for me to open my eyes, we're inside the island's center and standing on the grassy plain outside the gates of Emhain Abhlach.

We're not alone.

An eight-foot-tall man with deep-set eyes and a wild mane of matted hair is staring us down. Wearing only navy leather pants and a Mr. T. amount of silver chains against his bare chest, he doesn't seem at all happy to have been disturbed from whatever underwater realm he was governing. "You will fix this," Manannan booms. "You have so sworn."

I glance around the clearing and take in the scene.

Time is frozen, and it gives us a second to see what we're dealing with.

There is, indeed, a red-skinned sorceress with scales, horn eyebrows, pointed ears, and ebony hair. She's hovering in the air with her arms outstretched. It's not the same woman we faced last time, but there is enough of a resemblance it must be a descendant.

The oxen beasts are back. There are hundreds of them this time instead of dozens. They look much the same, and I take comfort that we might know what we're dealing with there. Many of them are embroiled in a battle with enormous, pink serpent beasts.

"What the fuckety-fuck are those?" Dillan asks.

"Ophidians," Eva says. "Very lethal. Very rare. They adapt to their surroundings like chameleons and are quite protective of their territory."

"What is their territory?" Calum asks. "I'll be sure to avoid it."

Yeah. Good call.

I've never seen anything like them. There are several on land but more in the river of prana, which seems to be drained in color as well as drained of power. What used to be a vibrant Barbie pink is now a shade of pale candy floss.

The chameleon comment makes sense. They are the exact color of the prana river and are impossible to see if they're underwater. You wouldn't think a pink snake thing could be so terrifying...but it is.

"Minions of the Prophetic Warrior," Manannan says, "I accept your pledge of aid. You will remain here to assist the serpents of The Source and restore my island to its former glory. Your master so swears it."

Our master?

Manannan disappears, and the world unfreezes. We're not in the thick of things and thankfully, we're undetected...but we won't be for long.

I take in our party. Not everyone here is a warrior.

"Shit. We should've secured the island before we invited people to join us," Dillan says.

He's right, but hindsight is twenty-twenty and all that. "Emmet, do your light weaver thing and shield Gran and the others so they're safe. It looks like the Ladies of Light two-point-oh will have to wait for their training until after we reclaim the island."

Emmet looks at me like I grew two more heads. "Fi, I can't make my clothes disappear. What makes you think I'm ready to make half a dozen people disappear?"

"I've got you, Jane," Dionysus says. "I'll shield the family and get them safely tucked out of the way. That way, the Prophetic Warrior can stay and help you battle."

"I heart you, Tarzan. Thanks."

"Who's with me?" he asks. As hands go up, he, Nikon's family, Gran, Granda, and Wallace disappear.

With that taken care of, I drop my backpack off my shoulders, unzip it, and take out my iron crown. Placing it on my head, I get ready for my first battle wearing it to command the troops.

"So, the scary giant god said we're helping the serpents. Let's hope the serpents know we're on their side."

"Who wants to tell them?" Calum asks.

"Not it," Dillan says.

"Not it," I say as quickly as I can.

Emmet raises his hand. "I'll do it. I hear their thoughts and will tell them who we are and why we're here."

"And ask them nicely not to eat us," Dillan says.

"Or spit prana water at us." Calum points as one of the serpents breaches the surface and spews a line of prana water twenty feet to catch a group of hairy oxen beasts in the face.

The moment the prana water hits them, the hair on their body singes and they recoil, screaming. A couple of them get the spray in the face and must swallow some because they drop to the ground and go deathly still.

"All right," I say, meeting the wide eyes of my family and friends. "Let's do this. Emmet, did you make contact with the serpents?"

"Yes. I gave them the lowdown, and they said something to the effect of feasting on the bones of meat sacks. I'm not one hundy percent sure if they're inviting us to feast on the enemy as their guests or if we are the meat sacks."

I blink at my brother. "That's a very important distinction, Em. Can we get a Clarica agent working on that one, please?"

There's no time. The oxen beasts have clued into our arrival and are coming at us in great force.

"Bruin, buy us a little time to get sorted, will you?"

"On it, Red." Bruin ghosts out and materializes between us and the horde of fighters coming at us.

Calum tosses his winter coat onto my backpack and calls his bow and quiver forward. "Someone, cover me. I need higher ground."

"Got you, bro." Dillan calls faery fire to his palms and Sloan follows suit. "Do you think you can get to that guard tower at the gate?"

"Abso-freaking-lutely. I bet you five bucks I can get there before you can throw ten fireballs."

"Challenge accepted." As Calum takes off, Dillan and Sloan start firing their flaming projectiles.

The oxen beasts don't like fire, which works for us because it's one skill all my brothers have mastered. There was something about throwing fireballs that had them working doubly hard to learn.

"Sloan, if Bruin can ghost out, can you and Tad do your portal *poof* fighting thing Dahir taught you?"

He disappears from where he's standing beside me, reappears, then is back beside me again. "Aye, it seems our powers are working fine here."

"Excellent. Then everyone have at it. Plenty to do." I call Birga to my palm and run at the hairy minions Bruin is cutting down.

With the crown on, my connection to our fighters syncs up, and I start getting a download of information—ours and theirs.

Fionn's right. This crown is amazing.

The hairy beasts are afraid of fire. I push the thought out to my party. *Work on forcing them back toward the river. With any luck, the serpents will jump out and chomp them.*

The serpents spray prana water, bite, or constrict themselves around foes. Da spins his staff and cartwheels. *Be careful not to get in their way.*

Emmet has called his ribbon of prana and is doing his gymnastic floor routine again. As crazy as it looks, it's amazingly effective and keeps the oxen beasts at a good distance.

Ciara is right there with him. I forget, sometimes, that she's been a druid-in-training as long as Sloan has and is almost as proficient. When I look at her with the crown on, I'm even more impressed.

She has power.

Nikon didn't hunker down to be safe with his family. He's picked up a sword and is cutting through the enemy with Bruin. Focusing on the blade of his weapon, I thrust my intention forward. *"Flaming Blade."*

In a *whoosh* that runs from the hilt to the tip, the steel of his sword lights on fire and now it's doubly effective. It stabs them and scares them.

Tad and Sloan are *poofing* in and out, confusing their opponents, and by the looks of it, having a lot of fun together. Who would've predicted that a year ago?

Certainly neither of them.

Rory flies by and swoops around the sorceress. Dillan and Eva are right there with her. Eva might be an angel, but she's a lethal fighter and seems to love chopping bad guys' heads off with her scythe.

A massive serpent breaks through the pink surface and beaches itself on the lawn like a long, fat seal—a forty-foot long, four-thousand-pound seal with twelve stubby legs…and claws… and a jointed jaw with a gazillion teeth.

Did I mention they're terrifying?

The ground trembles with the impact of the thing beaching. Then it races across the ground and joins four other serpents going after the sorceress.

When it arrives, one of the other four falls back and slither-skitters back to the river.

"Are they taking shifts?"

"That's what it looked like," Bruin says. "Maybe that's how they've held her back as long as they have."

I don't know how long this battle has been raging, but the devastation to the ground and the riverbank as well as the accumulation of the dead makes me think it's been a long while.

Sloan, did you ever come up with a portal jamming spell? I swear this sorceress is the great-granddaughter of the woman we faced last week. If she fights using the same playbook, I don't want uninvited guests.

On my way, a ghra. Emmet, if ye can, meet me by yer sister, I'll take a spell boost to give us the best chance at success.

On my way.

Dayam, I love this crown. To be able to communicate and coordinate on the fly is baller.

I grunt as I swing Birga, catching an opponent across the belly and changing his innies to outies. He manages a powerful lunge with his dying breath and rams me with a weird, glowing blue blade.

Last I checked, I'm not an orc, so I don't know what the blue glow is about, but the important thing is that while it's unusual, it doesn't penetrate my armor.

With a hollow *thunk*, it glances off my ribs as I spin to evade. I knock it from his hairy paws, and it falls along with its dead wielder.

Man, there are a lot of these beasts.

Dart and Saxa, if you can hear this and access the hidden city, we have a few hundred hairy oxen creatures you could fry for us.

We're trying to find our way to you. Dart says. *We can't see anything in front of us, but I'm following your voice, so keep speaking.*

Okay, I'll try. Make sure to focus on protecting the island from trouble. That should give you a pass into the hidden areas.

Got it. I'll tell Saxa.

I rush over to back up Bruin and turn to face two opponents. *Ninety-nine oxen beasts on the wall, ninety-nine oxen beasts. Strike one down, onto the ground, ninety-eight oxen beasts on the wall.*

I'm not sure I keep an accurate count as I'm battling, but by the time I'm at ninety-four oxen beasts, Saxa and Dart streak through the sky above and have joined us in the island's inner sanctum.

I finish with my opponent and reassess the situation. The key is the sorceress. If we take her out, we win.

I glance back to see if Emmet will have another one of his power tantrums to clear the playing field. Doesn't look like it. He's busy with Sloan amping up the spell to block opening a portal.

Wait? Will blocking portals negate his ability to *poof*? Is that a form of portaling? Damn, I need to start writing down my questions to get answers later.

Another massive serpent breaks through the pink surface of the prana river. It lands on the ground with a heavy *thunk* and scrambles toward the other four serpents going after the sorceress.

Like before, when it arrives, one of the other four falls back and slither-skitters back to the river.

The serpent that arrives for his shift spews a forceful stream of prana at the hovering red-skinned woman.

The liquid power hits her shielding and deflects.

My head cranks around on a pivot as I follow the trajectory of the splash zone and scream inside. Bruin has his back to the danger, fighting two oxen beasts.

He'll never get out of the way in time.

Digging my boots in, I turn back and book it hard. I launch myself at my bear, my mind racing, skimming through spells more on instinct than a decision.

"Impenetrable Sphere." The shielding bubble encapsulates the two of us as I land on Bruin's wide, muscled back. "Drop right."

He responds without question, and we roll out of the way of the prana spray.

Some of the pink liquid hits the sphere, but much more of it hits the two opponents Bruin was fighting.

Their scream is shrill but short-lived. Before long, they fall still like the others.

Bruin is lying on his belly with me flopped on the ground beside him and my crown askew. "Are you okay, Bear? None of the prana got you, did it?"

Bruin chuckles and licks the side of my face. "It's adorable ye thought to tackle me instead of simply tellin' me to ghost out. Yer a kick, Red."

I grunt, get back to my feet, and adjust my crown so it's not over one eye and one ear. "Glad I amuse you. Gotta keep my peeps safe. Lurve you, Bear."

The deep bass of his amusement vibrates in my lungs. "Lurve ye right back, ye nut."

I check what's happening outside our bubble of protection and get back in the game. *How's everyone doing?*

We need to take down the sorceress, Calum says.

End the red bitch. End the battle sitch, Dillan adds.

Agreed. I stare at the sorceress and try to assess where we are and what we need to do. *With my crown on, I can see her aura. She's not wearing down.*

I haven't been here long enough to know how her energy readings looked like hours or days ago, but from what I see, she's not being taxed toward exhaustion even with four massive serpents spewing at her, ramming her shielding, and trying to chomp her.

She must be drawing from a source, Sloan says. *With the island broken, that's not it. Find her source and target it. Take that out and wear her down.*

I run through my lessons about powerful sects. Sorcery is the use of power gained from the assistance or control of evil spirits. The power source is almost always external and bound to the caster somehow.

Two more oxen beasts target us and—not realizing we have a protective sphere in place—run straight at us at full speed and practically knock themselves out.

"Och, that was funny." Bruin laughs. "Why haven't we done this before?"

I ignore his amusement and stay focused on the sorceress. She doesn't have a jeweled staff or an amulet or anything that would be obvious as a source of power, but there is an odd glow coming off the bodice of her armor.

"Hey, Bruin? Have you ever seen armor like that before? What's it made of?"

He stands up on his hind legs and sets his paw on my shoulder. "Looks like bones."

"You think?"

He tilts his boxy head to the side and drops to all fours. "Aye, I think so."

Could bones be her source? I ask. *I don't see anything else, but her bodice is glowing, and Bruin thinks the ribbing is bone.*

Bones carry a lot of power, Da answers. *Even more if there's a blood connection to the one in possession.*

Like, say, an evil great-grandmother if she wanted to follow in her footsteps.

Aye, like that.

How do we counter that?

Separate her from the bones, salt them, burn them, Emmet says breathlessly.

That's what the Winchesters would do. Dillan adds.

I chuff. *That's for ghosts and is on* Supernatural*. This is for reals, you guys.*

Ignore yer brothers, Da says, *but unfortunately, Emmet's not wrong. Get the armor off her and destroy the bones to break the connection.*

All right. We're on it.

CHAPTER TWENTY-ONE

"Are you ready to do this, Bear?"

"Och, Red, this will be the stuff of legends."

I laugh at his enthusiasm and wish I shared half as much confidence. "Be careful, buddy. Evil bitches come and go, but there's only one you."

"Right back atcha, Red. Now, big girl panties. Let's do this."

With a deep breath and a prayer for luck, I drop the protective shield of our impenetrable sphere, and we strike off in opposite directions. My boots dig in, and I push off, racing across the mulched ground.

It's a classic offensive of face and trigger.

I'm the face. He's the trigger.

Okay, maybe it's not a classic—I learned it by watching *Hanna* last week on Prime—but if it works for teenage supersoldiers it can work for a druid and her battle bear, amirite?

Hells yeah.

Getting in front of the sorceress takes effort.

There are four massive serpents writhing like worms and head-butting her shielding. To get her full attention, I need to get in between them to distract her from our play.

Ophidians are forty feet long and four feet around, so going over them is faster than going around them.

"Feline Finesse." They're too tall to hurdle, so I call a little druid magic and Bo Duke hood-slide over them to get where I'm going.

Okay, that part is pretty cool.

What isn't cool is how touching their scales eats through my jeans on my left leg.

One minute I'm fully dressed, and the next, my skin is exposed from hip to calf. As I up and over the second Ophidian, I try to clear its body so I don't end up having an undies adventure like Emmet.

Costume malfunction aside, I'm in position quickly and raise my hands to the sky above. My call to elemental power gets an immediate answer.

I don't know if you can understand me, I project to the serpents, *but when I give you the signal, go at her with everything you've got.*

Understanding isn't the problem. Her shielding is. The words echo inside my mind and leave a chilly aftertaste. *Yes. We're working on that.*

Potential energy rumbles and rolls in the sky above, and the power of lightning builds fast. My cells ping to full awareness as an influx of energy bombards my body.

At the very least, a bolt from the heavens should distract the sorceress long enough for Bruin to do his thing.

I close my eyes, drawing as much power as I can harness, coaxing it to grow, fighting to keep it from breaking free too soon.

Are you ready, Bruin?

Ready.

Don't go in until the lightning grounds. I don't want you caught in the charge.

Got it. Let's do this.

I hear the impatience in his voice and stop stalling. He knows to stay out of the blast zone. I worry too much. "I hope you have your affairs in order, bitch."

Her taunting laughter grates on my nerves.

Raising my hand over my head, I grasp the power charge and yank it to the ground. The lightning bolt *cracks* directly at her. It strikes her shield hard above her head, and for the first time, she doesn't look so cocky.

She adjusts her stance, raising her hands.

There are definite fissures in her shield, and now she's scrambling to repair them.

"Hit her hard. Now!"

The Ophidian serpents double their efforts, and I join the fight. The noise of their attack is deafening, but that's good. We have her entire attention, and with her trying to close the cracks in her shielding, she doesn't realize it's already too late.

Because one tiny fissure is all my bear needed.

Bruin materializes inside her shielded area and attacks hard and fast. He swipes her with his mighty claws, and I don't care how tough a person is. When a massive mythical grizzly hits you full force, you feel it.

I give her credit, though—she doesn't give up.

She twists away, bracing her hands against her shield and exposing her ribs and back.

That's exactly what we need to happen.

Bruin swipes his claws down the tough material of her body armor. It's no match for his force, and he tears the chest plate free. It swings loose and drops to the ground. She realizes our play and grabs for the ancient bones…but it's too late.

Bruin lunges forward and wraps his mouth around her throat.

Abandoning the shielding is her only chance at survival, but even then, there's no chance. Bruin grips her throat and flings her at the serpents.

Two of the Ophidian beasts rear up to snap onto her. Both of them get hold and pull. Tearing a person in two is nasty business and makes one helluva mess.

They don't seem to care.

The serpents chomp and the crunch of her bones signifies how abruptly the tide has turned. Saxa and Dart are razing hundreds of her minion companions in fiery bursts. At the same time, dozens more serpents writhe out of the pink river to end this.

Trying to ignore the sounds and smells of death, I make my way over to where Bruin is standing bloody and panting. "Great job, Bear. Are you all right?"

"Never better. There's nothing like taking down a big bad. Do ye think that's the end of it?"

I take in the chaotic mayhem of oxen beasts trying futilely to flee. "Yep. I think we're good."

It takes another few minutes to sort through the chaos and for everyone to finish the skirmishes they're involved in. I scan the battlefield, and from what I can see, everyone is upright and whole.

Dillan is cradling his wrist under his cloak, Nikon is limping, and my leg is seriously burned and stinging like a bitch from where I contacted the Ophidian, but it seems the wounds suffered on our side are superficial.

Unlike the early days when I was always being rushed to the clinic with a knife in my side or a hex overtaking me, a little contact burn isn't so bad.

Sloan and Da jog over and both of them look at my leg as if they are thinking the same thing.

"Not too bad, then," Da says.

"Och, no. I'm grand." I lay on the Irish lilt. "Savage craic."

Sloan kneels next to me and scowls at my leg. "What did this, *a ghra?*"

"I rubbed against the serpents. I think they're prana radioactive or something. Doesn't matter. I'm fine."

Da accepts that better than Sloan and grabs a swatch of cloth left from the sorceress's sash. Stepping to where she'd shielded herself, he drapes it over the bone bodice. "We'll destroy this right away, so it doesn't cause anyone any more trouble."

Yes, do, one of the serpents says. *We are appreciative of your aid.*

"Hopefully, we can continue to help," I say. "We've been tasked with restoring Emhain Abhlach and re-establishing it as a primary conduit of The Source power. There are troubled times upon us, and we believe this island is a key element for the side of Light."

In days past, it was that way. That was long ago.

"It can be again. Do you know what we need to do to repair the connection to the primary power?"

There is nothing you can do.

I look at the pale pink water and sigh. "I don't accept that. The magic is still there. It's just not strong enough to power the island. There's a pipe broken in the plumbing somewhere, and we need to fix it."

It is not for you to fix.

I don't want to start an argument with the forty-foot pink snake, but we didn't go through all of this—in both timelines—for nothing. "I reject that answer. Someone sent us back in time to learn about the island and save it then. We're supposed to save it again now—I feel it. If it's broken, we'll fix it. It's what we do."

It is not for you to fix.

"It *is* for us to fix," I counter.

Da squeezes my shoulder. "I don't doubt yer instincts about resurrecting the island, *mo chroi,* but maybe yer not hearin' what he said." He looks at the serpents. "Ye say it's not fer us to fix...is it fer *you* to fix? Is there somethin' *you* can do to—as Fi says—fix the broken pipe?"

Nothing is broken. The power is disconnected. Without a guardian for the island, dark-intentioned people came. They tried to control the power.

"So, ye severed the feed," Sloan says.

"The state of disconnect is intentional?" I catch on. "It's something done to protect the power from being misused?"

Correct.

"Excellent. If you did it with intention, you can undo it. If it's not us meant to fix it, I ask you to please do it."

Without a guardian for the island, dark-intentioned people come. Disconnected is better.

"No. It's not," I say, exhausted by this whole situation. "Fixed would be better."

"What if the island had a guardian?" Emmet joins us. "What if someone with a strong connection to The Source committed to keeping watch over the island? Would you repair the disconnect then?"

The four serpents regard one another and look back at us. *If a suitable guardian pledged to oversee the island, we would repair the connection, yes.*

I'm looking at Emmet the whole time he's talking, and I'm getting a rock in the pit of my stomach. "No, Em. You don't need to do that. We'll figure out a way to fix the island without you making any crazy promises."

He looks at me and winks. "There's nothing crazy about it, Fi. For the first time, I know exactly where I belong and exactly what I need to do."

A wave of nausea hits. I look at my father. "Da, tell him not to jump into something. You know how he gets. He's impulsive."

Da's sad smile makes the ache in my belly grow. "Yer brother knows his mind. If he's found his purpose, he's man enough to make his own decision. I tried to decide fer all of ye once before, and the universe found a way around me. Ye came here and made yer choice. Let him make his."

I search Ciara's expression for any sign that she's against this. "You don't want to commit to this island, do you? No malls. No concerts. Tell him not to do this."

Ciara doesn't look pleased, but she's not on my side. "I loved remodeling Tad's place. Maybe fixin' up an entire ancient city would be fun. Besides, if Em is here and we take it on together, I'm game fer any adventure."

Why is everyone going along with this?

I swallow and try again. "Em, this isn't like you moving across the road. You'll be in Ireland, and not only in Ireland but on an island locked inside a hidden city. You can't just walk across the road and eat our cereal. We won't see you. You won't see the kids grow up. It'll change everything."

Emmet takes my hands in his and squeezes. "Breathe, Fi. It's going to be all right. This is where I need to be. Yes, at first, I'll likely have to stay here a lot and get things straightened out, but after that, I'll be able to step away briefly to visit at Gran's and at home if Sloan or the Greeks don't mind coming to get me."

"Anytime, my friend," Nikon says.

"I'll get you a pendant," Dionysus adds.

I swipe at the tears blurring my vision. "Why does it have to be you?"

Emmet smiles. "Because I know it's what I'm supposed to do. Ever since I fell into the river of prana, I've been uncomfortable in my skin—almost out of phase with myself. I don't feel like that here. On this island, I feel alive and whole and happy. That's what you want for me, isn't it?"

"Of course, it is, but—"

"Shh…" He presses against my mouth and wriggles his fingers all over my face being an ass. "Don't say another word. Everything works out as it's supposed to. You know that."

I do. But I hate this.

I check in with Calum and Dillan. Neither of them is putting up a fight.

That's because the battle is already lost.

Emmet's going to stay here. I don't even know how to wrap my head around that.

Sucking it up, I turn back to the serpents. "Okay, you have your guardian. Now, how soon can we get the disconnect in the prana power fixed?"

While the Ophidians do what they need to do, the rest of us stand around and stare at the demolition zone. "I gotta tell you, bro," Dillan says. "This place gives a whole new meaning to the term fixer-upper."

Emmet chuckles. "No argument."

Dionysus releases the protection spell keeping our families safe from the battle, and I go over to hug Gran. "Did you hear? Emmet's going to stay. He volunteered to be the guardian of this island." As I speak the words, new tears sting my nose and gloss my eyes.

This one hurts so much not even a Gran hug is fixing it. "Aye, luv, I heard. I also heard him say he feels he's found his place."

"I know but holy hell I'm going to miss him."

She eases back and cups my cheeks. "That's true. Take it from someone who's been through it. There is a great deal more consolation in knowing the person ye love is happy and livin' their truth than ye think at first."

I see the pain that Da's break from their life caused her and my emotional dam breaks.

This has been a shit day. From Patty, to Sloan, to Emmet, to Gran...why is my heart so mulched up today?

"*A ghra*? Come here to me, luv. Let Da and I have a look at yer leg."

I turn from Gran's hug to Sloan's and hold on tight. "Emmet's leaving us. Da's moved away. Brenny's gone. How am I supposed to hold the world together when I can't even hold my family together?"

Sloan's arms are strong and familiar, and I'm quite sure that without them wrapped around me, I would break apart and fly away in the breeze. "I'm sorry yer sufferin'. I know how deeply it hurts ye to think of yer daily life without them in it."

It does. I was okay with moving next door with Sloan because they were all still with me.

Now that won't be true.

"Hey, Red," Nikon says, stepping in behind Sloan. "Whatever we can do to help. Any time, day or night, if you need to be here, Dionysus or I will make sure you can get here and get straight back."

"Thanks, guys." I swallow, my throat thick with tears. "I'm sorry I'm being dumb."

"You're not being dumb." Dionysus steps around us to hug me from behind. "Every empowered person has a source of strength. Yours is the love of your family...and hopefully your extended family."

I smile and twist around to hug him. "Definitely. Thank you for keeping everyone safe from the sorceress and her hairy henchmen."

"You're welcome." Dionysus kisses my forehead. The contact is warm and spreads a sense of calm through my system in a matter of seconds.

For the first time since I sat down to tell Patty about his sister's gift, I breathe fully into the depth of my lungs. "Thanks, Tarzan."

Dionysus winks. "Anytime."

I give him one last squeeze and hug Nikon. "I heart you hard, both of you, so much. Thank you for always being here for me."

Nikon hugs me and kisses my temple. "I can't speak for Dionysus, but there's nowhere I'd rather be."

He steps back and winks. "On that note, we're being beckoned for our Ladies of Light lesson."

I chuckle. "Well, I don't want to keep you. See if you can unmask the hidden city, would you? I'd like to know my brother has a roof over his head."

Dionysus and Nikon stride off to join Papu, Andromeda, and Emmet. The five of them have a lot of work to do if they're going to learn the skills Kyna and her sisters taught Emmet to unveil the city.

Or maybe the city isn't there anymore.

It's impossible to know.

"How about I take a look at yer leg, Fi?" Wallace asks, smiling down at me. "Even with yer armor in place, it looks like ye've contracted a nasty burn."

I break out of my emotional funk and get back to the moment at hand. "It stings pretty badly. I vaulted over a couple of the serpents, and either their scales or maybe residual prana on their scales tried to eat me."

"What spell stones do ye have with ye? Have ye got an amethyst?"

"I do." I slide my hand into my pocket and pull out the precious crystals I've collected over the past year and a half. The collection of gemstones in my palm is a reflection of my path.

I have my peridot Patty gave me after the dragons hatched, the swirly psychedelic Ostara poop, the beginner crystals Sloan helped me pick out the day we went shopping and met Myra...

"Take yer amethyst and focus on the intention of my energy," Wallace says.

I do as he says and let the familiar signature of his healing take hold. How many times has Wallace had to patch me up after a druid misadventure? I don't think I could recount them all.

It stings a little as he works, but the pain is nothing compared to the pressure sitting on my chest. It feels like during Emmet's declaration to stay on this island, a Humvee parked on my chest and stayed there.

I'm not sure how to get it to move on.

This is neither the time nor place to have a complete emotional fall apart. No matter how much I want to.

"He'll be all right, luv." Sloan brushes his thumb across my damp cheek. "I know yer bond with Emmet is especially tight, but ye must allow him to find his path."

I blink fast and try to breathe. "I know that—I do. I've always believed he was destined for something amazing. It's just…now that his quest is beginning, I'm not ready."

"That's the funny thing about destiny, luv. Sometimes it's a sacrifice ye make fer the betterment of the world and sometimes it's an unexpected moment in a back alley when a wee hellcat grabs yer balls and drops ye to the ground."

I chuckle. "It's a crazy thing, destiny."

"Aye, it is at that."

CHAPTER TWENTY-TWO

"Hey, you two," Dillan shouts from over by a heap of dead oxen beasts. "When you see everyone around you cleaning up a kill site and doing yard work, that's your cue to pull your shit together and help."

Sloan scowls at my brother, but I squeeze his arm and chuckle. "That's just Dillan's way to say enough tears have fallen. There's work to be done."

"I know what he's sayin', *a ghra*. I think he could be gentler with yer feelings when sayin' it."

"Ha! Well, if that's what you're expecting, you're bound to be disappointed. I grew up with five brothers, remember? Gentle with my feelings wasn't a thing."

Wallace finishes up with the triage treatment of my leg, and I glance down at the damage. It's still quite raw and pink, but I suppose it's tough to use fae magic to heal a burn of fae magic.

"Do ye maybe have a change of clothes, Fi? If not, ye run the risk of more irritation and maybe infection."

"Yeah. In my backpack." I hug Sloan's father and turn, searching for the pile of belongings we tossed on the ground before all this began.

A quick change from dead jeans to clean cargo pants and I'm ready to roll again. Wow, this place really is a disaster.

Calum and Da are dragging bodies into piles of ten or twelve, Granda is opening the earth, so the heaps fall beneath the surface, and Gran and Ciara are spelling the remains to avoid any negative aftereffects. At the same time, Dillan and Tad are gathering weapons and making another pile up by the gates.

"What do you want us to do?" I ask.

"If yer not afraid to go near the water, settling the soil and healin' the land would be helpful," Da says.

"Afraid to go near the water?"

Da chuckles. "It seems Calum, Dillan, and Tad are all a bit weirded out about goin' within forty or fifty feet of the riverbank."

Dillan snorts, unaffected by Da's amusement. "Did you see them coming up out of the river and chomping the enemy?"

I chuckle. "We're not the enemy. We're the people dedicated to restoring the island."

"Sharks mistake surfers as seals. That doesn't mean their legs don't still get bitten off."

All righty then.

I wave away their paranoia and head toward the riverbank. It's not that I give any credence to their theory about getting chomped by the pink Source serpents, but I do stop a few feet back from the edge and watch the surface of the water. "Do you think they were there in the past? Were they swimming under the surface, invisible to us?"

"I don't know, luv," Sloan says beside me. "I'm not familiar with Ophidians. Eva said they're quite rare."

I glance around, searching for our Shirley Temple reaper. "Where is Evangeline?"

Dillan straightens. "She said there were many displaced souls here. When Emmet said he'd be staying on, she thought it best to help clear out some of the dead so he's not dealing with vengeful spirits and hauntings."

"Aye, that would be nice, wouldn't it?" Ciara snaps.

Despite what she said earlier when I asked her about staying here, I can't see Ciara thriving as the guardian queen of a deserted island. Maybe I'm wrong, and she'll surprise me. Maybe...but I don't think so.

"Good call." I drop to my knees to place my hands on the mulched divots and chunks. "The fewer ghosts, the better. Right, hotness?"

Sloan flashes me a surly scowl. "I know what yer doin' and yer not funny."

I chuckle. "I don't know what you're talking about. Oh, right, you're afraid of ghosts, aren't you?"

"Ye know full well I am, now focus on smoothing out the damage of the land."

I chuckle at how riled he gets at the mention of ghosts but don't tease him any longer. Focusing on the task at hand, I gather my intention and start healing the damage. *"Mold Earth."*

From one moment to the next, the terrain around me shifts. The pocked and battered land smooths out, the grass springs up to cover patches of dirt, and all evidence of the battles fought gets erased.

How long have the Ophidian serpents been fighting to keep the island's power out of the hands of ill-intentioned people? I have no idea, but I'm thankful they were here to do it.

I sit back on my heels and study the river. It's like a flowing river of Pepto Bismol. Except it wouldn't make any of us feel better if we drank it.

Staring at it, I try to see any shift in color toward bright fuchsia. Nothing so far.

I don't know how far away the disconnect is to the main conduit or what it's going to take for them to fix it. Hopefully, it won't be too long. We're just over a month until the beginning of the Culling period.

I finish restoring the riverbank and brush my hands off as I move to the next section of the grassy clearing.

Sloan finishes his area too and goes in the opposite direction.

The cute buildings and the open palapa with the thatched roof are all gone. There's nothing but an area of beat-up ground covered in the debris of battle.

"Howeyah?" Gran asks as I finish my third area.

"I'm fine." I brush off the knees of my pants as I move to the boundary of the area I just fixed. "Are we getting anywhere?"

"Aye, without a doubt. It's better by the moment."

Good. "I want that for Emmet. If he has to be here protecting the conduit of power, I don't want him living in a war zone."

"No. Me either."

Gran reaches down and touches the ground where I'm working, and a sapling pops through the turf and begins to stretch toward the sunny sky. In the span of a few moments, it grows fifteen feet tall, the trunk broadens, and the branches reach out and start budding and filling with leaves.

I watch as the tree blooms heavy with pink cherry blossoms and draw the fragrance deep into my lungs. "It's beautiful, Gran."

"Thanks, luv." She lifts the hem of her skirt and settles on the ground, allowing the fabric to fall around her.

I watch in wonder as she moves her hands in graceful sweeps, each arc of hand and fingers playing a harmonic rhythm with the air and the twining vines and reeds answering her call.

It's mesmerizing. The tender reeds twine themselves together, weaving over and under and back again until we're sitting there looking at a Gran-crafted wicker bench.

When she's finished, she holds her hand up, and Sloan is there to help her to her feet. "It's lovely, Lara."

"As it should be fer my boy. If Emmet is to stand as the gatekeeper to the isle of Emhain Abhlach, he deserves a lovely place to meditate and contemplate."

I draw a deep breath. "He does. Thanks, Gran."

She winks and gestures at the areas yet untouched by our restoration. "Back to our task we go."

"Absolutely. Let's getter done."

Even with as many druids as we have, it takes most of the day to bring the clearing back to a point where devastation isn't the first thing you think of when you pan a gaze across the grassy grounds.

Gran's cherry blossom tree with a meditation bench isn't the only addition she makes. On either side of the city gates, she grows and blooms a spectacular lilac tree with pretty green bushes running along the length of the ebony stone walls.

"Do you think the city is there?" I ask Da, staring at the nothingness beyond the gates.

"It's hard to say. I can't imagine the Ladies of Light ye met, no matter how powerful, were able to shield the city from view in their absence. If they were, that wouldn't negate it from physically bein' there."

"So, who makes an entire city disappear and how?"

"Maybe it's not gone but displaced from this plane." Wallace stares at the void beyond the gates.

"Mind bendy," I say.

"Magic often is."

We try not to disturb Emmet's lesson with Dionysus, Nikon, Andromeda, and Papu. He erected a bubble of privacy, so it's cut them off from what we're doing by sight and sound.

I have a feeling they'll be surprised by the transformation when they come out and join us.

"And a small orchard, too, I think," Gran says.

"Don't ye think ye've done enough, Mam?" Da asks. "We don't have to decide all of it now, and ye've expended a great deal of energy already."

She smiles up at my father and pats his hand where he has hold of her arm. "Nature work isn't work at all. It's my pleasure."

"I'm aware of that, but it still costs ye."

"How about you let the younger generation take a go at the orchard?" I ask. "You tell us what we're doing, and Calum, Dillan, and I will give it a go."

"Och, I can show ye what needs doing," Sloan says. "Trees, plants, bugs, and animals were my childhood chores. Tendin' to the family grove at Stonecrest Castle and helpin' Lara in her garden filled most of my days."

I grin and hook my arm with his. "Then it's settled. The kids will take on the orchard while Gran rests."

Gran rolls her eyes but doesn't fight us. "Very well, I'll just sit here and call the bees and bugs."

I chuckle. "That's not resting."

"Nothin' we've done here will thrive without bees and bugs."

Granda chuffs. "It's no use to argue. She's as stubborn as rocks."

Gran sits on the bench she made outside the gate beside the lilac tree, crosses her ankles, and closes her eyes, smiling a contented smile.

"She's not resting, is she?" I ask.

Sloan looks over and chuckles. "No. She's callin' the bees, as she said she would."

"From outside the protective field?"

Sloan shakes his head. "Most bugs, including bees, live beneath the soil."

"Hubba-wha? I thought they live in hives?"

"Honeybees do, but seventy percent of the others live in the earth. They'll be here, in stasis, waitin' for the magic to return and awaken them."

I meet his gaze. He's blown my mind once again. "How do you know so damned much?"

He chuckles. "I'm a nerd, remember? Ye tell me so often enough."

I do, but the truth is—I love my nerd.

We're twenty minutes into the development of a small citrus grove when Emmet lowers the veil of privacy, and we get our first glimpses of the five of them.

"So?" I close the distance to meet up with them. "How did it go?"

Nikon shrugs. "It was weird, actually. The sensation of fae prana in my cells has always been part of me, but before now, I've never activated it. Allowing it to gain purchase is a bizarre sensation."

"I rather like it." Papu chuckles. "It's nice to feel my cells ignite."

"I like the tingles," Dionysus says.

"No surprise there," Dillan says.

Dionysus grins wider. "I also like that it's a kind of power that doesn't count as god powers. Me helping you guys is always a little dicey because the gods of pantheons aren't supposed to influence the outcome of man."

"This way, you can?" I ask.

He nods. "I haven't cleared it with Themis, but yes, I think so."

"What about you, Andy? As the only actual Lady of Light, what did you think?"

Andromeda holds up her hands and her image ripples in waves until she disappears.

"Okay, cool. You picked that up quickly."

"She even disappeared her clothes, Em," Calum says. "She didn't need to strip down for the full effect."

Emmet shrugs. "Pick on me all you want. I taught four people an arcane method of magical camouflage. I'm the bomb."

"That ye are, luv." Gran moves in for a hug. "Yer grandad and I couldn't be prouder of ye."

"The question now is, can we put ye to the test?" We all turn to Granda. "It's grand to have the ability to go invisible, but can ye make the city reappear?"

Dillan chuckles. "Otherwise, you and Ciara will be pioneers on the frontier and living rough for a long while."

Ciara grunts. "I consider living rough having cotton sheets on the bed, a space heater on the dresser, and sharin' a closet."

Emmet frowns. "We already have all those things."

"Exactly," Ciara says. "That's pretty much my limit. I'm bankin' on you five findin' me a golden palace and an enchanted city."

Or what? Or she's *not* going to stay here with Em?

Richer or poorer, amirite?

"Don't worry, babe. You'll be sleeping in the golden dil—uh, palace tonight." Emmet's cheeks flush pink, and it takes him a moment to get his thoughts together. "Ladies, take your positions."

The five of them spread out along the black stone wall, and Emmet stands in front of the massive golden gates. They face the vacant expanse where the city should be, and the rush of power they give off makes the hair on the back of my neck stand on end.

But nothing happens.

After a few minutes, everyone looks around. "Should it be happening by now?" Calum asks. "I'm not trying to rush the process. I'm confused."

Emmet exhales a heavy sigh. "It should've been happening. I mean...I did everything they showed me. Did I forget something?"

"What about the blood oath to the island?" I suggest. "No one has bloody palms the way you did after your training with Kyna and her sisters."

"Right you are, sista. More than a pretty face." Emmet grins and withdraws the knife sheathed against his thigh. "The blood ritual strengthens the bond to the conduit power."

I don't want to be the one to burst his bubble, but the river wrapping around the city is still Pepto Bismol pink, not Barbie doll.

"Those of us fighting in the Culling should take the blood oath, too," I say. "Fionn and Bodhmall made it clear that to utilize the power-boost we'll get from the island, we have to connect to the conduit."

Granda nods. "That makes sense…although the conduit isn't repaired yet."

I glance at the river and frown. "It will be. I've got a good feeling. We have to give the Ophidians more time. They'll come through for us."

They have to.

"Do ye remember the ritual of blood oath, lad?" Granda asks Emmet.

He pulls out his phone, calls up something in his gallery, and hands it to Granda. "Got it."

Granda plays it once for himself and once facing out to the rest of us. "Very well, ye know what we need. Dillan and Calum, gather wood fer the bonfire. Emmet, oversee that we do everything how ye remember. Wallace, yer on healin'. The rest of ye, prepare to bond with the island."

CHAPTER TWENTY-THREE

With the preparations made and the bonfire crackling, the ten of us taking the oath stand around the circle of flames, readying for the big event.

"I've already made the pledge," Emmet says, "so I'll lead the ritual, and Granda can double-check that I'm doing it right. I wouldn't want you pledging your fealty to the wrong island or anything."

I can't see how that would happen, but with Emmet, I suppose anything is possible.

"All right," he says, getting everyone's attention. "Grip a blade, yank, and clench your dripping fist over the fire."

Those of us with sharp weapons have called them forward, and those who don't will use Emmet's knife or Wallace's or Dillan's spare dagger.

Here goes nothing.

I press Birga's spear tip against my palm and slice. *Yowzers.* I hiss as a scarlet line rushes to fill the slit in my skin and hand her to Sloan. "Watch her. She's wicked sharp and likes blood."

Sloan does the same and hands her to Nikon.

And so, it goes.

I hold my clenched fist over the fire. Blood drips into the flames as we wait for the others. Once we're all bleeding for the island, Emmet gets things rolling.

"Repeat after me: *By the goddess of earth, air, and water, and the god of this fair land, Manannan mac Lir, I swear to be faithful and true to the power of Emhain Abhlach.*

I shall nurture and protect these domains with rightwiseness and discretion, mercy and truth, and according to the principles of Light, never, by will nor by force, by word nor by work, do that which would be considered loathful.

I pledge this oath on condition that thou wilt strengthen me with might and power and bond me with the essence of my peoples' source magic. So mote it be."

"So mote it be," a gruff voice says, joining us.

"Manannan mac Lir." Emmet bows his head. "We are honored."

The ancient Celt towers over us, but this time when he looks us over, he seems to have tempered the haughty annoyance. "You have surprised me, druids. Over the past centuries, many have come to lay claim to what I once loved—Romans, Vikings, Nazis —anyone who valued the power of might."

"We aren't here to lay claim," Emmet says. "We want to restore the island to what it was and what it could be again."

"Their motives were not so different from your own. They too wanted to harness the power of the conduit."

My mind trips on that. How can he not see the difference? "Our intention of what to do with the power is very different. Our interest lies in harmony and justice, not dominance."

He flicks his hands through the air. "The whims of man hold no interest for me. The truth is you want the power of this island for your purpose the same as the others—to strengthen troops for an upcoming battle."

"Looking at it from a broad scope it might look the same, but it's not."

"It is."

"No. It's not." I grip my fist around the cloth soaking up the blood from my vow. "Sacrificing ourselves to fight for the sake of the innocent and those who aren't strong enough or informed enough to fight for themselves is nothing like power-hungry hordes wanting more power to dominate people. If you can't see that, you're blind."

There's a hiss of whispered curses behind me, and I catch myself. "Sorry. I get passionate about things and my mouth gets away from me."

"Is that how you justify disrespecting me?"

Okay. Tough crowd. "My point is, we care about this island. Emmet has pledged to become the guardian of the conduit. Surely, you sense his connection with The Source and can read his intention."

"I can and do."

"Then why are you busting our balls? We took the blood oath to defend the island and the power within. Indirectly, that means we pledged ourselves to you and will ensure people don't abuse your island. We are here to help make things better."

He stares at me stone-faced and arches a brow. "Do you not know enough to fear the gods, female?"

I shrug. "Not really. My cousin is Boann, Goddess of the Boyne, and I'm friendly with Themis and her daughters, the Greek Fates, and Dionysus and I are besties. Aren't we, dude?"

"Yeah, we are," Dionysus says.

I lean into him as he steps in beside me. "I've met my fair share of gods who are arrogant dicks, but mostly they want things just like everyone else. I try not to judge or pigeonhole people. That also means I'm not going to kowtow to you simply because you were born from a magical pantheon."

Manannan frowns at me and looks at Dionysus. "God of Feasts and Wine?"

Dionysus nods and holds up his sliced hand, which of course, is no longer bleeding and fully healed. "And newly inducted protector of your island, which, if I'm being honest, got away from you. It was a dump until we arrived. You're welcome."

The two meet gazes, and I get the distinct sense that they're measuring each other up. I know Dionysus is one of the most powerful gods in the Greek pantheon, but I'm not sure how that translates to the Celtic pantheon.

"Is this going to end in a pissing match?" I glance between them.

Dionysus chuckles. "No, Jane. We were having a sidebar chat on the god wavelength."

"You can do that?"

"Sure. I'm amazing." He wraps an arm across my shoulder and kisses the side of my head. "You couldn't have a better family of custodians for the island. Seriously, five stars."

Manannan seems to accept that, and his frame relaxes. "Where is the bear who destroyed the sorceress?"

I glance around the area and find Bruin lying on his back in the sun by the orchard with Manx and Doc. "He's the brown one there sunning his bear bits."

"Fetch him here."

I blink at the god and draw a breath. Rude. "Sure, I'll invite him over. Not a problem."

Focusing on Bruin, I reach out across our connection. *Buddy? Sorry to disturb you. The big brute who runs this joint would like to speak with you a moment.*

Without rolling onto his feet or getting up, he shifts his head to look at us. He's upside down, but I have no doubt he can guess which one is the big brute. *About what?*

No idea. He asked for the bear who destroyed the sorceress.

Accolades, maybe.

Maybe.

Och, well, if the powers that be wish to praise me, I suppose I can make myself available.

I chuckle. *It's nice that you are humble enough to make yourself available to the people.*

I try. He rolls onto his belly, pushes up onto his feet, and plods over to join us.

By way of introductions, I gesture between the two of them. "Manannan mac Lir, this is Bruinior the Brave, also known as Killer Clawbearer."

Both of them take a moment to study one another.

"I appreciate how effectively you dispatched the sorceress. The Source serpents were fighting her for days, and as effective as they were at holding her back, they were not winning the battle until you intervened."

He lowers his chin and grunts. "My pleasure. There is nothing I enjoy more than a righteous kill...well, except a good helping of whiskey and rutting a round-assed female."

I press my lips together, trying not to laugh.

Manannan grunts and his head bobs in agreement. "A sound sentiment. I share yer sensibilities."

Funny, the only person Manannan seems to have common ground with is my bear who wants to kill people, drink, and get busy with curvy girl bears.

Gods are a funny lot.

"I have a token to bestow upon ye." Manannan steps over to face Bruin. "Yer clan here have bound with the island, and if they manage to restore the conduit power, they will have that as their token. Fer the warrior who took the enemy down, I offer this."

He rests a hand on Bruin's head, and a surge of light comes off him. It's brilliant enough that I turn to shield my eyes and when I turn back, it takes a moment for the spots to clear.

"Holy shit, Bear," Emmet says. "That is seriously dope. You look badass."

I take in my bear and yeah, Em's not kidding. Bruin is wearing custom battle armor and looks like a tank. Segmented plates cover his haunches, back, and shoulders. Metal spikes run the line of his spine and up onto his forehead. A metal-trimmed face guard protects his cheeks and eyes.

"You look more badass than ever, buddy." I run a hand over the brown plating and knock on it to test its strength. Is it heavy?"

"No. I barely feel it."

Emmet pulls out his phone and takes a picture so he can show him. "Check it. You're rocking the look."

Bruin studies the picture and breaks out in a cocky grin. "Yeah, I am."

"Yeah, you are."

"Yeah, I am."

I laugh at the two of them and stop the ramble before it continues. "Your gift is generous and very much appreciated. We will think of you fondly as he puts it to use in the battles to come."

Technically, Bruin is a mythical immortal bear, but it's the thought that counts because even though he's never been injured enough to cause alarm, I don't want that to happen.

Manannan accepts my thanks. "I shall leave you now. I wanted to accept your oaths in person and reward the bear. Despite having given up on humanity and the hope Emhain Abhlach would ever again be what it once was, I am curious to see how these new revelations end. Young man, I wish you well. Treat my island with the respect it deserves."

Emmet nods. "I will. You have my word."

Manannan mac Lir vanishes, and we're left standing around our bonfire, blinking at one another.

"So, I think that went well," Emmet says.

I meet the gazes of my family and friends, and the consensus is the same. "It did. We did well."

"Who would like some attention on yer hands?" Wallace asks.

He and Sloan shuffle around the fire to heal Papu, Andromeda, and Nikon. We, the druids, all have enough magical healing to stop the bleeding of a simple cut.

"This armor is spectacular." I give Bruin's gift another look.

Manx and Doc are both admiring Bruin's new duds, but it's obvious they're feeling a little left out.

"You guys did great in the battle too. Don't take this personally. A win for one of us is a win for all of us."

Dionysus meets my gaze. "They're sad."

"Yeah, I know. As the youngest of six kids, I know what it feels like to live in the shadow of my older siblings who are out there taking the world by storm."

Dionysus nods. "As do I. It's not something I would wish on anyone."

Me either, though in Dionysus's case, the people comparing him to his siblings were also trying to kill him, so it sucked even more.

I wrap my arm around his hips and lean against his shoulder. The surge of his energy signature flares, then Manx and Doc are wearing matching armor.

I hug Dionysus tighter and kiss his cheek. "Point to you, Tarzan. You rock."

He winks and hugs me back. "I don't like it when anyone in our family is sad."

Such a sweetheart.

"Nice duds, boys," I say. "Super snazzy."

Manx's armor is gray with black metal and spikes.

Doc's is black with silver metal. I try not to giggle at Doc in armor. He's only as big as my arm from elbow to fingertips, so his armor is cute and tiny.

Doesn't matter. He loves it.

"Look at our handsome warriors." Gran comes over to admire them. "Ye look fearsome, my boys."

Sloan finishes the healings and comes over to join the armor fashion show. As he studies the companions up close, he frowns.

"How difficult will it be to get ye in and out of the armor, *sham*? I don't see any straps or latches."

"They don't need to take it off," Dionysus says. "It will activate by thought and need as Fi's armor does."

Manx swings his attention over to me. "How do ye do it, Fi?"

"Oh, it's super easy. I think about my armor, envisions it on me to call it forward and release it to recede when I don't."

Like that, Bruin and Manx are furry and armor-free. Doc, however, still has his on.

"Are you having trouble taking it off?" Emmet asks.

"No trouble," Doc says. "I'm not ready to wish it away. In fact, I might never be ready."

Emmet chuckles. "I totally get that. You look wicked cool. Be the tough marten as long as you want."

I laugh. "Yeah, when Dillan first got his Cloak of Concealment, he didn't take it off for weeks."

Dillan lifts his hand and scratches his eyebrow with his middle finger.

I'm readying for his response when my skin tingles and my body fills with a sudden rush of energy. The only time I've felt something like this was when we were in the Fianna fortress, and we touched our statues.

That moment when our base skills and druid knowledge downloaded into us held a similar sensation of power. I haul a rush of oxygen into my lungs, and my cells ignite. The ambient magic in the air has increased twentyfold.

"They did it!" I shout, rounding the fire and running toward the river. "They fixed the conduit to The Source."

Footsteps fall in beside me, but I don't turn. My gaze is locked on the pastel pink of the waters, searching for the increase in prana power.

"Is it getting pinker? Does anyone think it's pinker?"

"It looks the same to me," Nikon says, "but I feel it. The difference is incredible."

I turn to check on Emmet. He was the most sensitive to the ambient magic back a thousand years ago and has the strongest bond to the island now. "What about you, Em? You feel it, right?"

He snorts. "Yeah, I feel it. It's like I've lived my entire life in black and white and now I'm suddenly getting OLED HDR."

"Okeedoodle. If you say so."

The river's surface flutters as currents swirl and that darker pink we've been waiting for finally starts trickling up.

"Yeah, baby." I point at one patch of fuchsia, then another and another. It's enough that it's intensifying the overall color of the river and darkening the waters. "Now we're getting somewhere."

"It's a heady surge of power," Gran says.

"It's like riding an amazing high," Nikon says absently. Andromeda pokes him in the side, and he clears his throat. "I expect. I wouldn't know myself."

I laugh and hold up my thumbs. *Great recovery, Greek.*

He rolls his eyes. *Give me a break. It's been a day.*

Thanks for sharing it with us.

Always. I'm Team Trouble, Red. You know that.

Man, I need to find him someone to love.

We watch the river of prana for a few more minutes as the serpents swim and the waters churn, all of us fed with the raw power of The Source.

"A great first day as the island's guardian, Em." I bump my shoulder against his and smile as his aura of power grows. "You're sure about this?"

His answer is written all over the contentment in his expression. "It's what I'm supposed to do, Fi. I know it."

"Then, I guess you should take another run at releasing the hidden city and see if you've got a place to live."

He smiles at me and nods. "Yeah. Let's do this. Is everyone game for another attempt?"

Papu, Andromeda, Dionysus, and Nikon all agree.

"All hail the Ladies of Light." Calum chuckles.

CHAPTER TWENTY-FOUR

While they stride off to get back into their places along the wall of the city gates, I go over and hug my father. "You've been quiet today. How you doing, Daddio?"

"Och, I'm fine, Fi. Ye mustn't worry about yer oul man. It's my job to do the worryin'."

That might be true, but I hate to see him suffering under the weight of his grief. It's been over a year since we lost Brendan and Da seems sadder and more distant now than he did when my brother was first killed.

It hurts all of us to see him so sad.

The two of us watch Emmet and the others work toward releasing the lost city. Connected as I am to the ambient power around me, and with my arms still around Da's waist, I press my cheek against his chest, close my eyes, and focus my intention.

Pain of loss and wounds of old,
I set you free; you have no hold.
Your heart will heal, the burden lighter,
Your love is strong. You are a fighter.

My father gasps and staggers back and away from me. His brows pinch down hard and fast, and he pegs me with an accusing gaze. "What did ye do, *mo chroi?* Did ye cast a spell on me?"

"I...uh, I wanted to ease your grief like I did for Myra and Garnet. They were buried under the weight of loss, and I helped them find happiness again."

He takes a step back, and I don't understand the betrayal in his expression. "Ye had no right. My grief was the last thing I had of Brendan, and ye took it from me without my permission."

His anger strikes me like the lash of a switch. "Grief isn't the last thing you have of Brenny, Da. We have hilarious memories and the joy of loving him and pride in knowing he made a difference in our lives and the lives of others."

He points at me and leans in. "Ye overstepped, young lady. Ye may take the lead in the druid part of our lives, but I'm still yer father, and ye don't make my decisions for me. If I wanted to clear my grief, I would've done it. Believe it or not, I know a fair bit more about these things than the rest of ye."

"Da, I'm sorry you're mad, but—"

"Not a word, young lady." He holds his finger up and cuts off my apology. "Calum, once yer brother finishes with the others, ask one of the Greeks to please come to find me on the beach. I'm ready to head back to my bride."

Calum looks twisted up. "Sure, Da."

Before I can explain and make him understand, Da stomps off toward the entrance to the inner city and leaves us behind.

"Shit, baby girl. What did you do?" Calum asks.

"I was trying to help. He's been so sad..." I press my hand over the ache in my chest, but it doesn't ease the pain. "I only wanted him to stop hurting."

I glance around. Thankfully, not everyone stands witness to my family *faux pas*. The only ones who did were Calum, Dillan, and Gran.

"Don't cry, luv." Gran wraps her arms around me. "Yer father will calm down, and he'll realize ye did what ye thought was right because ye love him. Fer right now, let him be."

"Why would he want to be sad, Gran? What's wrong with him? He loved the force and resigned. He loved Toronto and moved away. He's all but shut us out of his life, and I know it's because he's hurting. Why would he want that?"

Gran pulls back from our hug and gives me a soft handkerchief with bunnies and clover embroidered on it. "I can't speak fer him, but it seems to me he's punishin' himself and believes yer brother's death is his failure."

"That's not true."

"Of course, it isn't, but men are proud beasts and sometimes see their responsibility to protect their young as a reflection of their worth as men."

"That's stupid. Brendan died a hero. He chose to save a woman and her daughter. How is that Da's failure? If anything, it proves Da taught us to defend the innocent, to sacrifice for what's right, and to stand up for what we believe, no matter the cost."

Gran nods. "That's all true, luv, but yer father is stubborn as rocks and doesn't see it yet. Don't you worry, he'll come around."

I want to believe her, but that doesn't help my leaden lungs fill when I try to breathe. "I didn't mean to hurt him. I wanted to help him."

"I know ye did, and somewhere beneath his anger, he knows it too."

I consider following him out to the beach, but it won't do any good. When Da gets like this, he needs time to cool off. "When you get a chance…will you tell him I'm sorry? Will you tell him I love him, and I only wanted to ease him a little and see him smile again?"

"I'll tell him, luv, but honestly, this is more about him than it is about you. Try not to take it too much to heart. It'll all work out. Things like this always do."

With a heavy heart, Gran and I go over to join the others, watching and waiting while the Ladies of Light work on finding the invisible city and making it visible again. I try to put what happened with Da out of my mind.

Maybe I was wrong to try to help release his grief, but I genuinely believe he'll heal better if he's not wallowing in it.

"What's happened?" Sloan asks when he sees me.

I shake my head. "A disagreement with Da. I don't want to talk about it now. This is Emmet's big moment."

Sloan studies my expression and nods. "All right. Come here to me, though. Ye look like ye need a little TLC."

I hug him tightly and absorb the rush of healing magic he sends me, then turn in his arms to watch the city gates. With his embrace still wrapped around me, I borrow his strength and focus on Emmet and what they're trying to do. "Have they made any progress?"

"Some. A few moments ago, the air undulated, and there was a flicker of buildings beyond the gates."

"That's exciting."

"It is."

"What do you think happened to Kyna and her sisters? How long would they have lived after we left?"

"I have no idea. Without knowing what happened to the island or what sect of empowered they belong to, I couldn't even hazard a guess."

They were unlike any other race of fae I've encountered. Maybe they weren't fae at all.

"Look, look." Calum points above the wall where buildings are flickering into sight.

The air surges beside me and Eva appears next to Dillan. "What did I miss?"

"Not much. Look, you're just in time to see the unveiling of the city of Emhain Abhlach."

"Oh, lovely. This is exciting."

I squeeze Sloan's arms around me, the excitement in the air taking the edge off my mood. "It was such a cute and colorful city. There, the foggy blur is lifting, and you can see the palace."

Eva giggles. "It does look like a giant golden dildo."

"Right?" Dillan laughs. "Now it's Emmet's giant golden dildo."

I chuckle. "We should try not to say that around Emmet and Ciara. If this is their home, we should be mature and supportive."

Calum looks at me and makes a face. "It was Emmet who said it first."

I'm not surprised.

"Ta-da!" Emmet holds out his arms as their weaving of light ends. "Behold the hidden city of Emhain Abhlach."

I start a round of clapping, and everyone joins in. "All hail the Ladies of Light two-point-oh. You did it."

Emmet hugs Nikon, Dionysus, and Andromeda and shakes hands with Papu. "We never could've done it without the Greeks. Thank you, everyone."

Andromeda smiles. "You don't have to thank me, Em. Our entire existence, we've had immortality, but we've never been able to do much with it. Teleporting, time shift, phasing through solid surfaces...they're great abilities, but learning to weave light and connecting with The Source power of the island is next-level. Thanks for including us."

I hug Andy, Papu, and Nikon. "Thanks for coming. I know it's been a long day. You're welcome to stay, but we have no idea what we'll find in the city."

Papu shakes his head and lifts my hand to kiss my knuckles. "As much as I appreciate the invitation for more adventure, I'm quite happy to return to my vineyard and call the day a success."

"I think I'll go with you and spend the night," Andromeda

says. "It's been years since I slept on the bluff and watched the sun come up."

Nikon looks at me and winks. "Always a magical moment."

It was. "Will you come back once you snap them home or will you stay in Rhodes?"

"I'll be back. I want to explore with you guys."

"I'm taking Gran, Granda, Niall, and Wallace home, then I'll be back too," Dionysus says.

"Da's out by the beach and sea." I point in the direction he stomped off.

"Gran told me. Don't worry." Dionysus squeezes my hand and sends me a rush of comfort. Obviously, Gran either explained Da is angry with me, or he picked up on it on his own. "I'll be back to explore. Dillan told me we could all explore the giant dildo palace together."

I chuckle. "Then we'll wait for you to get back before we explore. Thank you both for taking everyone home. We're so incredibly blessed to have you in our lives."

Dionysus grins. "Yes, that's true, but life is definitely more fun with you in ours."

We finish our goodbyes, then Nikon and Dionysus snap out to escort everyone who's leaving back to their homes.

"I guess that leaves us." I pick up my backpack and shrug it onto my shoulders. I hand Calum his jacket and pick up one of the sleeping bags from the pile of camping equipment.

As tired as I am from the day, I'm proud of us too. We freed the island of Emhain Abhlach from siege, reinstated the conduit of power, established our connection, and revealed the hidden city.

If Fionn and Bodhmall are right about the island giving us access to a backup generator of power to draw upon when we need it, Team Light leveled up today.

Bigtime.

"Check them out." Dillan points up at Dart, Saxa, and Rory

flying the skies. They must feel the high of the ambient power in the air too because they're doing acrobatics and letting loose. Good for them.

Handing Sloan the cooler and another sleeping bag, I straighten and face the gates. "Emmet and Ciara, since you two are the guardians of the city, lead the way."

Emmet grins and strikes off through the tall, golden gates and raises his arms into the air. "Welcome, my friends, to Fantasy Island."

We follow them inside the city walls, and I draw a deep breath and exhale.

"Are ye all right, Fi?" Sloan asks.

"Yeah, it's just…it feels like there's still so much to do and only a short time to get it done."

Dillan wraps his arm around Eva's hips and shrugs. "Yeah, well, what else is new? We'll deal. Clan Cumhaill works best under pressure."

I chuckle. "Yeah, we do."

THANK YOU

Thank you for reading *A Culling Tide*. While the story is fresh in your mind, and as a favor to Michael and me, please click HERE and tell other readers what you thought.
A quick star rating and/or even one sentence can mean so much to readers deciding whether or not to try a book, series, or a new-to-them author.

Thank you.

And if you loved it, continue with the Chronicles of an Urban Druid and claim your copy of book fifteen:
A Danger Destroyed

NEXT IN SERIES

The story continues with *A Danger Destroyed*, available now at Amazon and Kindle Unlimited.

Claim your copy today!

AUTHOR NOTES - AUBURN TEMPEST

JANUARY 17, 2022

Thank you for reading *A Culling Tide*, and for sticking with Fi and the Clan Cumhaill through fourteen books, so far. You rock!

So, here's the Chronicles of the Urban Druid news.

Book fifteen, *A Danger Destroyed*, will take us to the end of the Chronicles of the Urban Druid series—the first series in the Urban  Druid universe. Michael and I consider these first fifteen books the stepping stones where Fi and the gang learn how to be druids and gather as Team Trouble.

We're still working on the series name for the next set of books, but they will be the **continuing** adventures of Fi and the fam jam after the Culling. You will find the same characters, the same off-beat humor, and the same crazy antics, just with a new starting point for those readers who have just discovered us and don't want to start fifteen books back.

We're so incredibly thankful for your fandom and the fact

that you've loved these stories as much as we have. There will be more. We just want to have a new starting point to freshen things up.

Soooo, my questions to you are...who is your favorite character? What characters would you like to know more about? What situations haven't you seen that you're dying for? What myth or place or idea would you love to see as part of the next set of books? And if there were side, spin-off books, who would you like to see starring in their own adventures?

You can put it in a review or email me or FB message me or whatever you want. Just let me know what you're hankering for.

Blessed be,

Auburn Tempest

AUTHOR NOTES - MICHAEL ANDERLE

FEBRUARY 21, 2022

Thank you for reading both this story AND these author notes here in the back!

As Auburn mentioned, we are about to end the start of the Urban Druid set of stories. We have two ideas about where to go next and would LOVE a little insight into what has been told so far that we have failed to close the door on, or about areas and mythos that you would like the door opened and stepped into.

In short, the world is about to get a whole lot brighter...and is that an explosion I see in the distance?

Probably.

However, regardless of the calamity of the world, you can be assured that Clan Cumhaill will continue supporting family, rocking the free world, and coming up with snarky antics while driving others to distraction.

It's what they do.

We would LOVE you to join us on our adventures as we continue with Fi and try to do her justice!

Thank you (always) for supporting our merry antics and providing a window into what an Urban Druid can be.

AND NOW A WORD FROM OUR SPONSOR

Not so much a sponsor as an alarmed human being. Would SOMEONE please pay the freaking world's heating bill? It's @#@#%!#% cold and getting colder here in the Nevada desert, and I'd like to believe I'll feel my toes sometime soon.

(*Editor's note: Perfect reading weather! I have my fuzzy blanket and my tea, and a new six-book series. Hope it stays cold for a long time!*)

Ok, back to your regularly sponsored reading. Enjoy your week or weekend!

Ad Aeternitatem,

Michael Anderle

ABOUT AUBURN TEMPEST

Auburn Tempest is a multi-genre novelist giving life to Urban Fantasy, Paranormal, and Sci-Fi adventures. Under the pen name, JL Madore, she writes in the same genres but in full romance, sexy-steamy novels. Whether Romance or not, she loves to twist Alpha heroes and kick-ass heroines into chaotic, hilarious, fast-paced, magical situations and make them really work for their happy endings.

Auburn Tempest lives in the Greater Toronto Area, Canada with her dear, wonderful hubby of 30 years and a menagerie of family, friends, and animals.

AUBURN TEMPEST - URBAN FANTASY ACTION/ADVENTURE

Chronicles of an Urban Druid

Book 1 – A Gilded Cage

Book 2 – A Sacred Grove

Book 3 – A Family Oath

Book 4 – A Witch's Revenge

Book 5 – A Broken Vow

Book 6 – A Druid Hexed

Book 7 – An Immortal's Pain

Book 8 – A Shaman's Power

Book 9 – A Fated Bond

Book 10 – A Dragon's Dare

Book 11 – A God's Mistake

Book 12 – A Destiny Unlocked

Book 13 – A United Front

Book 14 – A Culling Tide

If you enjoy my writing and read sexy/steamy romance, my pen name for the books I write in Paranormal and Fantasy Romance is JL Madore. You can find me on Amazon HERE.

CONNECT WITH THE AUTHORS

Connect with Auburn

Amazon, Facebook, Newsletter

Web page – www.auburntempest.com

Email – AuburnTempestWrites@gmail.com

Connect with Michael Anderle and sign up for his email list here:

Website: http://lmbpn.com

Email List: http://lmbpn.com/email/

https://www.facebook.com/LMBPNPublishing

https://twitter.com/MichaelAnderle

https://www.instagram.com/lmbpn_publishing/

https://www.bookbub.com/authors/michael-anderle

OTHER LMBPN PUBLISHING BOOKS

Sign up for the LMBPN email list to be notified of new releases and special deals!

https://lmbpn.com/email/

For a complete list of books published by LMBPN please visit the following page:

https://lmbpn.com/books-by-lmbpn-publishing/

www.ingramcontent.com/pod-product-compliance
Lightning Source LLC
LaVergne TN
LVHW041755060526
838201LV00046B/1006